Praise for Carolyn Brown's Christmas Cowboy Romances

"Sassy and quirky and peopled with an abundance of engaging characters, this fast-paced holiday romp brims with music, laughter… and plenty of Texas flavor."

—*Library Journal*

"A story with a cowboy always hits the target, but add a little Christmas flair and a saucy heroine and you have a winner… Hot, humorous, and a great time."

—*The Long and Short of It Reviews*

"Sassy contemporary romance… with all the local color and humorous repartee her fans adore."

—*Booklist*

"This book makes me believe in Christmas miracles and long slow kisses under the mistletoe."

—*The Romance Studio*

"Carolyn Brown creates some handsomefied, hunkified, HOT cowboys! A fun, enjoyable four-star-Christmas-to-remember novel."

—*The Romance Reviews*

"Full of sizzling chemistry and razor sharp dialogue."
—*Night Owl Reviews* Reviewer Top Pick, 4.5 Stars

"Brown has once again delivered a well-rounded group of characters you will wish were your neighbors."

—*Thoughts in Progress*

"A great book for a Christmas warmup, it makes you want to believe in Santa. Throw your hats in the air and stomp your feet for Carolyn Brown."

—*BookLoons*

"A sweet romance that really stresses the chemistry that builds between two highly likable characters... a more mature, slower-paced relationship that continues to deepen. Readers... will enjoy this cozy bright contemporary romance."

—*RT Book Reviews*, 4 Stars

"Carolyn Brown is a master storyteller! Mixing the twang and love of country music, setting it to the charm of the old Honky Tonk bar and a love between two people that will enrapture and capture your heart."

—*Wendy's Minding Spot*

"The spark that I love so much is better than ever... Honky Tonk Christmas is the perfect Christmas gift."

—*Cheryl's Book Nook*

"Carolyn Brown's final installment in the Honky Tonk series will knock the country boots off of any Christmas romance fan."

—*Romance Fiction on Suite 101*

Also by Carolyn Brown

MISTLETOE COWBOY

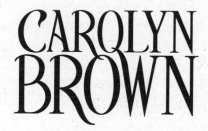

sourcebooks
casablanca

Published by Sourcebooks Casablanca, an imprint of Sourcebooks, Inc.
P.O. Box 4410, Naperville, Illinois 60567-4410
(630) 961-3900
FAX: (630) 961-2168
www.sourcebooks.com

Printed and bound in the United States of America
VP 10 9 8 7 6 5 4 3 2 1

To Joanne Kennedy,
my fellow smut peddler

Chapter 1

"DAMMIT!"

Sage's favorite cuss word bounced around inside her van like marbles in a tin can, sounding and resounding in her ears.

She had slowed down to a snail's pace and was about to drop off the face of the earth into the Palo Duro Canyon when two men dragged sawhorses and a "ROAD CLOSED" sign toward the middle of the road. She stepped on the gas and slid between the sawhorses, slinging wet snow all over the highway workers.

The last things she saw in her rearview mirror were shaking fists and angry faces before the driving snow obliterated them. They could cuss all they wanted and even slap one of those *fines double where workers are present* on her if they wanted. She didn't have time to fiddle-fart around in Claude waiting for eight to ten inches of snow to fall and then melt. She had urgent business at home that would not wait, and she was going home if she had to crawl through the blowing snow and wind on her hands and knees.

She'd driven all night and barely stayed ahead of the storm's path until she was twenty miles from Claude and got the first full blast of the blinding snow making a kaleidoscope out of her headlights. If she was going to stop, she would have done so then, but she had to get home and talk her grandmother out of the biggest mistake of her life. With the snowstorm and the closed roads into and out of the canyon, Grand wouldn't be making her afternoon flight for sure. Maybe that would give Sage time to talk her out of selling the ranch to a complete stranger.

"Dammit!" she swore again and didn't even feel guilty about it. "And right here at Christmas when it's supposed to be about family and friends and parties and love. She can't leave me now. I should have listened to her."

What was Grand thinking anyway? The Rockin' C had been in the Presley family since the days of the Alamo. It was one of the first ranches ever staked out in the canyon, and her grandfather would roll over in his grave if he thought Grand was selling it to an outsider. Had the old girl completely lost her mind?

"Merry freakin' Christmas!" she moaned as she gripped the steering wheel tightly on the downhill grade. The van went into a long greasy slide and she took her foot off the gas pedal and gently tapped the brakes to hold it back. She didn't have to stay in her lane. The roads were closed and no one in their right mind would be driving in such a frightful mess with zero visibility.

Sage could find her way to the Rockin' C with her eyes closed, and she might have to prove it because she couldn't see a damn thing except white. From the inside of her house, it might have been beautiful, but from the inside of her van, it was eerie.

Sage laid her cell phone on the console, pressed the button for speakerphone, and hit the speed dial for the landline at the ranch. Nothing happened, which meant the snow had already knocked out the power for both the landline and the cell towers. Grand kept an old rotary phone that worked when the electricity was out, but if the phone power was gone, nothing worked.

Neither surprised her. The next to go would be the electricity. She just hoped that Grand had listened to the weather report and hooked up the generator to the well pump so there would be water in the house.

She was crawling along at less than five miles an hour when she turned into the lane leading to the house at the Rockin' C, and the van still slid sideways for a few minutes before it straightened up. She slowed down even further and crept down the dirt lane, the engine growling at the abuse.

"Don't stop now," she said.

The quarter mile had never seemed so long, but if the van stopped she could walk the rest of the way. She'd even ruin her brand new cowboy boots if she had to. A warm house and her own bed were right up ahead and she was meaner than the storm anyway.

She kept telling herself that until she came to a greasy stop in front of the porch. She unbuckled her seat belt and clasped her hands tightly together to make them stop shaking, but nothing seemed to help. The adrenaline rush had brought her almost twenty miles into the canyon and now it was fading, leaving jitters behind.

Sage Presley was not a petite little woman with a weak voice and a sissy giggle, so she shouldn't be sitting there shaking like a ninny in a van fast losing its heat. She was five feet ten inches tall, dark haired and brown eyed, and there wasn't one small thing about her. But Sage didn't feel like a force right then. She felt like a scared little girl.

The small two-bedroom square frame house was

barely visible even though it was less than ten feet away when she stepped out. Her feet slipped and she had to grab the van door to keep from falling square on her butt. She found her balance and took short deliberate steps to the porch where she grabbed the railing and hung on as she climbed the three steps one by one.

If the storm really did stall out over the Palo Duro Canyon for three days, it was going to be one helluva job just digging out. It was a good thing she'd blown by those highway workers because Grand was going to need her help. She pulled her key ring from her purse and finally found the right key and got it into the lock. How on earth could anything as white as snow make it so dark that she couldn't even fit a key into a door lock?

Stepping inside was similar to going from an air-conditioned office into a sauna. She dropped her purse and keys on the credenza right inside the door and flipped the light switch.

Nothing happened. The electricity had already gone out.

The only light in the house came from the glowing embers of scrub oak and mesquite logs in the fireplace. She held her hands out to warm them, and the rest of the rush from the drive down the slick, winding roads bottomed out, leaving her tired and sleepy.

She rubbed her eyes and vowed she would not cry. Didn't Grand remember that the day she came home from the gallery showings was special? Sage had never cut down a Christmas tree all by herself. She and Grand always went out into the canyon and hauled a nice big cedar back to the house the day after the showing. Then they carried boxes of ornaments and lights from the bunkhouse and decorated the tree, popped the tops on a couple of beers, and sat in the rocking chairs and watched the lights flicker on and off.

She went to the kitchen and opened the refrigerator, but it was pitch-black inside. She fumbled around and there wasn't even a beer in there. She finally located a gallon jar of milk and carried it to the cabinet, poured a glass full, and downed it without coming up for air.

It took some fancy maneuvering to get the jar back inside the refrigerator, but she managed and flipped the light switch as she was leaving.

"Dammit! Bloody dammit!" she said a second time using the British accent from the man who'd paid top dollar for one of her paintings.

One good thing about the blizzard was if that crazy cowboy who thought he was buying the Rockin' C could see this weather, he'd change his mind in a hurry. As soon as she and Grand got done talking, she'd personally send him an email telling him that the deal had fallen through. But he'd have to wait until they got electricity back to even get that much.

Sage had lived in the house all of her twenty-six years and very little had changed, so she didn't have any problems going from the kitchen, across the living room floor, and to her bedroom without tripping over anything. There had been a couple of new sofas, but they'd always been put right where the old one had been, under the bar and facing the entertainment unit located to the right of the fireplace. The kitchen table was the same one that had been there when Sage and her mother came to live in the canyon. Grand wasn't one much for buying anything new when what was already there was still usable. She made her way down the hall to the bathroom and out of habit tried the light again. It didn't work either.

"That was stupid," she whispered.

The propane heater put out enough heat to keep the bathroom and the bedrooms from freezing, but it meant leaving the doors open a crack. Grand's door was ajar and she wanted to see her so badly that she was on her way to peek when she stopped. If Grand woke up there wouldn't be any deciding about when the fight would take place.

Grand was not a morning person even though she crawled out of bed at six every single day, Sunday included. Sage had learned early on not to approach her until she was working on her second cup of coffee, so there was no way in hell she was going to start the argument right then.

She turned around and went straight to her bedroom, kicked off her boots, and hung her wet shirt and jeans over a recliner in the corner of the room. She pulled an extra quilt from the chest at the end of her bed and tossed it over the top of the down comforter before she slipped into bed wearing nothing but her panties and bra.

She was asleep before her body had time to warm up the sheets.

The wind was still howling like a son-of-a-bitch when Creed awoke at daylight. Why in the hell had he decided to buy a ranch in the middle of the winter? Sure, he'd liked the land when he looked at it a week ago and he'd seen potential for raising Longhorns and growing hay come spring. No sir, it didn't look bad at all at fifty degrees and with the sun shining on the winter wheat.

And God only knew the price was right. Right, nothing! It was a downright steal and he'd felt an inner peace that he hadn't known in a long, long time when the owner had showed him around and made the deal with him. But he hadn't planned on the canyon filling up with snow on his first night in the house.

The weatherman said that the blizzard was going to stall out right above the canyon and wouldn't move on toward the east for at least three more days. That was the last thing he'd seen on the television the night before because the electricity had flickered and then gone out for good.

The phone service had gone out before the electricity. His cell phone's battery would soon be dead and the battery in his laptop would have bit the dust during the night. So there he was all alone in a blinding blizzard with a hundred head of cattle corralled in a feedlot behind the barn.

He wasn't very well acquainted with the house, so he moved slowly when he slung his legs out of the bed and made his way across the bedroom floor. He shivered and opened the door wider to let in more heat. At least he had the little two-bedroom house all to himself until the blizzard came and went and things thawed out.

He put on three pairs of socks, long underwear, jeans, and a thermal knit shirt. He topped that with a thick flannel shirt and peeked out the window. There was nothing but a chill from cold glass and thick falling snow beyond that. But rain, snow, sandstorms, or heat, cattle had to be fed and taken care of, and the lady had said that if he wanted to buy her ranch, he'd have to take good care of it for the next three weeks. She'd be home the day before Christmas to see if he qualified as a buyer. If she liked what he'd done, she'd sell. If she didn't, he'd only wasted three weeks.

Her words, not his!

It was December so he didn't expect eighty-degree weather, but he sure hadn't figured on eight inches of snow coming down in blizzard-strength wind either, and that's what the weatherman predicted. Two inches of snow or sleet crippled folks in Texas as much as two feet so they'd be a while digging out from under eight inches for sure. At least he wouldn't have to contend with the granddaughter. No way could she get into the canyon in a storm like this. She could just hole up in her fancy hotel in Denver where the gallery was showing her paintings. *La-tee-da*, as Granny Riley used to say about all things rich and famous.

The stipulation for the sale was that Sage Presley could live on the ranch as long as she wanted. Well, Creed could live with the painter in her own house on the back forty of the Rockin' C to get the ranch for the price Ada Presley quoted. She could play with her finger paints and take them up to Denver and Cheyenne every year. Their paths might cross once in a while and he'd tip his hat to her respectfully. He'd never heard of her, but that didn't mean much. In Creed's world a velvet Elvis was art and pictures torn out of coloring books held up with magnets graced the front of his mother's refrigerator.

Creed didn't care what Sage did for a living or what she looked like as long as she stayed out of his way. Miz

Ada had said that he'd best be prepared for a shit storm as well as the big blizzard because Sage did not want her to sell the ranch. At least the storm had kept her away from the canyon, and by the time she could get to the ranch she would be cooled down.

He made it to the bathroom, illuminated only by the fire in the open-face wall heater, and then down the hall way and halfway across the living room before he stumped his toe on the rung of a rocking chair.

"Shit!" he muttered.

His coveralls, face mask, and hat were hanging on a rack beside the back door, and his boots waited on a rug right underneath them. He zipped the mustard-colored canvas coveralls all the way to his neck, pulled the face mask over his head, and pushed the bottom behind the collar of the coveralls. Then he stomped his feet down into his work boots and crammed an old felt hat down on his head. It was a tight fit with the knitted mask, but a cowboy didn't even do chores without his hat.

He leaned into the whirling wind on the way to the barn located only a football field's length from the house. He'd run that far lots of times when he was quarterback of the Gold-Burg football team and never even thought about it. But battling against the driving snow sucked the air out of his lungs and by the time he reached the barn he was panting worse than if he'd run a fifty-yard touchdown. The barn door slid on metal rails and they were frozen. At first he thought muscles, force, and cussing wasn't going to do the trick, but finally he was able to open it up enough to wedge his body through.

The air inside wasn't any warmer, but at least it didn't sound like a freight train barreling down the sides of the canyon. He shook off a flurry of white powder, grabbed his gloves from the bale of hay where he'd left them the night before, and pulled them on.

"Won't make that stupid mistake again," he said.

He hiked a hip onto the seat of the smaller of two tractors and planted a long spike implement into a round bale of hay and drove it up close to the double doors at the back of the barn. He got off the seat, opened the doors, and ran back to get the hay out before the cows came inside. They had crowded up under the lean-to roof and eaten the last of the bale he'd put out the morning before. It took a lot of hay to keep them from losing weight in the winter. He just hoped he'd hauled enough big round bales from the pasture into the barn to make it through the storm.

The feeding job that should have been done in half an hour took twice that long. The two breeder sows holed up in the hog house were so cold that they barely grunted when he poured a bucket of food in their trough. One rooster was brave enough to come out of the henhouse and crow his disapproval before he hurried back inside. When Creed finished feeding, it was time to milk the cow. Glad to be back inside the dry barn, he filled a bucket with grain and gave it to the cow. While she got started on her breakfast, he fetched a three-legged milking stool and a clean bucket from the tack room. His hands were freezing, but he couldn't milk with gloves.

"Sorry about the cold hands, old girl," he apologized to the cow before he started.

When he'd finished that job he headed toward the house. Steam rose up from the top of the warm milk, but

it didn't do much to melt the snow coming down even
harder than it had been.

"And it's not letting up for three days!" he mumbled.

When he opened the back door into the kitchen, a
scraggly mutt raced in ahead of him. Ada hadn't mentioned a dog and he hadn't seen the animal before, but
there he was, ugly as sin, shaking snow all over the
kitchen floor.

—∿∿—

Sage was an early riser so sleeping until eight o'clock
had given her a stinging headache. She grabbed her forehead and snuggled back into the covers, but the pain
didn't go away. She needed a handful of aspirin and
a cup of strong black coffee. She seldom won a fight
with Grand when they were playing on an even field.
A blasted headache would give her grandmother a real
advantage. She jerked on a Christmas sweatshirt printed
with Tweety Bird all tangled up in a strand of lights on
the front and pulled on a pair of gray sweat bottoms.
She finished off the outfit with fluffy red socks from her
dresser drawer.

Grand hadn't even stopped long enough to get a fire
going. That could wait. Coffee came before warmth.
Sage passed the fireplace and went straight to the
kitchen. She filled the electric coffee maker, added a
filter and two scoops of coffee, and flipped the switch.

"Well, shit!" she exclaimed.

Old habits sure died hard. If the lights wouldn't work,
neither would the electric coffeepot. And that left out
the washing machine, the clothes dryer, and the electric
churn to make butter, too.

The fact that the electricity was out wasn't anything new in Palo Duro Canyon. If the wind blew too hard, and it did real often in the winter, the electricity went out. Grand said that if someone sneezed too loud up in Silverton or in Claude it went out, so no electricity in a blizzard was no big surprise. That's why they heated the house as much as possible with the fireplace and cooked with propane.

Sage opened a cabinet door and removed the old Pyrex percolator, filled it with water, put a filter in the basket, added coffee, and set it on the back burner of the stove. She wasn't as good as Grand about knowing just how long it needed to perk, but it would be coffee in a few minutes even if it might taste like mud from the cow lot.

She found the aspirin bottle to the left of the sink and swallowed four with half a glass of orange juice. While the coffee perked, she chose several good-sized logs from beside the fireplace and got a big fire going.

"Bless Grand's heart for bringing in wood to dry," she said.

She sat down in one of the two rocking chairs pulled up to the fireplace and warmed her hands by the heat. And a sudden pang of guilt twisted its way around her heart. Grand was out doing chores in this godforsaken weather and she was lollygagging around getting warm. She dug her cell phone out of her coat pocket and punched in the speed dial for her grandmother to see what she could do to help and a message popped up immediately saying there was no service available.

Of course there was no service. Damn storm!

At least Grand would come inside to a good fire to warm her cold feet by and a pot of coffee all perked and ready. Poor old girl would be miserable cold and she hadn't even had one cup of coffee yet. It was going to be a long morning for sure.

At seventy she had no business out in weather like this without any help. If Sage knew exactly where she was in the process, she would suit up and go help. But those pesky hogs wouldn't tell her they'd already been fed and neither would the chickens, and starting an argument with Grand already pissed because Sage had wasted chicken scratch or hog feed wasn't the smartest thing.

The living room soon warmed and the smell of coffee filled the house. Maybe she should whip up some pancakes for breakfast. Grand loved them and that would sweeten her up to see Sage's point of view. She had just set the mixing bowl on the cabinet when the back door swung open.

"It's about time you came in from the cold," she said as she turned.

Her hand flew up to her pounding heart and she backed up against the cabinet.

The abominable snowman pushed his way into the house behind something that was either the ugliest dog on the face of the earth or an alien from a faraway planet. The huge thing set a galvanized bucket of milk on the table and a basket of eggs right beside it before he stomped his feet on the rug under the coatrack. The dog stopped in the middle of the kitchen floor and shook from shoulder to tail, sending even more snow flying everywhere in her kitchen. When it melted there would be water everywhere and her socks would be soaked.

"Who the hell are you? Get out of here and take that miserable mutt with you," Sage said.

Creed removed his old felt cowboy hat and pulled off the face mask. His nose was scarlet and his dark eyelashes dusted with snowflakes. And of all the crazy things, there was a spring of mistletoe stuck in the snow on his shoulder as if it had grown there.

"I'm Creed Riley, ma'am, and I reckon if you want to throw your dog out in the snow that's your business, but I'm not that mean or cruel to animals. And I'm here to stay since I'm the cowboy who bought this ranch. I guess you'd be Sage Presley. I didn't think you'd make it home in this blizzard. I heard the roads were closed off."

He was well over six feet tall because Sage had to look up to him. His brown hair was a bit too long, and his mossy green eyes were rimmed with black lashes topped with heavy dark brows. His deep voice held a definite Texas drawl.

She backed up to the cabinet and braced herself against it. "Where is Grand? Is she behind you?"

"No, left a day early since the storm was coming in. I expect she's in Pennsylvania by now where it's fifty degrees and sunshiny today. Crazy, ain't it? We get a blizzard and the East Coast is downright pleasant. At least it was yesterday when she called to tell me that she'd made it fine and to tell you so when you got home. Guess her cell phone's battery was dead and her sister didn't have one so she called on a pay phone from the airport."

Sage rolled her eyes. "You have got to be kiddin' me!"

"No, ma'am! That's the truth and that's really not my dog. I'm bringing my two huntin' dogs out here soon as we make this sale legal, but this old boy just appeared out of nowhere this morning and rushed right in with me. I figured he belonged on the property. He wasn't none too pretty when he was covered in snow, but it was covering a multitude of ugly, wasn't it?"

Sage crossed her arms over her chest and glared at him.

He ignored her and started peeling away layers of clothing, taking the time to hang them on a coatrack just inside the back door. He didn't stop until he was down to jeans, socks, and a red and black flannel shirt.

What have you done, Grand? she thought.

The blizzard would end. The sun would come out and melt the snow. Electricity would be restored along with power lines and cell phone coverage. And Sage could have talked her out of the sale a hell of a lot easier face to face than over the telephone—if they ever got service back in the canyon.

This was Sage's home and it wasn't supposed to be sold to some rank stranger, even if his green eyes were sexy as hell with snow hanging on the lashes like that fake stuff out of a can that she and Grand sprayed on the windows when she was a little girl.

"Coffee smells good. Reckon it's about ready?" he asked. "Thank goodness for a full propane tank. Miz Ada told me that she has a standing order with the propane company out of Claude. And you can wipe that mean look off your face, lady. We're stuck here together until this ends. I'm not real happy about being holed up with you either, but it's the way it is and we might as well make the best of it."

Her eyes narrowed and her brow wrinkled.

You want your face to freeze with that nasty look on it? Her grandmother's words came back to haunt her.

"Number one, Mr. Riley, you don't tell me how to look or what to do. Number two, Mr. Riley, Grand won't ever sell you this place, so don't get too comfortable."

"Rule number one, lady, I speak my mind, so get used to it. Rule number two, I'm settling in and getting comfortable because I think she will sell the ranch to me. The deed will say that you get to live on the ranch as long as you want when the sale is sealed, signed, and finished. And back to rule number one, darlin', if you want your face to freeze like that, then just hold on to that nasty look," Creed said.

Her face softened, but she wasn't ready to smile and welcome the damn cowboy. Not yet, probably not ever.

"She wasn't supposed to leave until today."

Maybe the blizzard was a blessing. He'd see right quick that life in the canyon was too hard and he'd be ready to get the hell out of the place as soon as he could. Sage didn't mind doing chores. She hated milking a cow, but she could do that too if the cowboy would ride on out of the canyon as soon as the roads were cleared. Hell, she'd call a helicopter and pay the bill out of her own money if he wanted to get out of the canyon before the snowplow arrived.

"What's for breakfast?" he asked.

"Whatever you can scrounge up. I didn't take you to raise," she said shortly.

He smiled down at her. "Miz Ada said you'd be a handful and you'd come in here mad as a wet hen after a tornado. She was dead on, but darlin', I am buyin' this place. You are welcome to live on it. We can be friends, barely acquaintances, or enemies. Your choice and you don't even have to make it today. But it's going to be a long three weeks until she comes back and in this storm we've got no one but each other, so it can be pleasant or pretty damn miserable. Remember as you drink your coffee that this house ain't very big and we are stuck in it together."

The arrogance of the man!

He went on. "She left because of the storm and because her sister needs her, not because she was a bit afraid of you. That woman gave me the impression that she could face down the devil and own half of hell before the fight was over. You wouldn't pose much problem."

"You got her right, but you got me all wrong. I'm every bit as mean as she is. She raised me," Sage said.

Creed wiped the snow from his cheeks as it melted from his lashes. "I like my eggs scrambled."

"I like mine easy over."

Creed raised an eyebrow. "Who's cookin'?"

"Not me," she told him. She wasn't about to start cooking for him or feeding that dog he'd brought in either.

The ugly mutt looked from one of them to the other. Finally, he ambled toward the fireplace, where he curled up in a ball, covered his nose with his paw, and shut his eyes.

Creed brushed past Sage and poured two cups of coffee. He set hers on the table beside the bucket of milk and leaned against the kitchen side of the bar separating the two rooms.

"You going to strain that and put it in the refrigerator or am I?"

"I'll do it. You probably wouldn't do it right anyway."

It wasn't his ranch or his cows or his milk. She'd wear Grand down with the sheer volume of her arguments even if she had to whine and pout. Like she had said, he probably wouldn't do the job right anyway.

She went to the huge walk-in pantry, then picked up a gallon jar and a piece of clean cheesecloth. She put the cloth on top of the jar, made an indention in the top with her fist, and deftly wrapped a rubber band around the edge of the jar. Then she carefully poured the milk through the cloth and into the jar.

When the job was finished she removed the cloth, tossed it into the empty milk bucket, and set the bucket in the kitchen sink. She squirted dish soap into the bucket and ran warm water in it, washed out the cheesecloth, hung it on the dish drainer, and turned the bucket upside down in the drainer.

"You don't waste time or motions. That's good," he said.

Sage picked up her coffee and carried it to the living room where she curled up in the rocking chair. Creed followed her and she did her dead level best to ignore him. He had no right to be sitting in Grand's rocking chair with his long legs pushed toward the fire that she'd built.

Sage was prettier than the picture of her sitting on the mantel and a lot bigger than he'd imagined she would be. She was almost six feet tall and there wasn't one thing delicate or dainty about her. She looked like she could take down a full grown bull with one hand tied behind her back. And yet, with black hair floating on her shoulders, eyes the color of milk chocolate, and those full lips, she was sexy as hell. Tall women had never appealed to him but he had to admit, she was a looker, alright.

Hearing that her grandmother had up and sold the ranch had to be the shock of a lifetime. He couldn't imagine what it would feel like if his parents sold the ranch he'd lived on his whole life.

Of all the scenarios he'd imagined, this certainly wasn't the way he intended to meet Sage Presley. Keeping his eyes straight ahead, he stole a sideways glance toward her. She looked at the dog as if she could wish him out of the house. It wouldn't work. If she'd wanted him out of the house, she'd have to grab him by his wiry fur and throw him out and then she'd better shut the door real fast or else he'd beat her back inside.

So much for visions of having a friendship with the woman; hell, he'd be lucky if she didn't try to murder him in his sleep. He'd have to start locking the bedroom door at night, maybe even putting a chair in front of it for extra protection.

He wiggled his toes and said, "Ah, that does feel good."

"When did all this happen?" she asked.

"What? The storm?"

"Hell, no! When did you come here and why did she sell the Rockin' C to you? The first I heard about this was yesterday morning, and I had no idea you were already here. At first I thought she was teasing, but then she made me understand that she was serious so tell me what you did to make her sell to you," she asked coldly.

He stared right into her eyes. "Are you asking or demanding?"

"I'm not asking or demanding. I'm wondering how

this all happened so fast." She stared back and it became a battle of wills as to who would blink first.

The dog growled and they both looked down at the same time. Poor old boy was probably fighting off a coyote in his sleep because his eyes were still shut.

"Okay," Creed said. "I can tell you when and what happened. I don't know why she sold to me and not to someone else. You was gone off to your artist thing when I called and asked if I could come to the ranch and talk to her. She showed me around. I liked what I saw and she gave me a price. We shook and I put up the escrow, but she says she won't sign the papers or cash the check until three weeks are up so we both have time to think about it."

The dog whimpered again and he glanced at him before going on, "I went back to Ringgold and got my things. When I arrived yesterday morning, she told me about the storm, showed me where everything was again, including the generator, and one of the neighbors came to take her to the airport in Amarillo. Said she was going to Shade Gap, Pennsylvania, and she'd be back in three weeks, just before Christmas."

Sage sighed. "Aunt Essie is sixteen years older than Grand and she's been trying to get Grand to come out there for years. She has a little place in one of those godforsaken valleys."

Creed stopped the motion of the rocking chair and stared at her wide-eyed. "And what do you call this big hole in the ground? Paradise?"

"I call it home," she smarted off. "I suppose we'd best set up some ground rules. First of all, exactly where are you sleeping?"

"This place only has two bedrooms and one is yours. You do the math."

Her eyes popped open even wider. "In Grand's room!"

He nodded. "She took all her personal things with her. Cleaned out the closet and the drawers. When she comes back she said she'll have a mover take her furniture to her new home in Pennsylvania and I'll make a trip over to Ringgold to get the rest of my stuff."

Sage's face lost all its color and her jaw set firmly. Her eyes went to the shotgun hanging above the mantel and back to him.

Lord, was he going to die on his second day on the ranch?

"It's just a bedroom, for God's sake!" he said.

"It's *her* room."

"I don't have cooties. And it's only for three weeks. And I like Miz Ada right well, but darlin', she ain't God. That place ain't holy."

She shrugged. He could see the gears working in her mind, trying to figure out ways to get rid of him. She could try her damnedest, but he wasn't going anywhere.

He smiled. "Glad we got that straight. Are you making breakfast?"

"Hell, no!"

"Well, I am and I'm willing to make enough for two people and one scraggly old mutt. Pancakes all right? There's sausage in the fridge and I make a mean pancake."

She nodded. "That dog really doesn't belong to you? Tell me the truth."

"One thing a Riley does whether it's painful or not is tell the truth. We're honest, hardworking, and we state what's on our mind. The answer is no ma'am. That dog does not belong to me. I'd never seen him before he ran around my legs and shot into the house, but I guess he's adopted us."

—⁓—

Us!

There wasn't going to be an *us* no matter what her grandmother said or did. She didn't care if Creed had a halo under that thick brown hair and wings tucked up under his flannel shirt; he was not going to take over the Rockin' C.

The dog whimpered and sat up when he smelled the pancakes cooking in the big cast iron skillet. He stood up, yawned, and rested his head on Sage's knee. She wasn't going to pet the critter, and he was going outside right·after breakfast. There was no way that ugly thing was staying in the house, and she was not changing her mind—right up until he looked at her with big brown eyes, whined, and wagged his tail.

She scratched his ears and decided maybe he could stay in the house until the storm passed and the sun came out. Grand had probably arranged for him to appear in the blizzard knowing that Sage couldn't throw him out to freeze. She'd been trying for years to bring a pet into her granddaughter's life. But Sage didn't want anything or anyone that would abandon her again.

She didn't even remember her father, who had been killed in some kind of black ops mission when she was two years old, but there had always been a gaping hole in her heart that wanted a dad. Her mother had moved home to the canyon so that Grand could help with the toddler and then she'd missed a curve coming home from work one night when Sage was four. The hole got bigger. And now Grand had forsaken her too. She damn sure didn't need a dog or a cat or even a hamster to remind her of just how big that black hole in her soul could get.

Creed piled three pancakes up on a plate and put them on the kitchen table. "Ladies first. I'll fix a couple for the new pet and then make mine."

Sage pushed herself up from the rocking chair and stretched, bending from side to side and ending with a roll of the neck that produced a loud cracking noise. "Thank you, but that miserable excuse for a dog is not my pet."

"Did that hurt?"

"What? Popping my neck?"

Creed grinned and his eyes twinkled. "No, ma'am. That probably felt good. I was talking about it hurting to say thank you."

The worst blizzard the canyon had seen in her lifetime looked like it would go on for three days past eternity. She was stuck in a house with no electricity and a cowboy she didn't know and didn't even want to like. And he was sexy as the devil when he grinned.

"Yes, it did. I speak my mind too, Creed," she said.

Grand had been talking about selling the ranch for years, but it had all been a ploy to make her find a husband and settle down, raise a canyon full of kids, and be happy. The old girl could never get it through her thick Indian skull that Sage didn't need a man to provide happiness. Her paint palette and easel did that job just fine.

Her cell phone rang as she smeared butter on her pancake. She recognized the ringtone as the one she'd assigned to her grandmother and jumped up so fast that her chair flipped over backwards. She didn't even take the time to set it upright but dived for her purse, which was still on the credenza.

They called it a credenza but it was really the bottom half of an old washstand that had belonged to Grand's grandmother. The bow that held the towel had long since broken off and probably burned in the fireplace, but the rest of the burled oak washstand was still as sturdy as the day it was made. She fished the phone from her purse and hiked a hip on the edge of the credenza as she answered it.

"Hello, Grand," she said breathlessly.

"Well, you did make it home," her grandmother said through a buzz of steady static. "Looks like the blizzard is messing with the lines. Just wanted to be sure you were safe."

"Grand, what have you done?"

Grand giggled. "I told you I'd sell when I felt like the time and the buyer were right. Well, Creed Riley walked up on the porch and I knew it was time. I could feel it in my bones and it was even an omen that his name starts with a C. He agreed to keep the Rockin' C brand, so that was another good sign. I gave him a good deal and he took it. Live with it or move out here with me."

Sage shouted into the phone, "To Pennsylvania in the mountains! No thank you!"

"I love it. Wasn't sure I would, but it's beautiful. And me and Essie are doing just fine in this big old barn of a house she's got. I'm going to take care of the two old milk cows and we've got this little fruit stand out in front of the house where we'll sell stuff in the summertime. And the neighbors stop in every day to buy what milk we want to sell."

"All that will wear off before long," Sage told her.

"I don't think so. I knew when I looked into Creed's eyes that he was the one. My sense never fails me. And Essie needs me. She's getting feeble, Sage. You are cutting in and out so bad that I'm hanging up now…"

The phone went dead in her hands before she could say good-bye.

Sage redialed but got the no service message again. She picked up the landline and got nothing. It was going to be a long day.

Chapter 2

SAGE PAINTED WHEN SHE WAS SAD. SHE PAINTED when she was happy. She painted when she was nervous, and she painted when she was antsy, like she was that morning.

Her supplies had been stored in the bunkhouse when she finished the last canvas and headed to Denver and Cheyenne to the two showings. There weren't many days in a year when she couldn't paint outside. Sometimes spring rains kept her inside, but that wasn't every single day. And bitter cold didn't last long in the wintertime, but the way the snow kept falling, it looked like it might go on until eternity.

She finished the pancakes, drank two more cups of coffee, and started toward her bedroom to haul her heavy coveralls out of the closet. She could stoke up a fire in the bunkhouse and do her painting there. She weighed the consequences. If she escaped to the bunkhouse, Creed would think he had run her off. This was her house, not his. Or she could ignore him and show him exactly who the boss of the Rockin' C was.

She might have to share space with him, but that did not mean she had to talk to him. Knowing his name was enough, and she'd have been quite happy not even to know that much. She could have referred to him as "hey, you" or simply "cowboy" for three weeks.

"What are you doing the rest of the day?" he asked.

She turned around in the middle of the living room. "I'm going to get my supplies out of the bunkhouse, take a shower, and then paint until the light fades so much I can't see. And FYI, cowboy, I do not like people to talk to me while I'm painting."

"In cold water?"

Was he stupid or what? An idiot knew you didn't paint in water.

He grinned. "Are you going to take a shower in cold water?"

Dammit! Why couldn't he have one of those big toothy grins that turned a woman off? Oh, no! Grand had to leave her with a cowboy who had a smile so sexy that it lit up the whole universe.

"The hot water tank runs on propane. Grand thinks a total electric house is a joke. The trick to having a hot shower is to keep the generator that runs the well pump filled with gas. That means twice a day, and I like hot water enough to do it myself if you don't want to."

If anyone had told her two days ago that she'd be explaining the workings of her home to a complete stranger, she would have thought they were crazy. Never in her wildest dreams did she think Grand would ever go this far in selling the ranch. But it happened and it hurt to admit it, but his green eyes were mesmerizing, his pancakes were good, he was good to the dog, and when he grinned her heart got a hitch in the beating process. She'd bet dollars to cow patties that if there were kids around they'd flock to him like flies on the kitchen table in the summertime. That must have been what Grand saw in him when he appeared on the porch.

Grand might have enough clout with God to get Him to send the storm to the canyon so Sage would have no choice but to spend days and days with the cowboy, but Ada Presley had met her match. Sage had three whole weeks to fire up her temper and work on her arguments.

"What are you going to do with yourself all day long?" she asked.

"Read until chore time and then afterwards read until bedtime."

"What are you reading?"

"I got a whole pile of books in my bedroom."

That is Grand's bedroom. Like I said before, don't get too comfortable, Creed Riley.

He stacked the breakfast dishes on the cabinet. "They'll wait until after lunch and then we'll run a sink full to do dishes."

"We?" she asked.

"I understand you don't cook. Some women don't. But darlin', you can damn sure help with the dishes. If you don't know how to do that, I will teach you."

"Don't you get all high-handed with me, cowboy."

He held up his palms and took a deep breath.

"Hey, what do you say that we start over? Hello, Sage Presley. I am Creed Riley. Your grandmother, Ada Presley, is selling me this house. She told me you'd pitch a fit and I realize it's a shock to you, but I will buy it. I can cook. I can take care of a ranch. Looks like we are stuck together in this house for a few days. What do you say we make the best of it?"

"Don't look like we have much choice. I will try to be civil."

A mistletoe cowboy and a dog so ugly that its face would stop an eight-day clock—her world had turned totally upside down.

Where in the hell had those words come from about her trying to be civil anyway? She didn't want to play nice; she wanted to kill something.

The dog crossed the living room and sat down at her feet. "Grand's wanted me to have a pet for years and I don't want one. He'll have to go to the dog pound in Claude soon as this storm lets us out of the canyon."

The dog whimpered in disagreement and rolled over on his back.

"Do you know what'll happen to him at the pound? No one will adopt something that looks like that. Can you imagine a little kid coming in and looking at that in the cage? Kid would cry and run the other way. He'd tell his momma that he'd do without a dog before he took that critter home. They won't even wait the two weeks or however long it is before they put him down. First little kid he scares they'll shoot him right between the eyes. You want that on your conscience, Sage? And just for the record, it's not a boy dog. I just didn't think anything that ugly could be a girl, and there's more."

"What?" Sage asked.

"If that dog ain't pregnant then I'll eat my socks."

"Shit!" Sage mumbled. "I couldn't let them kill a momma dog about to have puppies."

"All that wiry hair and snow on her made her look like a fat old boy. But it's a girl and she's arrived with baggage. Hey, my coveralls are already wet with snow. Ain't no use in you gettin' layered up to go back out in the weather. Tell me what you want from the bunkhouse and I'll bring it in while you shower. Then you can paint the rest of the day."

"You'd do that?" she asked.

"We started all over. I wouldn't have a little while ago when I was still mad because you were mean and before we found out we're going to be grandparents." He grinned.

"I was not mean! And that dog isn't…" She stopped abruptly. "Thank you. My easel is in the corner. It folds up. Please bring the big black box beside it and as many stretched canvases as you can carry. It might take two trips."

"You *were* mean. The dog *is*, and you *are* welcome. I'll rap on the bathroom door between the trips in case you think of something else."

∼

The house was so small a cowboy couldn't cuss the pregnant dog without getting a hair in his mouth. And Creed didn't feel like spending his days in so much tension that a machete couldn't cut through it, so making nice was the only other alternative.

He'd been engaged. He knew women could be temperamental, and from what he had heard, artists were the worst of the lot. A trip thirty yards out back to the bunkhouse wasn't too big a price to pay for a nice quiet peaceful afternoon. Besides, when she got over the shock of the whole idea, Sage might be a right good neighbor. She was already coming around. It might take a while before she was ready to roll over on her back like the dog, but hey, a few more pancakes and a miracle or two and who knew what would happen.

It was the Christmas season, snow and all. A miracle could happen.

He trudged through wet snow up to his ankles and broke a layer of ice from around the bunkhouse door to get it open. Once inside he located the easel and the black toolbox. He tucked the easel under his arm, picked up the box, and started back toward the house. The temperature kept falling steadily, and the snow stung when it hit his face. He should've put the face mask back on, but he'd figured it would be a fast trip.

Sage was standing in the kitchen when he shoved the door open. She wore a chocolate brown sweatshirt with paint smudges all over it. Her hair was still wet and pulled up into a ponytail, and all her makeup had been washed away.

The sweet smell of soap blended with the aroma of burning logs and coffee and he had the sudden urge to bury his face in her dark hair, just to get a better whiff of her shampoo. Tall women had never attracted him and he'd never been particularly drawn to brunettes with brown eyes, but Sage Presley was a beautiful woman. One that probably had no time at all for a rough-edged cowboy who was gun-shy when it came to commitments.

He set the paint box on the kitchen table and rested the easel against the wall. "That was a quick shower."

"You don't linger when it takes a generator to keep the hot water coming," she told him. "Thanks for bringing that stuff in for me. I paint outside as often as I can so I can get the light just right."

"And in the winter?"

"In the house mostly, but I store my stuff in the

bunkhouse. Like you said, the house is small and it's not that far to go get what I want. At least it isn't when there's not a blizzard blowing outside. I appreciate you going after my stuff so I can work," she said.

"Does that mean you'll put in a good word with Miz Ada for me?"

"Hell, no! I'm going to do my damnedest to talk her out of selling the ranch. Does that mean you won't go get my canvases?"

He shook his head. "It doesn't mean that at all. I said I'd get your things so you can work and I'll do it. A Riley does not go back on his word. You just watch over Miz Chris."

"Miz Chris?" Sage asked.

"You know, our new pet. Chris for Christmas since she came to us during the season and all," he said.

"That's a girl's name, not a dog's name."

"She is a girl. I ain't never seen a boy dog yet with puppies wiggling around in his belly," Creed said. "And both of my dogs have girl names—Reba and Wynonna."

"Noel," she said.

He ran a hand down his cheeks to cover up the victory smile.

He'd forced her to name the animal and now it would belong to her. She could take it and all the puppies to her trailer when Miz Ada had one hauled into the canyon in a few weeks. And his two hunting dogs wouldn't be mad at him for letting another mutt live in the house when they had to stay outside.

Merry Christmas to Sage!

"Noel it is. I like that better than Chris anyway," he said. "I'm getting too warm with all these clothes on inside the house. Easel and paints are here. Now one more trip for canvases. How many, and anything else?"

"I'll take as many as you can carry, and bring that gallon of turpentine, please. It's sitting against the far wall beside where the easel was."

Snow blew in as he left, so she grabbed the broom and swept it into the dustpan along with the piece of mistletoe that had fallen off his shoulder earlier. She dumped the icy water into the kitchen sink and turned on the water to flush both dirt and snow down the drain. And there were two sprigs of mistletoe left in the wake.

Grand would find some kind of omen or magic in the fact that Creed had had mistletoe on his shoulder and that he'd tracked even more inside. But it just meant that the wind had blown a bunch from the top of a scrub oak tree and it had stuck to him. There was no reading a happily-ever-after into a couple of sprigs of mistletoe.

She peeled a paper towel from the wooden roller beside the toaster and dabbed at the green leaves and berries before placing the sprigs on the windowsill. If he kept hauling it in with every trip outside, she wouldn't have to climb a scrub oak for a bunch to hang up with the holiday decorations.

That turned her thoughts toward putting up the tree, the lights around the barn, and all the other decorations. She'd have the whole house decorated when Grand came home on Christmas Eve. There was no way in hell Grand could sign the ranch over to a stranger when she saw the tree and the sparkling lights. They'd remind her of all the good times that had gone on during Christmas on the ranch and any notion of selling would be gone.

And then there was the three weeks with Aunt Essie. That woman was an old sweetheart, but she'd drive a person to whiskey if they had to live in the same house with her. Her house at that! She was so set in her ways that the biggest John Deere tractor on the market couldn't budge her. And Grand was just as set in hers. Aunt Essie's house might be nothing but splinters and chunks of age-old linoleum at the end of three weeks because the two sisters argued and fought about everything. One thing was for sure: when Grand got off that airplane in Amarillo, she would be tearing up anything that she and Creed might have signed before she left. And Sage would never hear any bullshit about selling the ranch again.

Creed took so long that she went to the kitchen window and squinted, but the snow blew so hard against the window that she couldn't see a blessed thing. Then a bright red cardinal flew up and sat on the windowsill. It stared through the glass pane as if begging for just a little bit of the warmth to take the chill off his fluffed-up feathers.

"Can't do it, bird. The dog forced her way in, but you'd be really unhappy in the house," she said.

The cardinal took flight and the snow swallowed him up. She looked at the clock. If Creed wasn't back in five more minutes she was going to suit up in her coveralls and go find him. He could have slipped and fallen. He could be lying out there halfway from the bunkhouse to the kitchen door with a broken leg, freezing to death.

Well, that would definitely solve the dilemma of selling the ranch.

Grand's whisper was so clear that she jumped and looked around the kitchen. In that instant, Sage convinced herself that Grand hadn't left at all, but there was no one there.

"I don't want him dead. I just don't want things to change," she said aloud.

The kitchen door swung open and the room filled up with Creed Riley. Cowboy, attitude, and force all combined together to make the whole house seem smaller. Snow drifted in behind him before he could shut the door with the heel of his boot. He set the turpentine on the table and lined the canvases up on the floor with their backs to the wall.

"That enough?" he asked. "Speak now or forever hold your peace because once I take these coveralls off I don't plan on putting them back on until time to feed this evening."

She counted eight in various sizes. "More than enough. That should keep me busy for weeks."

He hung up his hat, brushed the snow from his face, and unzipped his coveralls. When they were removed for the second time that day, he kicked off his boots and left them on the rug beneath the coatrack.

"Well, let's hope the weather lets up before you get them all painted or we'll be covered up in it. It's turned even wetter; it's coming down so hard that you can't see your hand in front of your face and the wind is bitter cold." He talked as he peeled out of the outer clothing yet again. "I'm worried about the cattle, and I'm very glad that your grandmother had the foresight to bring them all into the feedlot right behind the barn before the storm hit."

"She's smart that way. She says it's her Indian blood. We don't get this kind of weather very often, but

Grandpa got prepared for it. That's why there's a row of cedar trees on each side of the feedlot. It breaks the wind and the snow coming from the north in the winter and the hard south winds in the summer. If we get as much as the weatherman is saying we will, there'll only be a couple of inches in the feedlot and the cattle will tromp that down pretty quick. They'll be cold, but they won't be standing in it up to their udders," Sage laughed.

Her face lit up like a Christmas tree when she smiled, but her laughter wasn't a girl's giggles. It was a full-fledged woman's laugh that echoed through the whole house and sounded even prettier than a good country music song.

"And that is funny why?"

"I love my grandmother, but she excuses everything by saying it's her Indian voodoo. She can smell a storm on the way, and if it doesn't arrive, then it bypassed us, but it didn't mean that she couldn't smell it. That kind of thing," she said.

"Well, whatever voodoo she has, I'm glad she's got the cows in one small enclosure and that they can huddle up under the shed roof on the back of the barn for a little protection." He kicked another piece of mistletoe with his toe as he started through the kitchen.

He picked it up and she reached for it. "I'll take that."

It was twice as big as the other pieces. Grand would say that was because she wasn't being mean anymore.

"Where are you going to set up to paint?" he asked.

She pointed. "Right there in front of the living room window to the left of the fireplace."

"What are you going to paint?"

She shrugged. After that comment about Indian

voodoo she couldn't tell him her deepest painting secret. That she depended on her painting gods to give her
inspiration and that she respected them enough to paint
what they offered.

"I'm going to paint a picture of that kitchen window
with a bright red cardinal on the outside ledge looking
in. While you were gone one lit there and looked like he
wanted to come inside."

"Smart bird. It's terrible out there. How in the world
did you ever get home? The last report I got before the
electricity went out was that all roads into the canyon
were going to be closed."

"They were just putting up the sawhorses and signs
when I drove up. I shimmied around them and kept on
driving. The men weren't real happy with me, but I
wanted to be home, not holed up in a motel somewhere.
I didn't have to worry about oncoming traffic."

"It was stupid! You were lucky to get here."

"I'm a damn good driver."

"Didn't say that. I said that driving down that twisting steep incline wasn't too smart."

The dog raised her head and yipped.

"Guess she don't want us to fight," Creed said.

"Guess she don't get to make the calls," Sage shot back.

"I'll put a pot of soup on for lunch and then I'm going
to have a hot shower to warm up my bones."

"You are changing the subject. Besides, the meat
is frozen and the microwave runs on electricity so you
can't thaw anything out that way," she reminded him.

"I took hamburger out of the freezer yesterday when
I heard about the storm moving in. And yes ma'am,
I am changing the subject. I don't like to argue and

fight. I got plenty of that growing up with a house full of brothers."

"Why do you cook?" she asked.

"Why don't you?" he fired back at her.

She frowned. "Because Grand does a good job of it and I didn't need to learn. Your turn."

"Because Momma said so. Seven boys make for a lot of work. So she made us all learn to cook and we had to do our own laundry and ironing after our twelfth birthday."

"Seven!" She carried the easel to the living room and set it up close to the window beside the fireplace.

He sat down in the rocking chair nearest the fire and shoved his feet toward the warmth. "You heard me right and I didn't stutter. Seven boys. She really wanted a daughter, you see. But she got three boys in about four years right after she and Daddy married. She waited a few years and tried again and got another boy, Ace. Waited a few more years and decided to give it another try. And got three more boys for her efforts. Me, Dalton, and Blake. She spoils her daughters-in-law and her granddaughters these days."

"I always wanted a brother or sister," she said.

The words were out and she couldn't put them back, but she wished she hadn't said them. She didn't want to share anything with Creed. That just led down a pathway that only ended in pain.

She chose a sixteen-by-twenty-inch stretched canvas. That would be the perfect size for a window painting. She looked at the kitchen window and her gods smiled on her that morning. For the briefest moment the snow blew in circles creating an angel in the upper part of the window.

Sage was known for her Western paintings that portrayed hidden animals in the rock formations of the canyon. She painted in earthy tones of umber, sienna, and ocher. But today she'd been given a new path: an angel looking down on a little red cardinal who studied three pieces of mistletoe lying on the sill just inside the window. She wanted to capture the cold and the way the bird eyed the mistletoe. She could hardly contain the excitement of something new and original as she set up the canvas and unlocked the paint box.

"What did you see?" Creed asked.

"What makes you think I saw anything?"

"You looked at the window and something changed in your face. All I saw was snow and mistletoe, but you saw something more," he said.

"I saw a cardinal," she said.

It was the truth. She had seen a cardinal earlier.

"Must've blinked at the wrong time. I didn't see it."

Sage could feel his eyes on her as she sketched and it created an itchy feeling like she'd been too close to poison ivy. She knew the very minute that he went to sleep. Trusting soul, he was, sleeping when she could easily get to the shotgun hanging over the fireplace or to the knives in the kitchen drawer.

The picture she was about to paint was etched firmly in her mind and she'd sketched in the beginning lines. So she stopped, sat down in the chair next to Creed, and stared at him.

Know thy enemy, is it? Grand's voice whispered.

She whipped around to look behind her and set the rocking chair in motion. She expected the squeaking rocker to wake Creed, but he didn't move.

That's right. I'll get to know him and find the very weakness that will run him off this ranch. You will not go through with this deal, Grand, she argued.

Thick dark lashes fanned out on his angular cheeks that sported a day's worth of black scruff. He was one of those men who had to shave every day and twice if he was going somewhere that night. He reminded her of her friend, Lawton Pierce, who owned the biggest spread in the whole canyon. Like Creed, Lawton had dark hair and long lashes and a beard. They could have easily been cousins, but Sage didn't give a rat's ass if he was Lawton's long lost younger brother and they'd been cut from the same tanned leather cowhide. She still wasn't going to like him.

Creed wiggled and sighed. She sure didn't want him to catch her staring at him, so she stood up so fast that she got a head rush. Her chair sounded like a bird chirping as it flipped back and forth several times. But then he settled back into a deep sleep and she sat back down. She had the strangest urge to run her fingers through all that dark hair and see if it was as soft as it looked. Would he be a tender lover or a demanding one? Would his kisses build a fire in her or would they turn her completely off?

Now where did that come from? I've only just met him and I'm determined that he won't be here more than three weeks, so there will be no kisses or sex. Besides, Grand would have a pure old hissy if she found out I'd slept with a man in this house, she thought.

"I couldn't face her," she whispered.

"You talkin' to me or the dog?" he asked without opening his eyes.

"I was just muttering while I decide how to paint that picture over there," she said.

His eyes opened slowly and he sat up straight. "Guess I'd best put the soup on if it's going to be done by dinnertime. That and a skillet of corn bread should do for dinner and supper both, right?"

"I'll make the corn bread," she said.

"You don't cook," he reminded her.

"I lied. I can cook. I just don't enjoy it. Grand made me learn enough to survive and I make a mean skillet of corn bread and the best Christmas sugar cookies in the whole canyon."

"You lied! What else did you lie about?"

Dammit! Was it a real lie if a person just omitted details?

"I saw the cardinal, but it was earlier in the day," she said.

"That all?"

She squinted at him and set her mouth in a firm line. "Did *you* tell any lies this morning? About that dog, maybe?"

"I did not. Your grandmother didn't say a word about a dog on the place and mine are registered redbone hounds. Two of them, Reba and Wynonna. They sure don't look like that mutt. So one more time, darlin'— that animal did not come from my neck of the woods."

She giggled. "Did you really name two bitches after the red-haired country singers?"

"You got it. They sing real pretty when they tree a coon or track a coyote."

She looked at the sleeping dog. "Think they'll like Noel?"

"They probably won't even think she's a dog. She looks like a big ball of tangled up yarn, don't she?"

The wiry dog did look like its momma had been a poodle and it's daddy a cross between a schnauzer and a ball of wool yarn. She opened one eyelid and whimpered.

Sage bent over and scratched the dog's ears. "It's okay, Noel. He didn't mean to hurt your feelings. Her fur is a whole lot softer than it looks, Creed. Do you think we should give her an old quilt? That hardwood floor is hard and cold."

"Might be nice." Creed grinned.

Chapter 3

CREED WAS A BIG MAN AND SAGE WASN'T A MIDGET. The kitchen was small, and every time he or Sage moved an inch they bumped into one another. A shot of her rounded fanny bending over to slide the corn bread inside the oven shouldn't have been sexy, not in sweat bottoms, but it was. Breasts brushing against his upper arm or plowing into his chest were a different matter. That he could understand stirring up things behind his zipper.

It had been a long time since he'd had sex, but his body could have behaved a lot better in his estimation. She'd made it very clear that she did not like him and intended to throw every obstacle she could in his way to keep him from buying the ranch. She'd lied to him about her cooking abilities, and now she was tempting him with every touch and move.

It wasn't fair. She was getting away scot-free and he was being punished. He'd gotten into scrapes. What kid didn't? He'd been drunk at rodeos. What cowboy hadn't? But God did not have to hate him so badly that He made his body respond to a woman who would shoot him stone-cold dead and never feel a bit of remorse about it.

He'd made several trips to the window to imagine lying naked, facedown in the driving blizzard. Thinking about something that cold on his bare skin and manhood usually shrunk it back down pretty fast, but each time it took longer than the last time because pictures of Sage lying naked next to him kept popping up. And the imaginary heat between them melted every bit of the snow for a hundred yards and turned what was falling into warm rain.

When the corn bread was almost done, he dipped up two big bowls of soup and put them on the table. While he did that, she bent over one more time to get the corn bread out of the oven and transport it to the table. He bit his lip to keep from moaning out loud and shoved his hands into his hip pockets to keep from cupping her fanny in his hand. He'd only met the woman that morning, for God's sake!

She put a container of homemade butter and the salt and pepper shakers on the table, and then looked around to see if she'd forgotten anything.

He rolled off two paper towels to use for napkins and joined her.

"Grace?" he asked.

"Grand usually does that," she answered.

"I'll do it since it's going to be my house," he said.

She bowed her head, said "amen" right after he did, and picked up her spoon.

"Mmmm," she said. "What's your secret? This is fantastic."

"Picante. I like to use my own, but there's no electricity and I have to have a blender to make it. I found that in the pantry and it worked pretty good," he answered. "You like it, do you?"

It shouldn't matter, but he wanted her to like the food. He wanted her to like him and for them to be good neighbors. He didn't want to feel tightness in his chest every time she smiled, but that was just a physical reaction to a very pretty woman.

"It's been a week since I've had good home food. Next week it might not taste nearly as good, but right now it's wonderful," she said.

"That's a left-handed compliment if I ever heard one."

One shoulder raised up half an inch. "I said it was fantastic, didn't I?"

Noel left her tattered old blanket Sage had rustled up from the linen closet and went straight to Sage's side of the table. She gave a little yip, her eyes on Sage's soup bowl.

Creed was glad that the dog had taken to Sage and not him. Reba and Wynonna would pitch a for real bitch fit if he let something like that live in the house and they had to stay outside.

"This is probably too hot for you, girl. I'll find something after we finish," Sage said.

Creed used the spatula to remove a piece of corn bread and crumbled it into his soup, saving one bite for Noel. She caught it before it hit the floor, gobbled it down, and wagged her tail.

"She thinks your corn bread is passable," Creed said.

"What do you think?"

He shoved a spoonful of bread and soup into his mouth and nodded. "I don't like sweet corn bread in soup or beans. This is perfect. We make a pretty good kitchen team, lady."

"Sweet corn bread is for dessert or for crumbling up and pouring milk over, not soup," she said.

"You got that right. What do you intend to feed this

hungry momma dog? I bet she'd eat the soup if it was cool. Without the bulge of those puppies she'd be bonier than a starving greyhound."

"We could try." She nodded. "I'll get a pie pan out and fill it. That way it'll cool faster."

Noel followed her across the kitchen floor to the stove and watched with hungry eyes while she dipped soup into the pie pan.

"Not yet, girl. It's too hot," she said.

Funny she should use that word because he was thinking the same thing about Sage. She was entirely too hot.

———ᴧᴧ———

Dammit! Sage thought but managed to keep from saying it aloud.

Half a day and she was already talking to the dog. Chances were that someone would come to claim the animal when the blizzard stopped and another living breathing thing would abandon her. It was so easy to get attached and so hard to let go.

She vowed she would not get close to Creed even if they were holed up together for the duration of the storm. Not even if he did have the dreamiest green eyes in the world and she'd always been a sucker for a man with green eyes and dark hair. Not even if he did fill out his jeans just right and it had been a very long time since she'd even been kissed.

After they'd eaten, talking only about Noel when either of them did break the silence, Sage said he could wash dishes and she'd dry them.

"Why don't you wash?" Creed asked.

"Because I know where they go and you'll have to ask."

"Okay, that's fair enough."

In the tiny corner where the sink was located, their bodies bumped together more often than they did when they had made dinner. She dropped the drying towel and he grabbed for it at the same time she did, their hands getting tangled up in the process. A plate slipped from his soapy hands as he transferred it to the rinse water and she quickly got a hold on it with one hand and his wrist with the other.

By the time they finished there were as many sparks hopping around the kitchen as there were snowflakes falling outside in the yard.

"You going to paint now?" he asked when the last fork was put away.

She nodded.

"Then I'm going to read." He disappeared down the short hallway and came back with a book.

Sage reclaimed her palette and began to work in earnest on her picture of the swirling snow angel. Creed was probably one of those cowboys who liked his women petite and dainty, with a little girl's voice and a clingy attitude that said, "Protect me, big old rough cowboy." Most men did. It made them feel all macho and needed. Tall women like her seldom got a second look.

Noel wolfed down the whole pie pan of soup and curled up on her warm blanket at Sage's feet. Sage wanted to talk to the dog and figure out how she'd gotten things so confused in less than twenty-four hours, but Creed would hear every word so she kept quiet.

She mixed just a dot of ivory black into a big glob of

titanium white and stirred it with her palette knife. Then she squeezed out a small amount of pure titanium white on the side. Glass wasn't easy to paint, with its glares and shadows, but snow was even harder unless it was lying on a tree or hiding in the crevices of the rock formations.

Next she put a tiny bit of cobalt blue in the corner of her palette. Snow was cold and the blue mixed with lots of white would create the icy shadows in the angel's wings. The cardinal would require red light hue and a dot of pure black for around his eyes and under his fluffed out feathers. She glanced at the window and added colors for the mistletoe and the valance that Grand had put up in the past two weeks.

Sage almost giggled out loud. There it was! Living proof in the form of a kitchen window valance. Grand wouldn't sell out, not when she'd put up the Christmas curtain, the one with the poinsettias embroidered on the border. If she was really going to sell, she would have taken that valance with her because her mother had done the stitching on it and it was one of her most prized possessions.

She dipped a brush into the paint and started working on the poinsettias in the valance, happiness filling her heart as much as the soup had taken care of her hunger. Painting was good for Sage's soul. That day she painted because she was all happy that the paint gods had smiled on her and given her an inspiration for a new picture and that she had no worries.

She felt a little bit sorry for Creed. It wasn't his fault. He wanted a ranch and Grand had set a price so low that any cowboy in the whole canyon would have jumped on it with both boots.

At least the painting had taken her mind off Creed and his sexy eyes.

"It's an angel," Creed said.

She jumped when he spoke. Did he read minds? If so, did he know that she'd been thinking about his sexy eyes?

"You can see it?" she asked.

"How could I not see it? It's an angel in the swirling snow and it's looking at the little cardinal on the outside and the mistletoe on the sill there. Where did you get three pieces, anyway?"

"You brought them in with you. I guess the wind blew a bunch down from one of the scrub oak trees. One piece was stuck on your shoulder when you came in the first time. Then you tracked the other two inside."

"We'll tie a red ribbon around them and hang them up for the holidays. When are we putting up the tree?"

"Well, it won't be today, will it?"

"Don't get all cranky on me, lady."

"Statin' facts. Not bein' cranky."

"You do put up a tree, don't you?"

"Yes, we do. A big real cedar tree and we decorate the whole house even if just me and Grand are the only ones who see it. She might be gone this year until the last minute, but I'll have the whole place decorated up by the time she gets home."

Creed laid his book aside. "I love Christmas. Momma sends me and Dalton and Blake to the woods the day after Thanksgiving while she and my brothers' wives do the Black Friday shopping. That night everyone comes home for leftovers from Thanksgiving dinner and we decorate the tree. I won't be there this year, but we can find a cedar tree and start our own tradition right here."

There was that word again, or at least a derivative of it.

Us. We. Our.

They all meant a joining of minds to form relationships, friendships, or otherwise. How could things change so quickly? Wasn't she fighting against it with all her soul and heart?

"If this wind doesn't stop we might have to dig a tree out from under the drifts before we could even cut it down," she said and went back to painting.

"It's doable. When it does stop we'll go find just the right one and we'll drag it in here, snow and all. These floors will mop up, and the branches would soon dry in the warm room. Did you ever wish you'd grown up in a big family atmosphere?" he asked.

"All the time," she said wistfully as she carefully dotted in the angel's eyes with her smallest brush. "You'll miss them if you stay, Creed. The canyon is a lonely place."

"But it's peaceful and that doesn't come cheap. And lonely is just a state of mind. Sometimes peace can override lonely if…" He stopped.

"Go on."

"I was engaged a while back. Head over heels in love with a woman named Macy. She went on a trip and when she came home she said she didn't really love me. She loved the idea of being in love, but she didn't think she'd ever really loved me. Turned out she'd met someone else that she did love on that trip. The engagement was over and I kept asking myself what I could have done different. This place has brought me the first peace I've known since then."

Sage's heart stopped. After that confession, how could she push him out of the canyon? Or maybe he was just playing her so that she wouldn't put up a fight for her grandmother to back out of the sale. He said he always told the truth and could be trusted, but saying and doing were often two horses of very different colors.

"Well?" he said.

"At least she was honest," Sage said.

"Yes, she was."

"It is peaceful here if you don't mind the solitude. Grand is an old hermit. She won't ever like being cooped up in a house with her sister or living in a congested part of the world."

"I thought her sister had a farm."

"Five acres. One old two-story house. A barn. Two cows, some chickens, and an apple orchard. Not much of a farm really."

"And is it in the middle of a big town?"

"Shade Gap is a rural community. Barely even anything left there except for a gas station and a picnic ground."

"Sounds like she'd be real happy there. As for me, there are cows, hogs, chickens, and when there is electricity there's good country music to listen to. And now Noel is here and there will be puppies."

"What happens when her owner comes to take her home?"

Creed looked at the poor skinny dog. "No one is coming to claim her, Sage. She's a castoff that someone tossed out before the storm hit. She's probably been living on field mice for a week and sleeping in barns. She's too skinny to have been thrown away just before the blizzard hit. She's found a home and a friend in you. Darlin', she ain't goin' nowhere."

Sage laid her brush down and scratched Noel's ears. "Stop callin' me darlin'. I'm not and I will never be your darlin'."

"It's just my way and I'm not changing," he said.

As if Noel understood that men were strange creatures who couldn't be reasoned with, she wagged her tail so hard that it sounded like a drumbeat on the hardwood floor.

"Look, Creed! I swear she smiled."

"Dogs do that when they're happy, just like humans."

Sage rubbed her fur and said, "You're a good girl. I bet you were raised on Venus with the rest of us girls and not on Mars with a bunch of mean old boys."

"I read that book," Creed said.

Sage turned her head so quickly that her neck cracked. "Why would a cowboy like you read that book?"

"Because my brother's wife mentioned it and because I wanted to understand why women are the way they are."

"Did you learn anything?" she asked.

He shook his head. "Not much. Just that y'all are temperamental. That y'all approach things you can't change with anger or tears. And that to really understand a woman is impossible."

He changed the subject abruptly. "Wonder what the puppies will look like? Maybe they'll have some old redbone in them."

"Not a chance. Noel wouldn't fall in love with a hun-tin' hound. She's going to have Irish setter puppies or maybe even beagles, but not an old coonhound, are you, baby girl?" Sage kissed the dog between the eyes and went back to her painting.

It was nearly time for chores and the storm had gotten even worse. Sage finished what she was working on and cleaned her brushes. She went to the kitchen and put a pan of milk on a burner to heat for hot chocolate, took down the cocoa and sugar and marshmallows, and then reached for two mugs.

She lit two oil lamps, carried one to the end table beside the sofa, and put the other one in the middle of the kitchen table. That brought precious little light into the room, but it beat trying to do anything in the darkness. After supper she'd scrounge around in the pantry for candles or more lamps so they could have one in each bedroom and the bathroom.

And matches! She'd need to put them beside the lamps so they could reach them without fumbling around and knocking off the lamp. Grand would be really mad if they wasted expensive lamp oil.

Creed looked up from his book when she set the mug of hot chocolate on the table beside him and said, "Thank you. That looks good."

"I thought we'd need a warm pick-me-up before we went out to feed. I'll gather the eggs and feed the hogs if you'll milk the cow. I hate milking and I'm so slow the milk will freeze in the bucket before I ever get the job done," she said.

"It's not in the contract that you have to help with chores," he said.

"You helped cook. I'll help with the outside work."

"I don't turn down willing help."

Willing or otherwise, she would help him because it

was fair. It wasn't fair at all that she had an almost instant attraction to the very man she had been determined not to like at all.

Sage was not innocent. She was twenty-six and she'd had a couple of relationships. There was Victor, a fellow art student in college that lasted at least six months before he accused her of being afraid of commitment. Then there was Justin who'd worked for Lawton four years ago who accused her of the same thing. True, it had been a long time since she'd been to bed with a man, but she wasn't a casual sex woman. If there wasn't something there beyond a one-night romp in the hay, she wasn't interested. But the honest truth was that she could never remember any man in her past that had created the stir in her heart like Creed had that day.

She finished her chocolate and Noel followed her to her room.

"You ready to go back out, are you? Well, you wear your fur coat. I have to get my insulated coveralls on before I can go," she said.

Sage removed her sweat suit, pulled on long thermal underwear, and then put her sweats back on, along with two pair of wool socks and a mustard-colored coverall much like Creed's. She zipped it up the front, jammed her feet down into work boots, and picked up her face mask and gloves.

When she reached the kitchen, Creed was putting on his boots.

"Ready to brave it?" he asked.

"I'm ready," she answered.

Noel barked and danced around the back door.

"Oh, no, young lady. You can't go out in that kind of weather," Creed said.

"You'd best let her go if she wants to. She's been inside all day. I bet her bladder is about to explode. Don't you know that pregnant women have to go a lot?" Sage said and then stopped before she opened the door. "You don't think she'll run away, do you?"

"She knows where the food is."

The minute she could get out, Noel disappeared in the snow, chasing around like a puppy.

Sage bent into the wind and went straight for the barn. She filled two buckets with feed for the hogs and carried them to their trough. It was easy to fill without going into the lot. Just open up a trap door on the back of their shed and pour the feed in. That done, she braved the biting snow back to the barn.

"Hey, give me a hand here. I'm thinking if we leave the back door of the barn open, we can shove one of these big round bales into it and it will stay dry longer. The lean-to will keep the snow from drifting up against it. If the barn was bigger, I'd just open it up and bring the cattle all inside."

"Poor old cows, but they are better off in the lot than they'd be out in the canyon," Sage said.

"At least this way their hay will be dry. Open the doors when I get close."

It was an ingenious idea. The hay was wedged into the space so the cows couldn't get into the barn. The lean-to kept the snow from blowing into it so the cattle at least had dry hay, even if it was cold. If they had Dutch doors they could shove a big round bale of hay in the bottom and shut the top doors. She'd have to remember to talk to Grand about that when she got home.

Creed hopped off the tractor and said, "Now to the milking."

"And to the eggs. Meet you in the house... did you hear that?"

"What?"

She cocked her head to one side. "It sounded like a baby crying."

The cattle were eating and the ones who couldn't get to the hay were fussing about having to wait. The milk cow was putting up a bawling fit about her full udder, and Noel had joined them in the barn. She cocked her head to one side and sniffed the air.

"Shhh, there it is again," Sage said.

Creed turned his ear toward the empty stall behind Sage.

"I don't hear a thing. You sure it's not the wind?"

She listened intently. "No, it's coming from the stall next to the cow."

Creed took a step in that direction. "I'd say it is kittens, but it's the wrong season. Cats don't usually have babies in the winter because they don't survive."

"We don't have cats."

Creed opened the door and pointed. "You do now. Those are newborn kittens right there. Recognize the big old yellow mother?"

Sage dropped down on her knees and moved the mother cat to one side. "There are three of them and I've never seen any of these animals before."

Noel plowed right into the stall and touched noses with the momma cat. She purred when Noel nosed each of the newborn kittens.

Creed smiled. "Would you look at that? She's not afraid of the dog and Noel isn't killing kittens. Those two are friends. There ain't no doubt about it. A normal momma cat would have scratched a dog's eyes out if she'd gotten close to her babies, but they know each other. They were probably hauled off at the same time. Looks like it's a two-for-one day for you, Sage. You get a cat and a dog and you're going to get Christmas presents early in the way of kittens and puppies. I can put some warm milk in a pan for her when I do the milking."

"They'll freeze out here, Creed. We'll have to take them inside or they'll be dead by morning," Sage said.

"They are out of season for sure. Cats usually don't have litters until the spring and then maybe another in the fall, but not in December. Looks of them, they were just born today, and you are right, they won't live in this kind of cold."

"The only thing to do is take them in the house. We can make a litter pan out of an old dishpan if you'll bring in a bucket of dirt from the barn floor. I wonder how long she's been in the barn."

Creed grinned. "Evidently she's been here long enough to have babies. Do you want to carry her and the kittens in the house or get the eggs?"

"I'll get the eggs. I'd be afraid I'd drop one of those little things in the snow and it would freeze to death before I could find it."

"Then I'll take her and the kittens inside and come back to finish my end of the chores," he said.

She'd gathered four eggs and was already in the house when she realized that she'd obeyed his orders without even thinking.

"Well, shit!" she said as she washed the eggs and put them into containers to go into the refrigerator.

What a day!

First no Grand.

Then a cowboy and a dog and mistletoe everywhere.

That was more than enough for one day, but then the angel appeared along with the cardinal. And now cats!

And this was just day one. There were twenty more to go.

Creed came in right behind her, a momma cat's head poking out of his coveralls at chest level. "She's a good cat. She didn't even scratch me when I zipped up to just under her chin. She knows I'm bringing her into a warm place."

"Noel told her when she bumped noses with her that we were good folks," Sage said.

"Got a basket and a towel or another old blanket?" Creed asked before he removed the cat from inside his coveralls.

Sage grabbed an extra plastic laundry basket from the pantry and hurried back to the hallway to find a blanket in the linen closet. When she returned he unzipped to his waist and handed her the yellow momma cat. She was nothing but an armful of bones and long fur.

"Good grief, Creed, she's skinny. Her hair made her look like she was chubby, but I can feel her ribs."

"She and Noel have been on the run for a while. I told you I bet they were dropped at least a week ago and they've been living on whatever they could scrounge up."

"Where are the kittens?" Sage asked.

Creed pulled two black ones from one pocket and a yellow one from the other. He laid them gently in the basket and Sage put the momma in with them.

"Think she's hungry?" Sage asked.

"Probably half starved, but we've got lots of milk. Give me a few minutes and she can even have it warm right from the cow. Whip up a couple of those fresh eggs to go in it for extra protein and she'll love it."

Noel checked out the cat and kittens, then went straight for her own blanket.

"Whoever dumped them should be shot," Sage grouched.

"It happens, but they've got a good home now, don't they? I'm going back out and milk before I get too warm in all these layers. See you in a few minutes," Creed said.

The door opened, a blast of cold air swept across the floor, and then it closed again.

"Yes, you do have a good home now. Don't you worry, momma cat. We won't let your babies die." Sage removed her coveralls and hung them up, cleaned the water from the floor again, and went straight to the living room. She shoved two more logs into the fireplace and sat down on the floor between the animals.

"I didn't even want pets. So what makes the difference?" she said aloud.

I wanted you to have a pet because you needed something to love that wouldn't leave you. Looks like you got them because they needed you. It was Grand's voice again but Sage just nodded in agreement. *Could be that the cowboy needs you too.*

Sage set her mouth firmly and said, "Now that is enough."

Noel looked up and whimpered.

"I wasn't talking to you. You can stay as long as you

like. There's lots of room on the ranch for your puppies. And your friend and her babies can live in the barn when the cold weather passes and it's warm enough to put them out there."

"What did you name her?" Creed asked when he returned half an hour later, a bucket of milk in one hand and a bucket of dirt in the other.

Sage looked from man to cat and back again.

"Well?" Creed poured the cold dirt into the old rusted dishpan.

"What makes you think I named her?"

"You did. I can see it in your face. Why didn't you have pets before now? You love animals."

"No I don't," she argued. "Pets just die and leave you all lonely again anyway. And who knows if these are really strays. Their owners might come looking for them soon as the weather clears up."

"I doubt it. Most folks wouldn't go out looking for a pregnant cat or an ugly dog, and you didn't answer me."

"Like I just said, pets either run off or die and I'd be left with the pain of it."

"Better to have loved and hurt than never to have loved at all," he quipped.

"Oh, so now you are a prophet?" she shot back at him.

"No, ma'am. Not me. I'm not that smart on a good day, and this one has been real strange in my world."

"You damn sure got that right." Sage whipped up several eggs and added warm milk to them. Noel saw her pick up the pie pan and came running so fast that she lost traction and slid the last five feet on her belly.

Creed looked at Sage and they both burst out in laughter.

"And that's why we have pets!" he finally said. "They

make us laugh and give us something to pet and to tell all our secrets to without worrying that they'll ever tell a living soul."

Sage was still giggling so hard that the milk sloshed when she picked up the pan. "You're going to have to set it down, Creed. I'll spill it."

He reached around her to pick up the pan and suddenly they were face to face, noses barely inches away from each other. She could have gotten lost in his green eyes, which were staring so intently into hers. His lips parted slightly and her tongue instinctively wet her dry lips in anticipation of the kiss. She was a boiling pot of desire just wanting to feel his mouth on hers.

———∞———

Creed wanted to taste those luscious lips more than he'd wanted to kiss any other woman in his life. When she moistened her full lips he could hardly wait for the sizzle that they promised. She had shut her eyes and was leaning in toward him when Noel jumped between them and her paws landed on Sage's hip bones.

Sage's eyes popped open.

Creed took a step back so she could see that he didn't have his hands in that place.

Sage blushed and mumbled something about Noel being hungry.

He set the pan on the floor and turned around to remove his coveralls for the umpteenth time that day.

"Guess she likes her milk," Sage said.

"Looks like it."

"How am I going to get Angel fed without Noel drinking her supper too?"

Creed chuckled. "I figured you'd name her Mary since she had babies in the manger because there was no room in the inn."

"I thought about it, but a cat shouldn't be named after Jesus's momma. I'm not one for making God mad in the middle of a blizzard. Besides, all that fluffy hair reminds me of angel wings."

He pointed. "Look."

The cat and dog were sharing the pan of milk.

"I told you they were friends," Creed said.

Sage was afraid the "almost-kiss" would be an elephant in the room all evening, but it wasn't. They had soup again for supper and she actually felt like she'd known Creed forever. He could be an outlaw or a serial killer. Just because he'd charmed his way past Grand didn't mean that he was the greatest thing since ice cream on a stick. She shouldn't trust him and it riled her that she did.

Before Sage trusted anyone she had to know them a long time, but there she was laughing and talking to him as if they'd both grown up on the Rockin' C. She was supposed to be making him miserable, not befriending him.

At the supper table, Noel begged and whined. When they set a pie pan of soup and corn bread on the floor Angel joined her again.

"She's even eating carrots, Creed."

He leaned over so he could see the animals. "Which one?"

"Angel is eating carrots and peas."

"She's hungry," Creed said. "Poor little thing probably thinks she's died and gone to heaven."

Grand's voice whispered into her ear, *He's a good man*.

She wanted to argue with her grandmother, but her heart said that Grand was right. Creed was a good man. He could be trusted. He just wasn't the right man for the Rockin' C.

When she slipped into her bed that night she laced her hands behind her head and stared at the dark ceiling. It had been the strangest day of her entire life. Maybe it was because she didn't have a telephone or a laptop, and the only person she could talk to was Creed. Maybe those three pieces of mistletoe really were an omen.

Whatever it was, she sure hoped the next day wasn't a repeat, because it was confusing the hell out of her. She touched her lips and felt cheated. She'd wanted that kiss to see if she really was attracted to the cowboy or if it was just a simple proximity issue. Close by. Nothing to do but think about those sexy eyes and dark hair. Cooking together. Working side by side. Cats with babies. Pregnant dogs. All combined, it would knock a hole in any woman's hormones.

Chapter 4

GOING TO BED BEFORE NINE O'CLOCK MADE FOR AN early morning. Creed looked at the clock beside his bed at four o'clock. He rolled over and pulled the window curtain back. The snow was still falling just as hard and fast as it had been when he went to bed. The wind whirled down the canyon walls turning the naked mesquite and scrub oak limbs into musical instruments that hummed something like Christmas carols.

There was no going back to sleep no matter how tightly he closed his eyes or beat on his pillow, so finally he crawled out, padded into the kitchen, and put on a pot of coffee. While it perked, he dressed for chores. He turned the gas off from under it just before he and Noel went out the back door. If Sage got up early, it would be ready. If she didn't, it would still be hot when he brought the milk inside.

The hay was half gone, but there was enough to keep the cattle happy until nightfall. He shoved the rest of the bale out into the lean-to and shut the doors tightly behind it. He fed the hogs, gathered the eggs, and then milked the cow.

Sage still wasn't awake when he took the milk inside, so he strained it and put it away. And that's when the cranky mood hit him. If he was home in Ringgold during a snowstorm, he'd spend time in the tack room or in the barn working on equipment. Or he'd go up to the

Chicken Fried Café and talk to the other ranchers in the area. One day was his limit when it came to sitting still all day and he damn sure didn't look forward to day two of it.

He poured a cup of coffee but didn't strip out of his outdoor clothing. Instead he carried the cup with him to the back door and turned to look at Noel. She'd huddled down into her blanket with a paw over her nose. It didn't look like she had any intentions of going back out into the storm, so he went without her.

He eased into the barn and shut the door behind him, lit two Coleman lanterns, and grabbed a wide push broom. Part of the barn floor was dirt, but the major-ity of it was concrete and it was strewn with hay. He leaned on the broom and noticed that the small hay bales needed straightening. He set the broom to one side and went to work on them. Anything to work the crabbi-ness out; and it had nothing to do with the fact that he'd missed getting a kiss he wanted or that he'd dreamed of Sage all night.

He'd come to the Panhandle to get away from all women, not to be mesmerized by one female.

Sage didn't have to wait for the grumpy mood to hit her. She awoke with it already in full swing. Not even hot coffee waiting on the back of the stove relieved the antsy feeling in her chest. Usually when she got like this she took her paints, and a bologna sandwich, and went to the back side of the canyon to paint from daylight to dark. But that wasn't possible in a snowstorm.

She rubbed Angel's fur and scratched Noel's ears, but

that didn't help. She wanted Creed to get up and talk to her. That's when she noticed the milk bucket in the dish drainer and the cheesecloth strainer was draped over it, so Creed had been up long enough to do the chores.

Where was he? If the chores were done, why wasn't he back in the house? Had one day with her been all he could stand? Was he inching his way up out of the canyon in his truck on his way back to greener pastures?

She stepped into her coveralls and put her boots on, picked up an old felt hat of Grand's, and slung the door open. Noel didn't make a move, so evidently she'd already been out that morning.

She found him stacking hay. The barn floor was clean enough to eat off of and smelled fresh instead of like two-day-old cow crap. "You plannin' on eatin' breakfast this morning?"

He didn't look around or slow down. "Is it ready?"

"Hell, no!"

"Then I don't guess I'm ready to eat."

"Who pissed in your coffee this morning?" she asked.

"Same four-legged critter that pissed in yours, I have a suspicion."

She popped her gloved hands on her hips and asked, "You are mad at the animals? What did they do?"

"Think about it," he answered without stopping work.

She grabbed him by the arm and swung him around. "I wanted that kiss too, but you damn sure didn't try a second time, so don't be blamin' the dog."

A smile tickled the corners of his mouth. He swiped his felt hat off with a flourish, tossed it on a hay bale, and drew her close with one arm. "If that pesky dog jumps up on us, ignore it."

"Yes, sir!" she said breathlessly as he ran the back of his rough hand down her cheek and tangled his hands in her dark hair.

His lips met hers in a fiery clash with enough heat to melt every drop of snow in the canyon. Tongue met tongue in a mating dance that left them both breathless and still wanting more. She'd had passionate kisses before, but Creed wasn't just kissing her, he was making love to her with his lips and tongue. She could actually feel her boots leave the cold concrete floor and float toward the rafters.

He drew back and she thought he mumbled her name, but it could have just been a moan like what came from her throat when he nuzzled inside the collar of the coveralls and strung kisses from her ear all the way back to her lips.

That kiss was even hotter than the first one. She tried to think of a kiss in the past that had turned her knees to jelly and erased every sane thought from her mind. But her mind had shut down and her body had taken over. The fickle thing wanted to sling all its clothing off and feel more than Creed Riley's hands on her neck and his body pressed to hers so tight that even the north wind couldn't find a way to get between them.

She'd had kisses, but she'd never had one that made her completely crazy with want. She'd have to keep her distance from him for sure because if one make-out session in a freezing cold barn could create so much heat, they'd burn the house down if they ever tumbled into a bed.

Or better yet, wrapped up in a blanket in front of the fire, she thought and then blushed at the visual of him naked with the fire reflecting in his green eyes.

When he pulled back the second time she inhaled deeply and laid her head on his chest. Even through all the layers she could hear his heart thumping like he'd run a mile in hundred-degree heat.

She tried to force her feet to take a step backwards, but her feet were glued to the barn floor. She was a grown woman, not a hormonal sixteen-year-old girl who chased down good-looking cowboys in the barn to steal a few kisses. And as such, she had to step back, walk away, and not look back. Falling for Creed Riley would be disaster.

One day, for God's sake! That's all I've known this man.

The argument began with common sense and her heart taking opposing sides.

You've been waiting for Creed Riley your whole life. How big is that hole right now? her heart asked.

Hush! He won't stick around here past Christmas, common sense said.

She never knew a heart could talk until she heard it say loud and clear, *I want Creed Riley for my Christmas present.*

Dammit! common sense yelled. *Don't listen to that worthless organ in your chest. You can't have Creed and Grand both, and remember who's been there for you your whole life.*

Creed hugged her tightly and said, "Well, that made me hungry. Matter-of-fact, I'm starving. Let's go cook breakfast and check on the livestock in the house."

Sage looked up at him.

Where in the hell had that crazy fool notion of wanting Creed for Christmas come from? It was just a kiss and she'd only known him for a day. The blizzard must have frozen the part of her brain that made adult, sensible decisions.

It wasn't until then that she realized she had unzipped his coveralls and her hands were warming against the warm flannel of his shirt. No wonder she could hear his heart beating so well! She withdrew them and brought a full load of guilt with her. She could not, she would not kiss him again.

"I'm not grumpy anymore." He grinned.

She removed her hands and he zipped his coveralls. "Me either, but I am hungry."

Creed's stomach growled, but food was the last thing on his mind. He could not fall for Sage Presley, not now. Maybe later on down the road it could happen, after he'd bought the ranch and they really got to know each other. And besides, Creed did not believe in that love at first sight shit.

It was the snowstorm causing all the crazy emotions between them. He was excited about finally finding just the right ranch and getting it for such a good price. He would just blame the whole thing on Christmas. For the past two years he'd searched for a ranch that he could afford and that had the right feel. And now he'd found it at the beginning of the season. It stood to reason that after growing up on a ranch with a big family, he'd get a silly notion like that in his head too.

The place had to have some kind of voodoo magic to make him fall prey to Sage's charms. There wasn't a doubt in his mind she had something up her sleeve that had to do with her grandmother changing her mind. He'd have to be very careful or else he'd be right back looking for a place of his own again if Ada Presley came home and listened to her granddaughter.

He'd just let things get to him. He'd been bored with only chores to keep him busy and it had been a long, long time since he'd wrapped his arms around a woman. Pregnant dog, new baby kittens, cooking together, and sharing meals—it all combined to put thoughts of a family into his mind.

Creed had a lot of work to do before he could entertain notions of a family. He'd arrived at the ranch with the idea etched in solid granite that he'd given up on all women. That he'd dance with them, do a little flirting, and enjoy a one-night stand a few times a year. But in the end, he'd be the old bachelor uncle who lived out in Palo Duro Canyon that all the nieces and nephews adored. There were six other Riley sons. The three older ones had families. Ace and Jasmine were already pregnant and it was going to be a girl, so Creed's momma was happy. And Dalton and Blake were out there scanning the mesquite bushes for a woman. It wouldn't be long until they'd have one cornered and wedding bells would be ringing. He didn't need to produce a Riley to keep the name going, and he didn't want another heartbreak.

He stomped what snow he could off his feet and slung open the back door. Noel danced around Sage's feet as she kicked off her boots and unzipped her coveralls. Angel peeked up over the edge of her basket and then curled up again. Sage reached over and picked a piece of mistletoe from off his shoulder.

"This stuff thinks you are an oak tree." She smiled.

"It must be blowing off the scrub oaks. I swear if they brought an instrument to measure the wind that would be a snow tornado out there. The wind is as bad if not worse than the actual snow."

She dried the mistletoe and laid it on the shelf with the other pieces. "It does feel like that with the hard wind, don't it? If you keep growing this, we won't have to go looking for any to hang up for the holidays."

Just moments before she'd unzipped his coveralls to the waist and slipped her hands inside to hug him tighter. His poor heart had about stopped in anticipation of where those hands might be headed, but they'd splayed out on his chest and stayed there. He'd wished she would go a layer deeper and pull his shirt out from his belt and put skin on skin. Frostbite would have been worth it to feel those long slender fingers all stretched out on his abs.

Now she was talking about mistletoe as if the kisses never happened at all.

"At least we'll have plenty to tie up with a bow and put over the doorway," he said.

If she wanted to ignore the kiss, then he could do the same thing.

———

When Sage painted she concentrated on the underlying message of her picture while she carefully built dimension upon dimension to bring out depth and character.

Anyone can color a page in a coloring book.

That's what her art teacher told them the first day she had walked into his class as a sophomore in high school. He'd seen something in her raw ability and had fussed at her for three years, critiquing and pressuring her to do better and better until she'd gotten the fantastic opportunity to study art in college.

Two years later she'd had all she wanted. She wanted to paint, not write creative English papers for the basic classes she had to take. So she quit and came home to the canyon. Grand supported her decision without a single negative remark. Four years later her bank account was substantial and she was doing exactly what she loved to do.

That morning she stood in front of the painting of the kitchen window and studied it. The angel was there, hiding in the snow. The little cardinal was on the window ledge, details in the way his feathers fluffed out against the cold. The next step was his eyes. She looked back at the window and either the original cardinal or one just like him flew out of the white flakes to land there again. Only this time he brought his mate, a female cardinal, with him to take a peek inside the house.

They stared into each other's eyes for several seconds before they took flight. Sage looked back at the picture on the easel. It wouldn't be difficult at all to put the female in the picture. The part of the picture where she would be was as yet unfinished. Sage picked up a tiny outline brush and painted the male cardinal's eyes. The critics might not see the love at first glance. They might only see four panes in each of the upper and lower windows with a snowstorm in the background. Maybe after close scrutiny, they'd see the whole story and it would touch their hearts.

She was tempted to rush, but she forced herself to slow down, to shut her eyes several times and get the female bird's part in the picture just right. Even though her colors weren't as brilliant as her counterpart's, and even though the wood between the panes separated them, she was his choice. And the angel was smiling down on them.

When both birds were to her satisfaction, she picked up the brush to paint in the mistletoe. She glanced back at the window and suddenly in her mind's eye the mistletoe wasn't lying on the sill but was tied up together with a bright red satin ribbon and hanging from the bottom of the poinsettia valance.

She blinked and it was back on the windowsill, but Sage Presley did not argue with her visions. If the gods said that she should hang the mistletoe then she would do just that. The times when she'd done what she wanted rather than what her visions gave her, those paintings had been a big flop. When she listened, the critics went wild with what she produced.

<hr>

Creed and Noel played tug-of-war with an old wash rag he'd found in the scrub bucket. Creed held onto the rag with his hand and Noel pulled against it with all her might using her teeth. Even while he played, he kept a steady watch on the picture's progress. He didn't know jack shit about good art versus bad art. But the canvas on the easel was alive with color and motion. Two birds on the windowsill, feathers fluffed out against the cold wind, the promise of warmth behind the thin glass, mistletoe and poinsettias and an angel floating in the background.

When Sage painted the mistletoe above the cardinal's

head, Creed could actually feel the painting. He couldn't have put a single thought into words, but it touched all the senses. He imagined one hand on the outside of the window and the other on the inside. One cold. One hot. He could taste the snowflakes on his lips, and the mistletoe reminded him of the kiss he and Sage had shared.

Lots of kisses were shared under the mistletoe during the Christmas season. He'd seen posters about Jesus being the reason for the season. If he turned it around maybe the season was the reason he felt such an attraction to Sage when she was definitely not the type that usually caught his eye.

—␣—

Sage signed her name to the bottom of the picture, removed it from the easel, and carried it across the room where she hung it on two screws in a bare spot.

"Why'd you put it right there?" Creed asked.

"That's where my work dries."

"Now what?" Creed asked.

She pulled the rocking chair away from the fireplace and parked it in front of the picture. "I study it to determine what I could have done better. I look at it through the critic's eye and the buyer's. Then I decide if I'm going to burn it or put it with my stash to take to the gallery."

"Good God, Sage! You've worked on that thing for hours and hours. Surely you wouldn't burn it," Creed said.

"What would you do if you were riding a horse, one that you'd raised yourself from birth, one you'd broken to the saddle and who'd carried you through a blizzard to a warm house, and he stepped in a hole and snapped his leg bone so badly that it stuck out of the skin and it could never be fixed? Would you shoot him to put him out of his misery or let him lie there in excruciating pain?"

"It would break my heart, but I'd shoot him," Creed said.

"That's my point. I'd rather burn it than take something that looks like a second grader's coloring book page to a gallery showing. And this picture scares me. I've never painted anything that quickly."

Creed gave the cleaning rag to Noel and pulled his rocking chair over close to Sage's chair. He reached across the distance separating them and laid his hand on hers and together they studied the painting.

"What do you see?" she asked finally.

"I'm not a critic. I don't know how long a masterpiece is supposed to take from start to finish. Hell, my momma thinks the prettiest picture in her house is a velvet Elvis that Daddy bought for her when they visited Graceland for their twenty-fifth wedding anniversary. It hangs above her bed and there's never a spot of dust on it."

"Surely you see something," she said.

Creed took a deep breath and told her the emotions it had evoked in him when she was painting the mistletoe.

"And you say you aren't a critic." She smiled. "It's just that I've never painted snow before. I'm building a reputation as a Western artist."

He pointed to the picture hanging above the credenza just inside the front door. "Like that?"

She nodded. "What do you see in that one?"

"I see the big rock formation over on the backside of the property. And the way the top is eroded, it looks like an old cowboy without his hat. His neck is sagging with age and his eyebrows have drooped. His face is fuller and wider than it would have been in his youth, but there's character there and lessons he could teach a grandchild."

"Wow!" She pulled her hand from his and hugged herself.

"Do I get an A?"

"A-plus. Are there any similarities in the pictures?" she pressed on.

"Oh, yeah!" He pointed to the one above the sofa again. "That one is fall and the end of life is near for the old cowboy. The one you painted is right now and there's a beginning for those two birds if they survive the cold. He'd like to kiss her under the mistletoe, but his little beak is frozen." Creed chuckled at his own joke.

"Then you could tell that the same artist painted them?" she asked.

Creed studied one picture and then the other. They were so different that his first thought was no one would ever know that Sage Presley had done both. But that first impression was totally wrong. It was very evident that she'd done both pictures.

"Well?"

"Give me a minute to put my words together. And while I'm doing that, Sage, you should be building a career as an artist, period, not solely as a Western artist. Paint life. It will sell because people will feel it."

"It's just that I've never finished a picture, even a small one, this fast and it scares me. I usually do six a year, maybe eight on a very good year."

"Okay, does size mean anything to a critic? Is bigger better?" he asked.

She giggled nervously. "Are we still talking about paintings?"

He laughed with her. "For now, we definitely are."

"Then the answer is no. Size is not a factor."

"You won't think I'm a sissy if I tell you my honest opinion, will you?" Creed asked.

She shook her head.

He ran his fingers through his dark hair. Men weren't supposed to see feelings or feel emotion or pain and they damn sure weren't supposed to discuss any of the above. That was women's business when they got together for a hen session.

He cleared his throat and started, "What I see is emotion, Sage. It's not just pretty pictures that you paint. It is feelings. Momma says that when she looks at her velvet Elvis she remembers the wonderful second honeymoon she and Daddy had. To her that is pure art. When I look at these two pictures, I see that old cowboy not caring that his days are up and time is short before the cold winter takes him away from this world. But there's a smile on his face and he's taking a whole passel of memories with him to the other side. In the other one I see the promise of spring, birds singing as they build a nest, and life buds once again in spite of the terrible storm. I feel warmth inside the window and sympathy for the poor little birds that are so cold. The angel promises protection if they'll remember the love of the season. That curtain thing is old so it's representative of the past. The angel is the promise of an eternal future."

When he looked over at Sage, tears were flowing down her cheeks. "Those are the most beautiful words I've ever heard."

Heat crawled up his back and he felt the sting of a blush on his cheeks. Creed could not remember the last time he'd blushed.

She squeezed his hand. "Thank you. I won't burn it and I'm going to paint more like it."

Angel hopped down from the window and ran across the room, landed in Sage's lap with a thud, and looked up at her. Sage pulled her hand away from Creed's and stroked the cat's long fur while she continued to look at the picture.

"She's purring, Creed. I think she's thanking us for the milk and food," she said.

———⁓———

Creed grinned.

Us.

She had said us.

Some miracles weren't instant. Some of them took a while in coming around.

Noel left the business of tearing up the rag and joined the family, putting her paws on the edge of Creed's rocking chair.

"Feeling left out, are you?" Creed scratched her ears.

"Didn't take them long to make themselves at home, did it?" Sage said.

"I think the children are asking you to do a portrait of them."

Sage laughed. "They aren't my children. I'm not even sure they'll be my pets. When the storm clears and they can go outside, they could easily go right on down the road on their journey."

"I doubt that Angel will leave her babies or Noel

either when she has them. Did you ever think about a husband and children?" he asked abruptly.

Sage bit her lower lip for several seconds.

Now why in the hell had he asked that question, Creed wondered. It was too personal and would kill the miracle that had barely gotten a foothold in her heart. Maybe she didn't even hear him ask. Hopefully she'd been studying her art so intensely she'd blocked out everything else.

Finally she answered. "That is a scary thought, Creed. My dad died and my mother's heart was broken as well as Grand's. Daddy was her only child. He and Momma were high school sweethearts and married before he went off to the Army. She went with him as soon as she could and I was born a few years later."

"So you have a fear of commitment?" he asked.

"Don't say that."

"Why?"

"I've heard it before and I don't have any fears. I'm just a careful woman. Fear is one thing. Caution is another. Besides, if I had a fear it wouldn't be of commitment, it would be of abandonment and Grand ain't helping one damn bit in that business."

"Well, I'm honest enough to say that I have the big C-word fear. It's the only thing that makes me shake in my boots. After my fiancée pulled off her stunt, I'm gun-shy when it comes to relationships."

"You? I don't believe it!"

"Believe it, darlin'. I'm a flirt but when it comes to trusting anyone enough to give them my whole heart to put through a meat grinder, well, that's another matter."

"Guess we make a pretty damn good pair to get stuck in a blizzard together," she said.

Chapter 5

"WELL, DAMMIT ALL TO HELL ON A RUSTY POKER," Ada fussed.

"Burned another pan full, did you?" Essie giggled.

"Damn sure did. Guess we'll only be takin' three dozen to the canasta game tonight."

"I reckon that'll be plenty. Everyone else will bring cookies too. You wouldn't burn them if you'd stop your worrywartin'."

Ada tucked her salt-and-pepper hair behind her ears. She and Esther had been born in southern Oklahoma to a father with Chickasaw blood and a red-haired Irish mother. Esther had gotten the red hair and green eyes, but she was as mild tempered as a gentle southern breeze. Ada inherited the dark hair and dark eyes and had a temper like a tornado and a hurricane meeting head-on with a Texas wildfire.

Essie had just passed her eighty-sixth birthday and Ada was over seventy. They hadn't grown up together or known each other as sisters until later in life because Essie married when Ada was only two years old.

It had been love at first sight between Esther and Richard Langston. He had come to Ravia, Oklahoma, for Christmas dinner with one of his buddies on the WPA project. That afternoon he'd met Esther who was literally the girl who lived next door to his buddy and three months later when he went home to Pennsylvania to take over the farm when his father died, Essie went with him.

Sixteen years later, Thomas Presley came to Ravia from Fort Sill with a friend for a long weekend. There was a birthday party that summer for his fellow army buddy and Ada had been invited. When Thomas finished his enlistment the following year, she went with him to the Palo Duro Canyon.

"Momma was a worrywart. She worried about you all the time," Ada said.

Essie tidied up a bun at the nape of her neck. It was smaller than it used to be in her youth and it was more gray now than red, but she still wore it the same as the day she put it up the first time.

"You ever wish you had done things different?" Essie asked.

"Well, hell, yeah! We all do. Right now I wish I hadn't left the ranch. I should be overseeing that young cowboy and my granddaughter. It wasn't too smart of me to up and leave them alone."

Essie's green eyes twinkled. "Good lookin', is he?"

"I would've pushed him into my bedroom if I'd been thirty years younger."

"That's a crock! You would've had to have been fifty years younger for him to let you push him anywhere near a bed."

Ada smiled. "I'm second-guessing myself. Momma said that I got the vision from Daddy. I knew the night that the cancer would finally take Tom away from me. And I knew that getting out of that canyon and making Sage face up to things was the right thing, but now I'm wondering if it was my own sight."

"Honey, there ain't no vision. It ain't nothing but common sense and intuition. Sage is a big girl, not just in size but in brains. Trust me, if she don't like that cowboy he won't even be there when you go back on Christmas Eve. And they'll never find a scrap of hair or a bone to get any of that DNA off of either."

"You watch too much of that damned *CSI* shit," Ada said.

"Good thing that wasn't on the television when Richard had his fling at forty or he wouldn't have lived to see forty-one," Essie said.

Ada laid her hand on her sister's shoulder. "Those were some bad times, weren't they?"

"Yes they were, but we lived through them and the boys never knew. The last words he said when he died was that he was sorry for hurting me. I was glad the boys weren't in the room."

"Ever wish you would have had a daughter?" Ada asked.

"I did want one but after three boys I figured all Richard could throw was boys and I stopped wishing. Maybe God knew what he was doing when he gave me boys. At least you'll get a son-in-law when Sage marries and you had a wonderful son. His only fault was that he didn't want to stay in that gawdforsaken canyon. If he had, he might have lived to see Sage raised up."

"Grandson-in-law," Ada corrected Essie.

"No, you raised her so she's yours. Sage is still young and this might not be the man for her. She might not be ready to settle down yet. I'm just glad you're either selling the ranch or putting it in her name when you go back. I'm not a spring chicken and I want you here with me."

"It's the right thing to do, isn't it?" Ada said.

"Yes, it is, and Thomas would be proud. Now let's go put on blinged-out sweat suits and go over to Idabelle's for canasta. Texas can have all that snow and wind. I'm going to enjoy this forty-five-degree weather and sunshine."

Creed awoke to the aroma of fresh banana bread baking in the oven. It was Christmas morning and his mother was in the kitchen making her traditional Christmas breakfast. They always had hot banana bread, cinnamon rolls, and a pumpkin roll with cream cheese filling on Christmas morning. All the nightmares about snow covering up the house had just been crazy dreams. He was in his bed at home on the family ranch. There wasn't even a real canyon that looked like a giant bomb had exploded in the panhandle of Texas.

He sat straight up in bed and realized in a split second that it was not Christmas morning and he wasn't in Ringgold, Texas. He was in a canyon fast filling up with snow, and it was not a nightmare that disappeared when he opened his eyes.

When he first drove out to that area it was the strangest sensation he'd ever known. Land met sky in every direction, and the ever-blowing Texas wind had picked up the remnants of a cotton crop on the side of the road and blew it around like big flakes of snow. He'd even gotten behind a cotton wagon taking a load from the field to the gin and then the wagon was gone, flat land was behind him, and he was following a twisting downhill road to the bottom of a big hole. It looked like someone had lobbed a nuclear bomb toward the Panhandle and it had landed between Silverton and Claude. It had been pretty that day, but the sun was shining and everything wasn't covered with almost a foot of snow and colder'n a well digger's naked butt in Alaska.

"All that cotton was trying to tell me that this was coming along pretty soon," he muttered as he jerked on a clean pair of jeans.

He didn't even stop to check on Angel and the kittens but followed his nose straight to the kitchen. Part of the dream had been real because there was a loaf of banana bread on the table with steam still rising from it.

"I couldn't sleep," Sage said. "Usually I paint when I can't sleep, but I had a hankering for Grand's banana bread so I made some."

She wore tight-fitting jeans and a sweatshirt with more paint stains on the front. The mistletoe he had tracked in was tied with a red ribbon and pinned to the curtain above the window.

He moved toward her. "Smells good. I thought it was Christmas morning. Momma makes this for our breakfast on Christmas morning."

"Grand makes it too. But I had to eat my eggs before I could have it," she said.

He settled a hand on the cabinet on either side of her. Her eyes met his and her eyelids fluttered. Then something changed and she turned her head to the left to stare at the coffeepot.

"Creed, I don't know…"

He tucked a fist under her chin and gently turned her back to face him. He looked up at the mistletoe and grinned.

"Can't waste it," he whispered.

His lips touched hers in a sweet, sweet kiss that ended too soon and left him yearning for more. He took two steps back and opened the drawer where the knives were kept. Before he could pick one up, her hand closed over his and forced him to shut the drawer.

"Chores first. Breakfast after."

"You are downright mean. It'll be cold by then."

"It will be perfect. The pecans will slice well instead of making a gummy mess on the knife, and the cream cheese will be softened to spread on it."

"You are killing me," he groaned.

"I'll help with chores."

"That's a poor second choice but I'll take what I can get." He started getting his coveralls on to go outside.

———⁂———

"Look!" Sage pointed. "I can see the outline of the barn. It's slowed down, Creed!"

"There is a God. I thought maybe He'd forgotten us and this whole canyon would be level with the rest of Texas before the storm moved on."

"It really is the worst storm I've ever seen. Grand talked about bad ones back when she and Grandpa first married, but this takes the cake for my generation," she said.

Going was still slow as they trudged through snow halfway to their knees. Noel bounded through it like she was running through daisies in the springtime and beat them to the barn by several minutes. The smell of hay, cows and warm cow patties greeted Creed when he opened the door. Noel dashed inside ahead of him and she ran to check on the milk cow before he could shut the barn door.

"Are you putting another big bale in the doorway?" Sage asked.

"That worked fairly well. If it quits sometime today or tonight, tomorrow I'll put the plow on the front end of the tractor and scoop any snow they haven't tramped into the ground to the sides of the feedlot so we can feed them out there. I'm just grateful for the lean-to roof that they could huddle under. If they'd been out in the far reaches, we might have lost a few."

"Grand wouldn't have been happy about that," Sage said.

"Neither would I. Soon as possible I'm hauling my stock out here. I've got Angus and a few Longhorns. My hope is to build up the Longhorns for rodeo stock. I've got a friend over the Red River into Oklahoma who raises them for the Resistol Rodeo down near Dallas. He makes a fair amount of money that way."

Creed started the smaller of the two tractors and ran the front spike into a big round bale of hay. "She told me to bring this many bales into the barn right before she left. Think they'll last until we thaw out?" he yelled over the hum of the engine.

"She's a smart old girl. When we get ice or bad weather she brings the cattle into this pasture and puts the big bales in the barn. She could use the little square ones to feed but says that she'd have to come out here three times a day if she did. She knows what she's doing so I expect she knows how many bales you'll need. It's also the reason she had that lean-to built on the back of the barn," Sage said with a smile.

"Okay, open 'em up," he said.

She pushed the doors back and he stuffed the bale

into the doorway. Before he could back away the cows were already chomping at it.

He killed the tractor engine and hopped down from the seat, picked up a clean bucket, and went in the stall to milk the cow. "How often during a winter does she do this?"

"Depends. Usually when we have a snow coming through. Maybe once or twice a winter. Sometimes not at all. Once the snow is melted, she turns the cattle back out into the whole ranch and brings in the big bales as she needs them."

"You always keep a milk cow?"

"Not always. Grand likes one in the winter so if we get stranded down here and can't get into town for supplies we have fresh milk and butter. She even makes cheese, but I have no idea how to do that. I do know how to run the electric churn and make butter."

"That's good. In the spring we'll be too busy to milk a cow twice a day," he said.

There was that *we* business again. And she'd almost used the past tense when she talked about Grand. That was enough to depress Jesus on a good day in heaven. She grabbed a feed bucket, filled it with grain for the hogs, and headed toward the hog pen.

She yelled at the hogs to drown out the niggling voices in her head. "Hey, pigs! You're going to be happy to know that the snow is slowing down and in a few days it'll warm up and your whole pen will be a brand new mud bath," she said, but it didn't cheer her or the hogs up. They snorted, ate the grain, and she knew they'd much rather have a big bucket of cornmeal softened up with hot water or warm milk.

The chickens were happier with their breakfast. Even the rooster flapped his wings and crowed. They gave her eight big brown eggs in exchange for the chicken scratch she'd spread out on the floor of the henhouse.

When the ranch was really Creed's, would he expect her to keep helping with chores? She'd always helped Grand and she'd miss not going out to check on the ranch every day, but when it was his, he would probably hire some help. The bunkhouse might even be full again and there could be cowboys all over the ranch.

"Dammit!" She shook her fist at the chicken coop.

She didn't want to think of Grand in the past and she wanted to think of "if" not "when" Grand sold the Rockin' C. And if Creed really did buy the property, she'd be damned if she helped do one thing. He and all his cowboy friends could feed his own hogs and gather his own eggs.

Noel bounded out of the barn and stopped when she reached the chicken yard wire fence. When she stopped moving, she sunk down until her pregnant belly was brushing the snow.

Sage let herself out the gate and secured it by turning the wooden latch crossways. "I'm okay, girl. I'm just mad. You going to be able to get out of that snow or do I need to give you a helping hand?"

Noel stuck her nose in Sage's hand.

"I'm really fine, but you'd best be getting back to the house. You'll have frozen puppies if you stay out here much longer."

With one jump, Noel was moving toward the house

and barely sinking into the snow at all. They were halfway to the house when movement caught Sage's eye. She followed the tiny tracks to the big cedar tree between the house and barn. She bent at the waist and pulled her dark hair back so she could see underneath the lower branches of the tree.

Two cotton-tailed bunnies stared up at her. They huddled together against the tree trunk, their light bodies sitting right on top of what snow had drifted under the tree. Her special paint gods had given her the next painting. It wasn't going to be the whole big cedar but just the bottom branches and the two brown rabbits surrounded by snow. She stood up and backed up slowly so she wouldn't spook them and imagined a bright red bow and a bunch of mistletoe hanging from the bottom limb right in front of them.

"Good Lord, I am besotted with mistletoe and holiday pictures."

Besotted! Shit! I've never used that word in my whole life. I don't even like that word. It sounds so formal. Erase that, Lord!

She made a motion in the air like she was erasing a big blackboard. "What the hell is the matter with my paint gods that all they are giving me are Christmas pictures with mistletoe in them? Will it be my best year ever next winter? Will they refer to this as the Sage Presley mistletoe season? Or will it put a screeching halt to my career?"

Maybe it wasn't paint gods. Maybe it was hormone devils making her see mistletoe since that was the first thing she noticed after the initial shock of Creed Riley bursting through the back door that first morning.

"Maybe they'll refer to this year as the year Sage Presley lost her edge and got all sappy." She opened the door and Noel bounced inside ahead of her. Angel met them, bumped noses with Noel, and then proceeded to wind herself around Sage's legs. The dog shook snow and dog-smelling water all over the floor.

Sage unzipped her snow-covered coveralls to the waist, removed her boots and set them on the rug to drip, and then finished removing her coveralls. She hung them on the rack and grabbed the mop from the pantry. Wintertime had its problems just like all seasons in the canyon. But at least there was Christmas to make it bright and cheerful.

"Is it your breakfast time, sweetie?" Sage crooned at the cat. "Well, that old slow cowboy will be here soon with warm milk…"

"Who's slow?" Creed pushed through the door, closed it behind him, and set the milk on the table. "Can I please have some of that bread now? I'm starving."

"Soon as I feed the house livestock and you get out of all those wet things." She broke four eggs into a bowl, whisked them into an orange froth, and poured fresh milk over it.

Angel hurried over to the pan and joined the dog when Sage set it on the floor.

"They're still sharing," Creed said.

"Looks like it. Let's get that milk taken care of and *we'll* share that loaf of bread," she said.

"Well, damn!"

She spun around. "What?"

"I thought it was just for me."

She smiled. "Too bad."

—••—

Creed settled in a chair at the table with a spiral notebook before him.

"What's that?"

"I usually keep the workings of the ranch on the computer, but since there's no electricity and the battery is down on my laptop, I'm making notes. When things are back up to normal, I'll get it all transferred into the computer. How'd your grandmother do things?"

"By hand. I offered to put it on the computer, but she'd have none of it. She doesn't even like banks," Sage said. "Didn't she give you the books?"

"Not yet, but she said she would when she came back."

Sage's giggle was soft but he heard it.

"What's so funny?"

"There's at least ten big boxes out in one of the bunkhouse bedrooms. You'll pull your hair out when you start to go through all that," she answered.

The canvas she fastened into the easel was smaller than the one she'd just finished. Creed figured it to be an eleven-by-fourteen, about the same size as his momma's velvet picture of the King. In no time she'd sketched in the lower branches of a cedar tree with a couple bunnies hiding underneath. It didn't look like much right then, but he'd seen her work magic with nothing but a kitchen window as a model.

From the corner of his eyes he watched Sage mix the colors and begin to work.

"I told you in the beginning I don't like people to watch me," she said.

"But you fascinate me. Bunnies, right?"

"I saw them when I was on my way back inside. They'd taken shelter up under that big cedar between here and the barn."

"You going to take a whole month to paint that one?"

"I don't think so. Must be the Christmas season that's gotten into my blood. Probably won't sell but I'm having fun."

"Then you are a success," Creed drawled.

"How do you figure that?"

"Granny Riley said that if you love what you do whether it's diggin' ditches or servin' as president of the U.S. of A., then you are a success. Your love comes through the paintings, so you are a big success. Take a snapshot of that window painting and send it up to your gallery owner. See what they think, but I'm telling you, they're going to love it," he said.

"You think I should?"

"Can't hurt. But if they say it is trash, don't burn it. I'll buy it to hang right where it is."

Ada tried to call the house phone at the ranch in Texas, but evidently the lines were still down. She tried to call Sage's cell phone and Creed's as well, but service wasn't available and with no electricity, they had no way to recharge their phone batteries anyway. The weatherman on the six o'clock news said that the storm was finally moving east but it was going slow. The last time the Panhandle had seen a storm that severe had been back in the thirties and thousands of people would be without power for several days.

She carried a bucket of milk in each hand from the

barn to the house. Essie did need her help, that was for sure. Until she got there, Essie had been doing all the work on the place, and at eighty-six she didn't have a bit of business milking two cows and picking apples. But convincing her to leave the five-acre farm was like getting St. Peter to open up the pearly gates and welcome Lucifer in for a double shot of Jack Daniel's.

Essie had always kept two milk cows. According to her, it was as easy to milk and feed two as one and she sold enough milk to the neighbors to buy her groceries. The small apple orchard produced abundantly and on good years she put quite a wad of money into her bank account, but last year she'd fallen off a ladder while picking apples.

Ada kicked the back door with the toe of her cowboy boot. "Eighty-six and still climbing ladders!"

Essie opened it wide. "Age don't mean I can't fix a roof or pick apples, so stop your bellyachin'. Idabelle called and said that blasted Texas storm is headed toward us now. Weatherman says it's going to build up force until it hits the East Coast and that by the middle of next week, we'll have snow."

"Long as my flight can get off the ground on Christmas Eve morning, I'm not too worried. I've fed cattle and milked cows in everything from a hundred and fifteen degrees down to ten below zero."

"You promise you'll come back the day after Christmas? I really like having you here, Ada."

"Got the ticket already bought and paid for. But you got to promise me that you won't climb any more ladders to pick apples. If I'm going to live here, you are going to have to trust me to do the work."

The wrinkles around Essie's mouth disappeared

when she smiled. "I didn't tell you that just before I fell, I climbed on the roof and fixed a few loose shingles."

Ada set the milk on the counter. "Great God Almighty, Esther! I'll have to live with you. Your mind has done left your body."

"No it didn't," Essie argued. "It's just that my stupid old body ran off and left it. Body is eighty-six. Mind is still twenty-six."

"Those boys of yours ought to be over here helping you," Ada fussed.

"Calvin is sixty-eight and he's had two heart attacks. Can't say how it's any big surprise with that woman he's been married to for more than forty years. She'd nag a normal man to death and Calvin ain't never been real healthy. He ain't got no business crawlin' up on a two-story roof and hammerin' shingles back on."

"Neither do you," Ada said.

Essie shot her a dirty look. "Omar is sixty-six and he just retired from over at Letterkenny Army Depot. His wife is a whiner and a hypochondriac. You just try namin' a disease and by golly she's either had it or has it ordered for next year. She's got him runnin' back and forth to that drugstore so often it's a wonder to me that his car don't have the place on automatic pilot."

Ada laughed.

The daughters-in-law had always been a sore spot and age hadn't improved any of them. Essie hadn't really liked any of them from the beginning, but then they hadn't liked her either.

"Well, Lester is only sixty and his wife is busy with her church stuff. He could help while she's off doing her charity work," Ada said.

Essie shook her head. "Lester got his grandpa's tongue. Not my sweet daddy's but his paternal grandpa's. He'd help but I'd have to endure a lecture about how this house is too big for me and how I should be lookin' at a nursing home. No thank you!"

Ada strained the milk and put it in the extra refrigerator in the pantry. Ten gallons were ready for sale. It would be gone by noon the next day. If they had ten milk cows they couldn't keep up with the demands for it.

She wiped her hands on the butt of her jeans and unsnapped a shirt pocket to take out her cell phone. Sage's cell phone's battery would have long since died, but there was a possibility that the landline would work.

Three rings later, Sage's voice came through.

"Grand! We've got service, at least on this old rotary phone you keep in the kitchen for emergencies. The storm has passed. It's still cloudy and cold. How are you? Are you ready to come home?"

"I am home, Sage. How's the cowboy working out?"

"He didn't lose a single cow and he's been doing the milking. You know how I hate to milk. And I painted a new picture. I took a snapshot and sent it to Marquee but then when I tried to call you the battery had gone dead and the service had gone out again. It's very different than what I'd done before…"

Ada butted in. "Is the cowboy naked in it?"

"Grand!"

"Well, shit! I guess that means you aren't bein' nice to him. Is he bein' nice to you?"

"He's standing right here, Grand."

"Is he smiling?"

"Yes."

"Then he knows we're talkin' about him. What do you want me to bring you for Christmas?"

"Just you. Come home and call this whole thing off."

"Essie needs me. You're a big girl. You don't need me, and you are beginning to cut out. Well, shit! I forgot to charge my phone. I'll call you tomorrow and we'll talk longer."

"Grand, I'll always need you."

That was the last thing Ada heard before the line went dead.

"Well?" Essie asked.

Ada sat down at the table. "Service is still spotty even on the old phone and the battery is down on her cell phone. Damned technology! Get used to it all and then it plays out."

Essie poured two cups of strong black coffee and carried them to the table. "Is he a serial killer or were your instincts right?"

Ada picked up her coffee. "She says she needs me and wants me to come home for Christmas and call it all off."

"And?" Essie held her breath.

"And her tone says something different. I was right. She just don't know it yet."

"What if she don't figure it out?"

"She will," Ada said.

Sage grabbed Creed by the arm and danced around the kitchen floor with him. Chores could wait. She'd talked to her Grand and the world was almost right again.

"I heard her voice again, Creed, and she's fine."

Creed pulled her to his chest and tipped her chin up with his fist. "Why wouldn't she be? She's doing exactly what she wants to do."

All the air left Sage's lungs. She wanted her grandmother to come home and never leave again, but after only three days she didn't want Creed to leave either. She wanted him to kiss her. She wanted to snuggle into his arms and listen to him describe her paintings to her. She couldn't have it all and she only had until Christmas to decide what she wanted most.

The movement stopped and she looked up at Creed. His lips were coming closer and closer. Warmth shot through her body like she was hooked up to a Jack Daniel's IV. The first touch made her lips so hot that his tongue felt cold when it gently probed her lips and begged for entrance.

It was the first time that she had experienced a kiss that was every bit as intimate as sex, and the feeling was so heady that she wondered if it came complete with a climax. She closed every inch of space between them and savored the touch, the taste, and the moment.

His hands found their way under her knit shirt and splayed out on her back. She wished he'd move them all over her body because they were frying her skin with blistering hot heat, but the only thing that moved was his thumbs. They made lazy deliberate circles right below her bra line.

If he hadn't stopped when he did she would have pulled the shirt off, shucked out of her bra, and stretched her body out on the kitchen table and whined for sex. But it all ended with a gentle kiss to her forehead and one more hug.

"I'm glad you heard from her. I'm sure she's been worried," Creed said hoarsely.

His kisses.

Her grandmother's voice.

She didn't want to give up either one. Was there a way under heaven she could have both?

Chapter 6

Sage had started with a fist full of snow and patted it firmly until it was big enough to roll and then she and Creed worked together. It went fast at first, but the last couple of rolls had taken all their combined strength.

"I reckon that's big enough," Creed said.

Sage huffed as she leaned against the round ball. "Now what? Even though the next one will be smaller, we won't be able to lift it up on this one, even if we work together."

"You start rolling one up and I'll go get the tractor. If it can lift a bale of hay from the back of a truck, it'll easily put that next ball up on that one," Creed said.

Sage picked up a handful of snow and patted it into a ball. She really intended to start rolling but Creed's wide back was just too tempting. She drew an imaginary bull's-eye on the back of his coveralls, drew back, and hurled it like a softball. It hit with a loud thud and if he hadn't grabbed the porch railing, he would have pitched forward into a six-foot drift.

She had another one formed and ready by the time he got his wits about him and turned around. He sidestepped to the right, caught it like an outfielder, and hurled it back at her. She giggled and hid behind the base for the snowman. He hid behind a cedar tree and sunk his glove into the snow. When he peeked around the tree, she got him right in the chest. He threw one and it whizzed past her ear. She reloaded her glove and stood up only to come face to face with him.

The grin on his face said that she'd lost the battle. The warmth spreading through her when she looked at his face said she hadn't lost a damn thing.

He grabbed her around the waist and wrestled her to the ground. From the hips down she was on bare frozen ground. From there up, the snow made a soft mattress. She wasn't aware of hard, cold, or softness because Creed was suddenly on top of her and his lips made their way to hers.

Cold lips tasted different than warm ones. She'd never realized that before or how they could send such a sensation down her entire body. His tongue slid through her parted lips. She dropped the snowball and wrapped her arms around him, pulling him tighter against her.

Damned old coveralls anyway! If they were gone she could feel all those muscles that had taken her down with hardly any effort at all. If he'd make love to her in the snow, she'd gladly die of pneumonia.

He drew back and tried to prop up on his elbows, but they sunk deep into the snow. He sat up and pulled her with him, settling her onto his lap.

"You lose, darlin'."

She tangled her fingers in his hair and brought his lips back to hers. He wasn't calling the shots and she hadn't lost. She was the winner of the whole war. Her hands went from his hair to his neck, down inside the coverall's collar. She wiggled out of one glove so she could feel bare skin, and she felt him shiver.

"God that feels good," he said.

"Mmm," she purred.

"You are something else, Sage Presley."

His warm breath in her ear traveled down her body like a lightning bolt, creating heat all the way to the deepest reaches. He nibbled on her earlobe and strung light, sweet kisses to her cheeks, her eyelids, the tip of her nose, and finally back to her mouth.

So she was something else, was she? What did that mean in cowboy language, anyway? She hoped it meant that he was as besotted as she was. And there was that blasted word again. *Besotted*. The last time she heard anyone use that was when Aunt Essie was telling the story for the nine millionth time about when she met her husband, Richard.

That nagging common sense voice that she hated reminded her that it would be even harder to watch Creed leave and never look back if they had sex. So when his lips left hers and he nuzzled the inside of her neck, she wiggled free. She almost made it out of his reach, but he got her by an ankle and brought her back down beside him, her cheek in the snow.

He stretched out beside her, kissed her one more time, and then sat up, pulling her into his lap. "It's my day to win, darlin'. Now I'm going to get the tractor, and if another snowball hits me on the way, I'm going to win a helluva lot more."

Her brown eyes twinkled. "Oh, yeah!"

"Remember what I said: I always tell the truth."

"Ever had sex in the snow?"

His neck jerked back with a crack and a wicked grin spread across on his face, lighting up his eyes. "What did you say?"

"Ever had sex in the snow?" she repeated.

"You offerin'?"

"I'm askin'."

He shook his head. "Don't believe I have. You?"

"No, I have not. Well, now that we got that cleared up, I'll start another snowball for the middle of our snowman. I believe we've got enough to build a snow momma and maybe a couple of kids."

"Darlin', there's enough snow to build a whole new town. What shall we call it?"

She laughed. "Mistletoe."

He raised one dark eyebrow, retrieved his hat from the snow where it had landed when he attacked her, and set her to one side. "Why Mistletoe?"

"You've got some stuck to your hat, Creed. Every time you go outside you bring more in the house."

"All right, then our town of snow people shall be called Mistletoe, Texas." He laughed, got to his feet, and offered her his hand. "I'll be back in a few minutes with the tractor."

He pulled her up like she was a feather. Not many men could do that without a grimace or even a small grunt, but not Creed. She felt like a princess standing there in her mustard-colored overalls, no makeup, and snow in her hair.

Creed had planned to hop on the tractor, drive it through the snow to the front yard, and use the hay spike on the front to help lift Mr. Snowman's midsection. But then he saw the scoop shoved up against the back wall of the barn. He grabbed the toolbox, removed the spike, and put it on the short trailer that could be affixed to the back of the tractor. He attached the trailer and put the scoop on the front of the tractor.

Noel hopped up on the seat beside him and he carefully backed out of the big double doors. Using the scoop like a snowplow, he cut a five-foot swath from barn to house, leaving a pathway with a ridge of slightly dingy snow on either side.

Sage shook her head when he got close and put up a palm. When he shut off the engine, she yelled, "Don't plow all the way up to them! I want them sitting in snow when I take pictures."

He nodded and hopped down off the tractor seat. Noel chased back and forth on the plowed pathway like a kid with a brand new toy. Angel sat in the window watching the whole affair and twitching her tail.

"We need to let her out. She's getting jealous of Noel," Creed said.

"But she might run away or get buried in the snow and die and the kittens wouldn't have a momma," Sage argued.

"She'll be fine, darlin'. Turn her loose to play with us."

"Promise she won't run away."

"Not a chance. Her babies are inside and she gets fed in there."

Creed could hardly believe it when Sage let the cat outside. The miracle was back on track. He was changing out implements when she crossed the distance from porch to tractor in a few long strides and helped him. "Good idea to plow out pathways. It'll sure make chores easier. Look, she's going to sit on the porch. She's not even interested in coming out into the yard."

"Got the idea from the ones we made when we made

the snowman's butt. We've never had snow like this in Ringgold. Noel might entice her out to play but she won't go far."

"I believe you are right. I wouldn't have thought of plowing pathways. Grand probably would have. She says when she first came here about fifty years ago there were some fierce winters. You about ready to give Frosty a big round belly?" She pointed to the big ball she'd rolled up while he was gone.

He looked down and nodded. "Perfect. But is that his jolly round belly or his wife's butt?"

She studied the size and shape and even the location. "It could be his wife, couldn't it? Okay, that is the wife's butt, but we'll have to move it closer to him. Let's make all the bottoms and the middles and then stack them. It will make fewer tire tracks with the tractor when we put them in place. That way there will still be snow all around them."

He grabbed a handful of snow and patted it.

The twinkle in her eyes when she looked up had him wondering if she'd start another battle. A part of him hoped she did because the next one was going to involve *him* touching bare skin. The only problem was that when he did, he might not have the willpower to stop.

"Want to go inside and warm up before we start?" Creed asked.

She shook her head. "I was going stir-crazy in the house. I can't remember ever being cooped up like that." She dropped her snowball on the ground and started rolling, patting the sides firmly as she did.

He did the same. When they were the perfect size he picked up the first one and carried it to the place where the two snow children would stand.

"Right here?" he asked.

"Wow! You are strong," Sage said.

He made fists and bent his elbows in a wrestler's stance. "Muscles of steel!"

He didn't need to posture to prove that to her. She'd felt those muscles up close and personal and would like nothing better than to feel them even more.

"You wrestle in high school or college?" she asked.

"No, ma'am, not unless you count wrestlin' a bunch of hay bales into the barn. I worked on one ranch or the other during the summer from the time I was thirteen. Even went over the river and helped throw watermelons the summer I was sixteen. I'd rather throw hay from the pasture to the trucks than watermelons into the haulin' busses."

"Why?"

"Because you can't break hay. You ever haul any?"

"Oh, yeah! This is where I grew up. I know all about hay. You about ready to put this family together?"

His eyes twinkled when he grinned. "I sure am and then we're goin' inside for something hot."

"Oh?"

"Hot chocolate. Get your mind out of the gutter, woman. We're about to birth a couple of snow children here."

He loved it when she laughed. It wasn't a sissy giggle but a full-fledged woman's laugh, and when he said something that brought that kind of happiness to the surface, his cowboy heart threw an extra beat into the rhythm.

She had the hiccups the whole time he stacked the snowballs together. While he was on the tractor he took it back to the barn.

When he returned she was standing back, hands on her hips, head cocked to one side.

"Please don't tell me that we have to build a lamb or make a whole nativity. I'm really getting cold," he said.

"Poor Mrs. Frosty. She looks naked."

Creed threw his arm around her shoulders. "Shhh, you'll offend her. She'll go shopping as soon as she can, but right now she's thinking about Christmas presents for the kids."

Sage laughed and patted the snow wife. "Welcome to Mistletoe, Texas, Miz Frosty. Hope you enjoy your stay."

Sage couldn't remember the last time she'd had so much fun.

Maybe it was because she'd been cooped up in the house for three days and cutting out paper dolls would have been a great distraction.

Maybe it was the text message she'd gotten that morning from the gallery owner. She'd said that the mistletoe pictures breathed life and joy and she should bring eight to ten to next year's showing. They were going to bill them as the Sage Presley Mistletoe Collection and start advertising two months before the showing.

Maybe it was Creed who brought out the little girl in her and made her laugh so much. Or perhaps it was a combination of all of the above after being snowed in for so long.

Her nose was numb by the time the snow family had arms of twigs, buttons for eyes, and carrots for noses. She'd found old scarves and hats, plus a purse with a sequined Christmas tree on the outside for Mrs. Frosty. But still there was something missing and Creed's nose testified to the fact that he really was cold.

She pointed at him and smiled.

"What?" Creed asked.

"Your nose is red. Is your middle name Rudolph?"

"Well, darlin', so is yours, and no, my middle name is not Rudolph. Can we go inside? I'll even make the hot chocolate and we can get warm by the fire."

"Not just yet. Something is still missing." She clapped her hands when she thought of what they needed for their new little icy family decorating the yard. "I know! Mistletoe. Frosty needs mistletoe hanging from his fingers. His beautiful wife will want a kiss when she comes home from the church social Christmas party."

"Well, this place seems to grow that stuff with no problem. Let's go hunt some up. I'll back the tractor out again and we'll take a trip over the river and through the woods." He grabbed her hand and jogged to the barn.

"And back to Grandma's house!" She kept pace with him the whole way.

"And back to my house, not Grandma's house," he said.

"Not until Christmas," she told him.

He didn't argue, which made her wonder if he was having second thoughts after living through a Texas-sized snowstorm.

"I thought you were cold," she changed the subject.

"I am, but you want mistletoe and you'll have mistletoe. Besides, I saw a big chunk of it not far out into the pasture. We could walk there, but it'll be faster on the tractor."

He motioned toward the snowy white field lying before them. "It seems like sacrilege to mess up something that pretty."

"Virgin snow is always beautiful, but you'll probably

turn the cattle back out of the feedlot before long and they'll mess it up and look, there it is. In that scrub oak tree and not too high up. There it is."

"Yes, ma'am. That's exactly what I was talking about and I'll use the tractor seat to reach that first limb. What do I get if I bring it all down and don't lose a bit of it?"

"A kiss. That's what mistletoe is all about, isn't it?"

He drove the tractor close to the base of the tree, stood on the seat, and grabbed the lowest limb. He threw a leg over it and was soon climbing to the top like a monkey. The way he moved from limb to limb made her gasp. He unzipped his coveralls and reached for the perfect ball of mistletoe, tucked it inside, and zipped up. Coming back down the tree took longer than going up.

"You sure are taking your own good time," she yelled up.

"Can't lose a single leaf or I don't get my prize," he hollered back.

When he reached the bottom, he unzipped, carefully pulled it out, and handed it to her. "I believe that is perfect, madam. It just needs a red ribbon tied around the top."

He sat down in the driver's seat, drew her even closer, and brushed a sweet kiss across her lips.

"Paid in full," he said.

Sage didn't think it was paid in full at all. She didn't want a kiss that left her aching for more. She wanted one that melted her insides and turned her legs to jelly.

―⁂―

The house smelled like a mixture of turpentine, burning logs, breakfast bacon, and wet dog when they went inside. Creed warmed a pot of beef stew, and Sage sliced thick slabs of bread from a loaf she'd pulled from the freezer that morning.

It was Thursday, which meant he'd only known Sage four days, but it felt as if they'd known each other since childhood. He could still taste her kisses on his lips and wondered if this was the way his friend Rye had felt when he tumbled ass over belt buckle in love.

Creed used the glass in the kitchen door to check his reflection. No, he wasn't love drunk. He didn't have that crazy look in his eyes that Rye had had all those years ago. It was simply being cooped up in the house with a beautiful woman that made things all haywire. Either that or she was working an angle to get him to leave.

If that was the case, she was damn sure going about it the wrong way because every time he touched her or kissed her, it deepened his resolve to stay. He looked at his reflection again. Nothing unusual there.

Maybe you can't see it. I bet if you were in Ringgold Ace could tell you if you have the look, the voice inside his head said.

He forgot about what he could or could not see when Sage started humming "White Christmas" behind him.

He turned and faked a cough to cover up the quick intake of breath. She had just finished pulling her dark hair from the rubber band holding it into a ponytail. As it fell to her shoulders, she shook her head slowly from one side to the other. That movement bringing all that silky black hair tumbling down to frame her face was sexier than anything he'd ever seen.

"If you really are dreaming of a white Christmas, I

figure you are about to have your dreams come true," he said hoarsely.

The movement stopped and a worried look crossed her face.

"Are you getting a cold? I told you we shouldn't stay out all morning," she said.

"Just a frog in my throat. I'm fine and you aren't remembering right, woman. It was me askin' you if we shouldn't come in out of the cold and get warm," he said.

"Doesn't matter who said what right now and don't call me woman. I've got a name. There's no way in or out of here for at least one more day and maybe more. Neither of us can get sick," she told him.

"Yes, ma'am. It will be so. The great Sage Presley has spoken," he said shortly.

"That's tacky."

"No, it's funny."

"You're making fun of me."

He smiled. "I was not making fun of you. I was teasing."

She held up a long bladed knife with a serrated edge. "You'd better be. All you got is a wooden spoon and look what I'm holding."

Noel growled from her blanket in front of the fireplace.

"She's tellin' us that the fire is getting low and that all that energy she used up out there helping plow a path and make snow people made her hungry too. And she's also saying we shouldn't be arguing when all we got is each other in this house until the snow melts. Dip her stew out before it boils and she won't have to wait for it to cool down. As soon as we can drive on the roads, we've got to go buy real dog food and cat food." Sage crossed the floor and tossed a couple of sticks of wood into the stone fireplace.

Sage's head bobbed one time. "Children do have to be fed."

She put a paper towel in a basket, shuffled the slices of bread into it from the cutting board, and carried it to the table. Her job was finished. The rest belonged to Creed, so she left the kitchen and went to the basket of kittens. She picked the yellow one up and held it close to her breast.

"At least they don't have to be clothed," she yelled over her shoulder.

He chuckled. "You sure about that?"

"Of course I am. Little girls might put their doll clothes on puppies and kittens but adults don't, do they?" She remembered seeing a picture of a movie star in a magazine. She had one of those tiny lap dogs and it had a bow in its hair and wore a pink sweater.

"I knew a woman who had a special walk-in closet for her toy poodle. It was completely full of clothing for each season and the critter had a different bed for days when it rained or the sun shined."

Sage put the kitten back and picked up a black one. "You're teasing again, right?"

He dipped out enough for the pets' dinner and set it on the cabinet. "I wouldn't tease about something that crazy."

"Did you date her very long?"

"Twice. Took her to a rodeo over in Wichita Falls one Friday night and the next week we went to dinner. She asked me in to meet her daughter, Fiona. She sure didn't act like she had a child, but what was I supposed to do? I couldn't think fast enough to make an excuse, so I went inside with her."

"And the daughter had a puppy right?"

"No, the puppy was the daughter. Imagine my surprise when Fiona had gray hair and four legs."

Sage laughed. "Don't make me laugh. I always get the hiccups and I don't hiccup or sneeze like a lady."

Creed held up a hand and crossed his chest with the other one. "I swear to God. It really happened. I'm not joking."

"What happened?"

"The dog got all excited and squatted on the floor."

Sage laughed harder.

Creed went on. "The lady grabbed some scented wipes, soaked it up, and told the poodle that if she wasn't good that she'd have to sit in the time-out chair. She pointed to a mink-lined bed in the corner of the room."

"Real mink?"

"Probably not, but it didn't look like much punishment to me."

"And you never dated her again?" Sage asked.

"Couldn't get out of there fast enough. So answer my question, are you going to buy clothing for these animals?"

"Hell, no! They'll do good to get cheap dog food and cat food."

Visualizing a big, rough man's-man cowboy like Creed cooking a pot of stew was stretching the imagination. Walking a toy poodle dressed up like a movie star and prancing along on a shiny pink leash brought on even more laughter.

She put the kitten next to Angel, gathered up the last one to give it some attention, and said between gasps of giggles, "You were a wise man, Creed. She would have made you be friends with that critter and you'd have had to walk her. I just can't see you walkin' a little bitty dog wearing a tutu and a pink bow."

Creed shook his head. "Me either. When she showed me the dog's closet, I about had a stroke. If the dog was that high maintenance, then what would she be? It'd take more than one cowboy to make enough to keep her and her pup happy."

"Well, I promise not to humiliate my animals with clothing. They can romp through the mesquite without having to worry if they tear their tutu, and they can sprawl out on the porch in the summertime strip stark naked. And you can bet your cowboy butt that I'm not having a real or fake mink time-out chair for them."

"Somehow I can't see Noel in a mink bed," he chuckled.

Sage put the last kitten back in the basket and scooted across the floor to Noel's blanket. The giggles had subsided and she didn't have the hiccups that time. "My girl is happy with her frayed blanket, aren't you?"

Noel wagged her tail and slurped her tongue across Sage's cheek like it was a snow cone.

"Snow ice cream," Sage said.

"A dog's slobbers reminded you of snow ice cream?"

"No, I just remembered that we've got to make it. The snow is clean right now, but in a day or two it'll all be nasty. We've got to bring in a bowl of good clean snow and make ice cream."

"Oh, yeah!" Creed agreed. "Just tell me when and I'll go get the snow for you. Do you have a special recipe?

My momma uses whipping cream, milk and eggs, and vanilla. Do we have all that stuff here?"

"I thought you were cold."

"I am, but I don't mind stepping out the back door and getting some snow. I'm just glad you weren't talking about building a snow cone stand for our snow family. I'm dishing it up, so come and get it while it's hot. I'm talking about this stew, not snow ice cream."

"My snow family would probably appreciate a snow cone stand. They do need something to keep them occupied other than kissing under the mistletoe all the time. And yes, I do have a special recipe. It's an old family one that we never share, so don't even ask. You might talk Grand into selling the ranch, cowboy, but my ice cream recipe isn't up for sale."

She left Noel, washed her hands at the kitchen sink, and sat down at the table. "This smells even better reheated."

He sat down across from her, pulled his chair up, and their knees bumped together. "Soup, stew, and beans all get better toward the end of the pot. Maybe we'll make a pot of beans and ham tomorrow. And fried potatoes."

She nodded because all the words in her head were suddenly gone. Only two layers of denim separated her knees from Creed's. The steaming bowl of soup in front of her was actually cold compared to the heat generated between them.

Then he shifted his chair and it was gone.

She moved her knee a little, couldn't hook up with his, and was searching under the table for his leg when she realized what she was doing. She jerked her hand back faster than if she'd touched a hot iron, and high color blazed in her cheeks.

Whoa, hoss! You've got to slow this buggy down. Four days, Sage Presley, and have you forgotten this is the man who's going to buy the ranch? You are supposed to hate him and discourage him from wanting to live in the canyon.

She blew on a spoon full of soup. *But maybe he could work for Lawton and I could still see him. There are other small ranches in the canyon that he could buy.*

She realized she wanted to have her cake sitting all pretty on the table and eat a big chunk of it too. Life didn't work that way. Either preserve the past and keep the cake, or get a knife and slice into it.

"Hey, what are you thinking about? It looks like you've got a war going on in your head," Creed said from across the table.

"Whether to buy Noel a pink or red sweater. Since it is Christmas and she does have a holiday name, I was thinking red. What do you think?" she joked to keep from spitting out what she'd really been thinking about.

"Ask her. She's the one who'll have to wear it," Creed said.

"How old are you?" Sage asked bluntly.

"I might ask you the same thing, but a gentleman never asks a woman about her age or weight."

"I was twenty-six in September. I went to college for two years, came home, and started painting full time, sold a few, and then got a fantastic break when my professor dropped my name to a gallery owner in Denver. What I weigh is between me and the bathroom scales and if they ever start talking, I will take the hammer to them. Your turn."

Creed laid his spoon down. "I was twenty-eight on

the first day of October. I have a bachelor's degree in agricultural business. All I've ever known is ranching and farming. Like you already know, I was engaged once, and I've sworn off permanent relationships. What about your love life, Sage?"

"I love painting. Seems that men have this crazy notion that I've got commitment issues."

"Imagine that."

Sage didn't want to talk about the big, dark *C* word so she changed the subject. "Don't eat too much. You'll want to save room for ice cream, and besides, Noel looks like she's still hungry."

"That's the first step toward a mink-lined bed in the corner. Feeding the dog," he quoted the last word with two fingers on each hand in the air, "the good stew and going hungry yourself."

"The bathroom scales would argue with you that I'm not about to waste away to nothing," she said.

"I think you are just right, Sage. Matter-of-fact, my Grandpa Riley had a way of describing a woman like you."

Sage didn't know if she wanted to hear what his grandpa would say about a woman who was too tall and who was too hippie and whose smile looked like a dental chart (compliments of a remark made by Triston Jones in the fourth grade).

"Well, do you want to hear it or not?" Creed asked.

She nodded even though she was telling her head to go back and forth, not up and down.

"He would have said that you were built like a red brick shit house without a brick out of place." Creed smiled.

She jerked her head up to lock gazes with him across the table.

"Thank you, I think."

"It's a compliment, I promise."

"Maybe so, but it won't keep me from talking Grand out of selling the ranch, and that's a fact."

He reached across the table and covered her hand with his. His knee settled against hers under the table at the same time.

"I meant what I said. You are beautiful. Whether I own the ranch or not, it doesn't make you any less gorgeous," he said.

"Thank you," she whispered.

Then his knee was gone and his hand left hers.

He picked up his spoon and started eating stew again, changing the subject and talking between bites. "I haven't had snow ice cream in at least five years."

"Well, finish up your dinner and bring in a big bowl of snow and you'll get the best you've ever had in your life," she said.

He wiggled his eyebrows. "Are we still talking about ice cream?"

"Creed Riley!"

"Just checkin' to be sure." He grinned.

"Yes, we are!"

He finished eating, grabbed a huge metal bowl from the pantry, and filled it with snow from a drift at the edge of the back porch. He was halfway across the porch when he noticed bird droppings in the snow. He dumped it and went to the other end of the porch, checked to be sure it was clean, and took it inside.

Sage swallowed her last bite at the same time he did and set their dirty dishes beside the sink. She grabbed a can of sweetened condensed milk from the pantry, hurriedly opened it, poured it into a mixing bowl, and grabbed a whisk.

When Creed returned she was busy stirring, scraping the sides, and stirring some more so he would think she'd whipped up several ingredients together. She stirred small amounts of snow into it until it was finally the right consistency and then dipped out two smaller bowls full.

He tasted it and shut his eyes as he groaned. "God, this is the best I've ever had. What is your secret?"

"Just the right mixture of eggs, sugar, and cream," she said.

There were some things a woman just kept to herself, right?

"Living room?" he asked.

"Oh, yeah! Warm fire, snow ice cream, and Christmas."

He sat on one end of the sofa. She claimed the other.

She grabbed her head with her free hand. "Oh, shit!"

Creed set his ice cream on the end table, scooted down the length of the sofa, cupped her chin with his hand, and kissed her hard.

"Wow, that worked," she said when he pulled back.

"Heat melts cold, darlin'."

He went back to the other end and started eating again.

In seconds Sage had gone from aching cold to boiling hot. How many times could a woman's body do that and not explode?

Chapter 7

A BRAND NEW BLANK CANVAS WAITED ON THE EASEL.
The window painting had been relegated to the top
shelf of the pantry to finish drying. The bunnies now
had the drying space on the living room wall and she
liked them even better the second day after finishing
them than she did at first. Two paintings in such a short
time did worry her, though. Was she color-booking or
was she really painting?

Sage eyed the rest of the canvasses and decided the
one on the easel was too big. She removed it and picked
up a sixteen-by-twenty-inch one and slid the top bar of
the easel down to hold it steady. She looked around the
room, but there were no angels swirling about outside
the kitchen window.

A flash of yellow leapt from floor to living room windowsill and caught Sage's attention. The snow people
seemed to fascinate the cat. Or maybe it was the birds
that lit in their tree limb arms that got her attention. She
made a deep guttural sound in her throat as if telling
them if they'd come on into the house, she'd tell them
a pretty story.

Sage had no doubt that the old fairy tale would be
a brand new jacked-up version of "Little Red Riding
Hood" if Angel could entice the birds inside. Sage
smiled at that idea and turned her attention back to the
canvas in front of her.

"The Mistletoe Collection," she said. "That sounds wonderful."

Still, nothing materialized. Maybe her mistletoe collection was going to consist of two paintings. One of a snow angel and one of two bunnies.

The back door swung open and Creed filled the space for a split second before he stepped inside. "Mistletoe what?"

"Cowboy. Mistletoe cowboy. Did you track more inside the house?"

She was not going to paint a cowboy with mistletoe on his shoulder or a cowboy boot with it frozen to the toe, either.

He looked at his shoulders and down at the floor. "Not today. I plowed the snow away from a third of the feedlot so the cows wouldn't be standing in it, but you were right. They'd stomped down most of what was in the lot so the job was easy. Those wind breaks your Grandpa planted sure work."

"Next thing you know, you'll ask me to knit socks for the cows."

He hung his heavy coat on the rack. "You knit?"

She stole quick glimpses of him without turning around to face him head-on. His jeans were snug and stacked up over his scuffed up boots. His denim shirt had two buttons undone showing an oatmeal-colored thermal shirt underneath.

"I do not knit. Grand does and she tried to teach me. That pesky yarn crawled up the needles and tried to strangle me. So don't ask me to make socks for your cattle."

He chuckled.

"What? It's the truth."

"I'm not saying it's not. You said *your* cattle."

"Slip of the tongue. I meant to say Grand's cattle." She folded her arms over her chest and turned her attention once again back to the blank canvas.

Nothing!

Nada!

Nil!

The PGs weren't giving her a thing that morning. Two small paintings weren't enough to make the Sage Presley Mistletoe Collection. Had her special gods forsaken her?

Then the sun peeked out from the dark clouds covering the skies and there it was plain as day. Angel's fur glistened as the rays flowed through the window and settled on the basket of kittens sleeping soundly. A snowbird with its dark feathers on top and white belly sat in the twig arms of Mr. Frosty, right at the top of the mistletoe ball. Sage moved the canvas one foot to the left. Mr. Frosty was barely showing in the side of the window and the mistletoe in his arm made of twigs hung right above Angel's head as she washed a paw.

Sage grabbed a sketch pencil and began to work as fast as she could before the sun rays shifted. Two long rectangular lines to denote the direction of the sun. The edge of the snowman's hat, his scarf blowing out in the wind, the stick arms, and the bird. And the sun's rays bringing it all to life.

Please, paint gods, let the sun stay out a few more minutes so I won't lose every little detail. It's the world coming back after darkness. It's the sun breathing warmth into a dark room, and it is a momma cat who

wants to go outside and play, and it is baby kittens bask-
ing in warmth they've never known.

She expected the sun to disappear as soon as she had
the major sketch done, but it didn't. Angel hopped down
and joined her babies. The snowbird flew away and a
chicken hawk tried to rest on the twig arms to peck at the
frozen carrot nose, but the twigs wouldn't support him
so he gave up and flew away.

"So that's the next one? Coffee, tea, or me?" Creed
asked.

"That's a hell of a choice there, cowboy," she said.

"Your choice, darlin'."

"Better be hot chocolate then. I've already had too
much coffee, and honey, right now even you couldn't
entice me away from this picture."

"Now I'm hurt." He threw a hand over his heart and
his chin dropped to his chest.

"You are not. You are a big flirt and you're used to
rejections. And marshmallows, please."

She chose her background colors and squirted them
onto the palette.

Creed headed for the cabinet. "I'm not a big flirt and
you'll have to stop all this shit about me not having the
ranch to make it up to me for hurting my feelings."

"You're one brazen cowboy," she laughed.

The phone rang and they both jumped. Creed had to
do some fast handwork to keep from dropping a whole
can of cocoa onto the floor. Sage did drop her brush but
caught it midair against her sweatshirt, leaving a yellow
blob right on her breast.

Sage crossed the floor in long, easy strides and grabbed
the receiver before Creed could get around the table.

"Hello!"

Creed set the cocoa on the cabinet with a bang.

"Yes, ma'am, he is right here. Yes, ma'am, the sun is out and I am Sage Presley."

He reached for the phone and she put it in his hand.

"Hi, Momma."

Sage finished making the hot chocolate he'd started, but the kitchen was small so she heard every word.

"Yes, ma'am."

A pause.

"Just fine."

Another pause.

He laughed. "I'm not answering that."

He listened for a long time and then said, "Bye, love you, too. Tell all my brothers that I'm surviving, but if they'd like to play in the snow to come out for a visit."

He'd barely gotten the phone back on the hook when it rang again. He picked it up. "Hello."

He held it out to her. "This one is for you."

Two long strides and she stood in front of him, her hand outstretched.

His fingers brushed her palm in the transfer and naughty visions danced through her mind. "Hi, Grand. Looks like we've got phone service but no electricity. Creed's momma just called and…"

Creed stepped around the table and took over the chocolate making process.

"Oh, I'm sorry, Marquee. I thought you'd be my grandmother. She's on a vacation trip to Pennsylvania. I didn't think about you calling the house phone."

Marquee's excitement came through the phone line.

"You wrote it down on the back of your business card. I love this new mistletoe idea, Sage. It's going to be every bit as big as your Western pictures. I feel it in my bones. I've already got it penciled in for the first week in December. I need a better photo of the one you sent when you have time. When I design the brochure I plan to use that one on the front page. It's... damn, girl, I can't even think of a word to describe it. Ethereal. Paranormal. I don't know, but it's not like anything I've ever represented," Marquee said.

"I'll have it to you as soon as I get electricity. Cell phone battery is dead. Internet won't be back until we have electricity, and my laptop battery has long since gone. If my grandmother hadn't kept this old rotary phone we wouldn't even have phone service."

"I can't even begin to tell you how much I like these," Marquee gushed. "The inspiration is still going, isn't it? I'd like ten or more."

"So far the PGs are smiling on me."

"Well, don't do anything to piss them off," Marquee said. "Call me if you need to discuss anything."

"Will do."

She put the receiver back on the wall base and two cups of hot chocolate were sitting on the table.

"Thank you," she said.

"PGs?" Creed asked.

Sage didn't want to tell him about her special gods. That was even more personal than scorching hot kisses.

"Personal gurus?" he asked.

"Paint gods," she said before she could bite down on her tongue.

"And they are smiling on you?"

She nodded.

"Well, that's good. I found a package of hot dog buns in the freezer. Reuben hot dogs for dinner?"

She nodded. One minute she's telling him the most personal thing about herself and the next he's talking about hot dogs? Her world got crazier with every passing minute.

He motioned toward the new canvas. "What's that one going to be?"

And now it was back to paintings. Talk about one complex cowboy.

"Wait and see," Sage said.

The phone rang again and Sage got it.

"Hello." Sage put her hand over the mouthpiece. "It's April. They keep an old rotary around for times like this too."

Creed went to the living room and settled into a rocking chair. Noel left her blanket and stretched out at his feet. Angel got out of the basket and with a single leap landed on his lap.

He hadn't liked the idea of being holed up with Sage at first, but it hadn't been so bad. She was easy on the eyes, had scorchin' hot lips, and she entertained him with her painting. Yep, he would miss her when she moved to the back side of the property, but maybe he could talk her out of one of the kittens. He peered over the edge of the basket and decided he wanted Rudy, the yellow one. He could catch any field mice that came into the house and sleep in his lap like Angel was doing right then.

At first Sage's voice sounded excited and happy as she told April about building the snow family and going off in a new direction with her paintings. But then after a few minutes of silence, it turned serious and worried.

"April, you've got to talk to them both about this. It's a big decision," she said.

She listened a while longer and then hung up, picked up her lukewarm chocolate, and slouched down into the rocking chair beside him.

"They love you more than me," she said.

As if she understood, Noel left Creed's side and went to stand beside Sage.

Sage reached down and massaged her ears. "Thank you, Noel. I need some love right now."

"All you had to do was tell me," Creed said.

"Oh, hush. I wasn't talking to you."

"Some days a lonesome old cowboy don't get handed nothin' but bad luck. Well, if we aren't going to talk about love then tell me what kind of trouble is your friend April into? I couldn't help but overhear," he asked.

"Big decisions. She wants to quit college and come home. The ranch will be hers someday and it's the biggest operation in the canyon. She thinks she's ready to start learning how to run it from the bottom up."

"If she's in college, she should already know the basics. By the time I was that age, Momma and Dad were leaving me and my brothers to run the place when they went places like rodeos and off to Graceland for their anniversary," Creed said.

"Lawton and Eva, that's her dad and mom, divorced

when she was four. Eva took her to Oklahoma and she only comes to Canyon Rose Ranch in the summers and for three weeks at Christmas. Sometimes she sneaks down for a couple of days during her spring break and maybe a day at Thanksgiving. When she's at the ranch she's the adored pet, not a working ranch rookie."

Creed whistled through his teeth. "Whew!"

"Yep! And there's more. Eva hates the canyon. Didn't like it when she married Lawton according to what little I know, but she managed to stick it out for a little more than four years. Story is that Lawton was the quarterback and Eva was the head cheerleader. They got pregnant toward the end of their senior year and married soon as they graduated."

"Mercy!" Creed said.

"April will have a hell of a lot to learn if and when she quits school. And she'll have to wade through Eva to get to the ranch."

"How old is she?"

"Twenty. She'll have two years of college finished in May."

Creed stopped petting Angel and she left him for Sage's lap.

"Fickle critter," he said. "Can I keep Rudy here when you get your own place and move to the back of the property?"

"You can take Rudy with you when you go home to Ringgold. Oh, and speaking of going somewhere, April says if the roads get cleared off that Lawton is going ahead with the Christmas party at the ranch."

"You are downright mean, Sage. I'm not going

back to Ringgold and you just don't want to share your kittens."

"You got it, cowboy!"

———~~~———

Time had stood still the past several days. Sage had painted. She'd lived, slept, ate, and gotten to know Creed. Minutes drug by like a slow old turtle in the hot summertime. Hours sped by with the speed of lightning.

Limbo. I feel like I'm floating around in space.

It was hard to believe that just a week ago she was setting up in Denver for her final showing, the excitement mounting as the first people arrived to look at her work. There had been a room full of canyon pictures, most of them at least two feet by three feet in size. She'd figured out that the massive size of the canyon required a big picture even if the central focus was nothing more than an eagle or a lone wolf.

One critic said that he felt like he could crawl into the picture and smell the heat off the canyon walls. She knew what he was talking about as she stole a glance toward Creed. She could feel the heat all the way across the room. She was a moth and he was an open flame. She should not go any closer or her wings were going to catch on fire. Keeping her distance was the only way that she'd ever talk Grand into keeping the ranch.

He caught her before she could blink. "What? Do I have chocolate between my lip and nose?"

"No," she said quickly and went back to work.

"Well, I've wasted enough time and I've gotten warm all the way to my bones so I'm going back out to plow some more snow. Maybe I'll push it out of the way up the lane next so we can get out when the roads are clear. I'll be back in time to help get some dinner on the table. Want some more snow ice cream this afternoon?"

She shook her head. "Grand says if you have it more than once a snow it isn't special anymore. I've got a chicken thawing out for supper. I was thinkin' dumplin's, but if you don't like that idea I could fry it."

"My favorite food in the whole world is dumplin's. We only talk Momma into making them on Easter and Thanksgiving. She's as stingy with her dumplin's as you are with your recipe for snow ice cream," he said.

"Then dumplin's it is. And honey, my recipe is so complicated that you'd never get it right."

"You'd better not leave it behind when you move or I'll find it!" He stretched the kinks from his neck and back when he stood up. Then he crossed the room and wrapped his arms around her from behind. "I like that picture best of all three."

"Thank you, Mr. Riley, and there isn't a written copy of my recipe. The only one in existence is in my head and it will die with me," she said.

"That would be Creed, ma'am. My friends call me Creed."

"Do you go around hugging and kissing all your friends?"

"Only the pretty ones who paint gorgeous pictures and make luscious snow ice cream. See you after a while." He kissed her on the neck, just below her ear.

It was a full five minutes after he left before she could steady her hands enough to touch the canvas with a paintbrush. Yes, sir! Just like the moth to the flame and Creed was one scorching hot blaze.

She'd barely gotten started when Creed burst in the back door. "You've got to come and see this, Sage. It'll be gone by morning. Do you have a camera in the house? My phone is dead or I'd use it."

She laid her palette and brushes down. "What is it?"

"Your next big thing." He grinned.

She didn't have the heart to tell him that Grand had taken her to see the next big thing dozens of times, but she could never get them to come out right on canvas. If the PGs didn't slap her with inspiration, she might as well not even try to paint it.

"I'll get the camera."

She disappeared into the bedroom and came out with a digital camera and hoped the batteries in it were still good. She seldom used it. If she saw a picture, it was imbedded in her mind permanently and refused to leave until she finished the job.

He held her coat while she slipped her arms into it. She stomped her feet down into her boots and followed him outside. He grabbed her hand to hurry her along the plowed path leading to the tractor sitting on the south side of the barn.

Sage didn't see a thing that was so wonderful, but warmth ran from his hand up her arm and into her body. Maybe the next big thing was that she would fall in love with the man.

Hell, no! She caught herself before she said it out loud. Sage Presley never made rash decisions. She weighed everything carefully, sometimes even wrote the pros and cons on paper, before she made up her mind. She'd known Creed less than a week, for God's sake!

When she had her first sexual relationship as a sopho-more in college, she'd gone into it thoughtfully and with lots of care. That was seven years earlier, so there was no way she was entering into something with Creed Riley after such a short time.

He stopped and pointed. "Look."

She stared, slack-jawed.

Sure enough. There was the next big thing and it had been delivered through him. That was a first, for sure. The PGs had never worked that way before.

"What do you think?" he asked.

"I think you should paint. You have an eye for it." She dropped his hand and brought the camera up and pressed the button. She moved a foot to the left and took another picture, two feet and another one. Not that she would need the pictures, but the vi-sion through the lens was like framing it after she'd painted it.

"Aww, shucks." He kicked a big pile of snow. "I can't even color without getting outside the lines. Just ask Rachel."

She lowered the camera. "Rachel?"

"Yep, she's the expert."

"Oh?"

"She's my friend's daughter. She's in preschool and she tells us all that we've got to stay in the lines or we can't color in her books," Creed said. "So you think you can use that in your new collection?"

"Oh, yeah!"

Sage stepped back and branded the moment into her brain. It was a scraggly old scrub oak tree with a big bunch of mistletoe near the top. The sun had melted the snow from the top branches and the water had dripped slowly through the mistletoe, making icicles all through the thick green leaves. Icicles as thin as hair even hung on the tiny white berries.

Sage stared until her head hurt. True, the berries and the mistletoe were beautiful, but the thing that made her know that this was an inspiration were the shadows in the branches. They formed a manger with a shepherd's hook leaning against it. No people. Nothing like a complete nativity scene or a baby kicking and wiggling in the manger. Just the wooden box of straw with the mistletoe hanging inside the hook's crook. One part of the mistletoe lay in shadows. The other parts' icicles glistened with the sun rays sneaking in from the edges of the dark clouds.

"It's wonderful," she whispered.

"I thought you'd like it. I just wish that pair of cardinals would have come back so you'd have had some more color."

"I see color. There's green in the mistletoe leaves and red in the berries and the clouds are throwing beautiful shadows."

"What clouds?" He looked up. "Oh, I didn't see those."

Sage smiled. He was the messenger, but the best had been saved especially for her. She shoved the camera into her pocket and kissed him on the cheek.

His arms went around her and he pulled her so close that the sunlight couldn't sneak between them. "I really do like you, Sage Presley."

Her heart came to a screeching, skidding stop. "Like" meant commitment and that was a big black cloud without a silver lining.

"Now back to the house," he said. "You've got one to finish and one to start. The phone is already working and the electricity will soon be on, which will open up cell phones and laptops. Your uninterrupted days are about to come to a halt."

"Creed, I…" she stammered.

He laid a hand over her lips. "No explanations necessary."

"Really?"

"Really. I think you know your way back inside. I'll be there in an hour to grab a Reuben dog and then I'm going to come back outside until dark. I've been cooped up so long if I go back inside I'm going to get so grumpy that you'll throw me out the front door and lock it."

―∿―

He watched her jog back toward the house, camera in hand and hair flowing in the wind. She hadn't said that she was sorry but she didn't like him, that his kisses were just something to ease her boredom.

That was progress.

Creed had broken lots of horses in his time. Some of them required a lot of care and attention before he put the saddle on their back and his foot in the stirrup. He knew how to be patient even if it wasn't one of his virtues.

"I'm not comparing her to a damn horse," he mumbled before the voice in his head had time to smart off to him.

―∿―

Ada was on her way back to the house from the mailbox when her cell phone rang. She dug it out of her coat pocket and answered it on the third ring.

"Grand!" Sage said. "I miss you horrible. Do you realize this is the longest we've been away from each other since I moved home from college? No, it's the longest ever because when I was in college I came home every single weekend."

"Slow down, kiddo! Tell me about the cowboy. Where is he?"

"Out making pathways for the cows so they will have dirt under their feet instead of snow. I'm glad I never learned to knit or he'd want me to make little socks for them," she said.

"So he cares for his cattle, does he?"

"He's a cowboy from the heart out, Grand."

"Okay. Now tell me about you. You got any painting done with all the snow?"

Sage went into a long detailed description of her mistletoe pictures and what Marquee said about them. She even told her grandmother about the latest one that Creed had found for her. "He's got an eye for seeing the unusual for sure. But he didn't see the shadows," she said and caught her breath before going into more detail about the newest picture.

"Heard from Lawton?" Ada changed the subject.

Sage launched into April's tale of woe and ended up with the fact that Lawton was still planning the Christmas party on the third Saturday in December. Since they'd missed the annual Hanging of the Green because of the storm, they were having it the next day after the Christmas party.

"I always enjoyed that ceremony. It moves the soul," Ada said.

"Come home and go with me. We've gone to the Hanging of the Green my whole life. I can't believe you are going to miss it."

"I wasn't kiddin' when I said that Essie needs me, Sage. She actually crawled up on the house to nail down shingles."

"Shit!"

"You said it! Her boys want to put her in a nursing home."

"Never! I won't have it, Grand. Neither of you are ever going to a nursing home. Aunt Essie can come here."

"She'd wilt in the Texas heat at her age. Speaking of the weather, don't forget to put flowers on the graves. Red poinsettias for the holidays."

Ada heard the catch in Sage's voice. "By myself?"

"Take the cowboy with you."

"It's not his momma and daddy and grandpa."

"But he'll own the cemetery when I sell to him."

There was a long pause.

"Sage, are you still there?"

"You are really going to do this, aren't you?"

"I think I am," Ada said.

"I'm going to cry and pitch a hissy and pout and whine," Sage said.

"That sounds like a crock of shit! I didn't raise you to be a sissy. If I sell that ranch you aren't going to shed a single tear. You're going to stand on the porch with a straight backbone and wave at me. Do you hear me, Elizabeth Sage Presley?"

"You second-named me. You haven't done that in years."

"Yes, I did. This is serious, and you're acting like a crybaby, so you deserve it. Change happens and you need to realize it don't kill none of us."

"But I damn sure don't have to like it."

"Nobody said that you had to like it, but you won't carry on like a lovesick coyote."

"You are a tough old broad," Sage said.

"And don't you forget it for a minute."

"Can I grow up and be just like you?"

Ada laughed. "I hope you do. Did you make snow ice cream?"

"Yes, I did, and Creed says it's the best he ever ate and wanted to know my recipe. I tricked him. Put the can of milk in a bowl and whipped it with a whisk like I had all kinds of ingredients in there."

Ada laughed even harder. "Did you tell him the truth?"

"I did not!"

"You know that once he eats snow ice cream from that recipe, he will never leave."

"Well, shit! I didn't think of that."

"Too late now. Tell me about the cat and dog."

"Creed says Noel is going to have puppies any day. It's a madhouse around here. When you left, you took all the sanity with you."

"Old place needs some life in it," Ada said. "No, I didn't say Sage was going to be a wife."

"What!" Sage yelled.

"I'm back in the house and Essie thought she heard something about a wife."

"Tell her I said hell, no!"

"Be careful, darlin'. Sometimes that *hell, no* business sneaks up and bites you on the ass. Essie's got her hand out. I guess you're going to have to talk to her for a spell before you get to hang up."

Essie's voice came over the line loud and clear. She didn't sound like she was feeble and needed anybody's help. "Hello, Sage."

"What's this about you crawling up on the roof? Don't make me come out there, Aunt Essie."

"Shingles were coming loose. Somebody had to fix them and if I thought you'd move out here, I'd crawl back up there again. You don't be worryin' none about me, child. You've got enough to worry about with a strange man right in the house with you. I don't know what Ada was thinkin' about, leavin' you there with him. He's been a gentleman, hasn't he?"

"Yes, ma'am."

Ada wrestled the phone from her sister. "Give me that."

"Grand, what are you two doing? Fighting like little girls?" Sage asked.

"You damn right we are. Don't you be buyin' her brand of bullshit! I knew exactly what I was doing when that cowboy walked up on my porch. I saw a vision of the future. My Indian senses get sharper with age. Don't you dare laugh at me. You got the vision too. You just call it your PGs and paint what you see. I know in my heart he's the right cowboy to take on the Rockin' C."

"I'm starving. Let's make Reuben dogs," Creed's deep drawl came through the phone line. "Oh, I'm sorry, I didn't see that you were talking to someone."

"Reuben dogs? He eats sauerkraut on hot dogs. He's definitely a keeper," Ada told Sage.

"It's Grand," Sage said.

"Hi, Miz Ada. The sun is out and we're diggin' out.

Didn't lose a single cow and we gained some inside livestock," he raised his voice.

"Go take care of your cowboy," Ada said.

"You and Aunt Essie both are losin' your minds."

"Call me tomorrow when you have time, and don't pay no mind to Essie. I wouldn't leave you with a serial killer."

Chapter 8

"THAT ONE IS TOO BIG," CREED SAID.

Sage walked around the enormous cedar tree and imagined it with lights and tinsel. "But it's shaped just right."

"Look up, Sage."

She threw her head back expecting to see something fantastic like shadows creating a phenomenal idea for a painting or maybe a ball of mistletoe the size of a church punch bowl. But there was nothing but a promising Christmas tree.

"Now look at me and compare the tree to my height. Remember the ceiling is eight feet," he said.

"Well, dammit!"

"They look a lot smaller in the pasture than they really are. That thing would take up more than half of our living room."

"You sound like Grand," she said.

"Does that mean you've always wanted a tree that wouldn't go through the kitchen door?"

"I love Christmas. It's my favorite holiday and we've got tons of ornaments. When I was a little girl, I was afraid if we didn't get them all on the tree that the ones left behind would get their feelings hurt. It's crazy but..."

His big hand closed around hers, dwarfing it in size. She liked that. She'd been the tallest kid in the kindergarten class and kept that title until ninth grade when the boys started catching up. By then she'd heard all the jokes about height—*How's the weather up there? Can you see the ground? Do we all look like toys?* —and had developed a complex about it.

He led her through the crusty-topped snow to another tree. "How about this one?"

She studied it carefully. "It's four feet taller than you, which means at least three feet would have to come out of the top to make room for the angel, and it would look like a blob."

They went another fifty yards across the pasture with the rock formation that Sage had painted so many times getting closer and closer. Finally, she stopped and stared at the rock. Answers were there. They always had been. She just had to stare at it long enough and they would surface.

"You see something to paint or are we still looking for a tree?" Creed asked.

She hadn't realized that she'd stopped or that she'd been gazing at the rock so long. Creed hadn't pressured her to go on and find a tree. He didn't tell her that it was cold and they were walking through snow that came almost to the tops of their boots. He hadn't even shifted from one leg to the other and sighed deeply. It was those things that he didn't do that she appreciated as much as all the things he had done that whole week.

"The first time Grand brought me to this spot I was about five years old. Grand and I were going to put flowers on the graves. I hated that. It made it so final that I didn't have a father or a mother like other kids.

"I saw Grandpa's profile in the eroded edges of the

top rock. Even though he was dead and gone before I was born, I recognized him from the picture that Grand kept on the dresser in her bedroom. The sky was cloudless with only the silhouette of a single bird high up in the sky on the opposite side of Grandpa. There he was with his heavy eyebrows, wide nose with just a slight bump on the top, moustache, lower lip, and chin that dropped into a saggy neckline. And I told her that I was going to paint that rock someday."

"How long was it before you actually painted it?"

"More than sixteen years. I went home that day when I was five and drew it on a piece of paper and gave it to Grand. She still has it somewhere."

"It's quite a formation," he said.

It rose up out of the floor of the canyon like a huge ocher-colored sand castle with a sloped side at the back where a cautious climber could make his way to the ledge. The top flattened out with a small mesa, barely big enough for a man or a dog to sit on. At the back of the floor it looked as if someone had haphazardly set a chimney stack down.

She had sold a dozen or more paintings of the rock, changing the subtle cuts and erosions to suit whatever theme she put into the picture. Her highest selling piece had been a profile of an Indian chief cut into the top layer. And then she'd painted the chief sitting on the ledge looking out over his world, meditating about the changes that were coming to his people.

Now snow hid in the deep shadows. The sun had melted most of the white cap from the top, but icicles hung from the edges like those hanging from the roof of the back porch at the house and bunkhouse.

"How many pictures have you painted of this place?" Creed asked.

"Several?" she answered.

"You going to paint one of it for your new collection?"

She shook her head. The vision she'd been given that day didn't have snow. The clouds had moved across the erosion on the side and Grandpa Presley was gone. Now it was Creed's profile and the tip of his cowboy hat. And around the base of the formation the mesquite trees had the first bloom of springtime with its minty green leaves.

She didn't even want to think about what that might mean.

Creed wondered if they were going to stand there all day staring at the huge formation. When he'd first laid eyes on the thing, he'd thought about what fun it would have been to have something like that in the part of the world where he grew up. He and his brothers, along with the O'Donnells and Slade Luckadeau, would have turned it into a castle or a fort or any number of things.

She pointed to a tree standing all alone about ten feet from them. "What about that tree?"

"It could work," Creed said.

They walked around it, still hand in hand. She cocked her head to one side and then the other and they walked around it again.

"It is perfect," she said.

He dropped her hand and pulled the small chain saw out of a canvas backpack he'd thrown over his shoulder.

He fired it up and the noise bounced around in the still quietness of the snow-frosted canyon. The saw cut through the base of the tree, but it didn't fall far when he yelled, "Timber!"

Her laughter was music echoing off the canyon walls and coming back to settle in his ears, his heart, and his soul. He picked up the six-foot tree and shouldered it. The limbs knocked his hat off and snow slipped down his collar, his body's heat melting it into a cold trickle down his backbone.

He shivered. "That is some cold stuff when it gets next to bare skin."

She picked up his hat and put it back on his head. "That should help."

"You might have to warm me up when we get in the house."

"Is that a come-on line?"

"Could be. I never used it before, so if it is, it's original."

Dolly, his mother, had told him for years that he was a romantic at heart. He thought that meant he was a sissy and he fought hard against such a title. But that morning, walking in snow with a tree on his shoulder and Sage Presley at his side, he felt what his mother was saying.

He really was a romantic. He wanted a home and a wife and a whole yard full of kids to go with the kittens and the puppies. Sage had opened his eyes to that and he would always love her for it.

Love! I didn't say I was in love with her. I said that I would love her for making me consider a family.

Sage held the kitchen door open so Creed could maneuver the tree into the house, around the kitchen table, and into the living room.

"That is one big tree."

"Yes, it is. That first one you picked out wouldn't have even made it through the door."

Noel sniffed the tree then went back to her blanket. Angel peeked up over the edge of her basket and settled back down.

"I bet they think human beings are crazy," Sage said.

"Just be glad they don't have the sense to call 911 or they'd have us both committed. In their minds cows belong outside. Trees belong outside. People and pets belong inside."

Sage quickly moved her easel into the kitchen to make room for the tree. Creed had been right. Even though the tree looked like the smallest one in the whole canyon, anything bigger would have filled up the entire living room and edged over into the kitchen.

"There's going to be a mess when this stuff starts to melt. I tried to shake the tree good before I brought it on the porch, but there will be puddles when the snow melts," Creed said.

"It'll only be melted water and the floor is hardwood so it'll mop right up. Now let's go to the bunkhouse and bring up the decorations. The tree stand is in the box with the lights that go around the house and the barn. We'll make sure we bring that box in first."

"The barn?" Creed asked incredulously.

"It's no big deal. We leave the clips around the outside edge of the front of the barn and across the fence between the house and the barn. It's just a matter of putting them up."

"Are you teasing?"

"I am not! That way there's lights to be seen from every window in the house. When I was a little girl, I'd run into Grand's room and jump on her bed. And lights would shine through the window."

"Does each cow get jingle bells around her neck?" he asked.

Sage stared at his boots, which were dripping water onto the floor right along with the Christmas tree. "No, just the bulls. I've got a special string of red ones for you."

Creed chuckled. "Do I get to choose where you hang them?"

Sage blushed crimson. "No, that's my decision."

"Some days a homely old cowboy just can't win for losing." He sighed. "Let's go fetch the box with the stand in it and get this tree standing upright."

The decorations were stacked neatly in one of the three bedrooms in the bunkhouse. Back when Grandpa Presley was still alive they'd had all three bedrooms filled up and the hired hands did their own cooking. But one by one Grand had let them go through the following years and by the time Sage was old enough to remember, the bunkhouse was used for storage. Later, after she'd come home from college, she'd used the big living room and kitchen combo for her spring, summer, and fall work space, but it had been years since the water and gas had been turned on to the place.

She wondered if Creed would bring the whole ranch back to its original status: five or six times as many head of cattle, hay fields, and much, much less mesquite dotting the land.

Creed read the writing on the masking tape stuck

to the top of the blue plastic bin. "Tree stand. Outside lights. I pictured cardboard boxes."

"That's the right one to start with. We used to keep them in cardboard boxes, but the mice kept getting in them so we replaced the boxes with bins."

"Okay, let's go get it upright so it can drip on the floor while we string the barn lights. Then we'll mop up the mess and start decorating," he said.

She picked up a second box marked *tree lights*. "Mr. Organization."

"It takes a fair amount of that to run a ranch."

They were almost to the house when they stopped at exactly the same time and turned their ear toward the highway.

"Snowplows!" she said excitedly. "That means the electricity will be back on before long and I can do laundry."

"Me too! I'm almost out of clean socks and there's a whole basket full of dirty clothes in my room. I dreaded washing by hand," he said.

His room! Grand's room!

The whole concept was so tangled up that it made Sage's head hurt, so she pushed it away. Today she was decorating the tree and putting up lights. When it was all done, she intended to send pictures to Grand. And when she saw the pictures, it would make her so homesick that she would come home, maybe even before Christmas Eve. She could bring Essie with her and Sage would look after both of them. Hell, she'd give Essie her bedroom and clean up the bunkhouse to live in. She liked to go there to paint in the spring and fall anyway, and with very little work, it could be a nice big comfortable house just for her.

"What's on your mind, Sage?" Creed asked when they reached the back porch.

"Decorating," she said.

"You've been pretty quiet all morning. Something happened out there at the rock formation. What did you see?"

"What is probably a glimpse of the future."

"And that makes you mad?"

"Why mad?" she asked.

"Because it did not make you happy or you would have reacted differently."

"Not mad, but sad. I don't adapt well to change. I like my rut. I love it, as a matter-of-fact. It is my stability, my rock, and I know what's happening next."

"That's not life, darlin'."

"I know, but I don't have to like it."

<hr />

Creed fastened the tree stand onto the trunk of the tree and stood it upright in front of the window. And like the sun coming out after days and days of dreary rain, Sage's mood turned from dark to sunny instantly. She clapped her hands and kissed him on the cheek in her excitement.

"It's beautiful. It's the best one ever and I mean it. Look how perfect the limbs are and it's just the right height for the angel. She won't even hit her head on the ceiling, and we don't have to trim anything off. I wish the snow wouldn't melt off."

Creed laughed. "Darlin', you can't have fire and ice both. Now let's go get that barn and fence ready to light up before we take off our coveralls."

Putting the lights around the barn wasn't an easy feat in the snow, but by noon they had them in place and the cord taped down to the barn floor all the way into the tack room. Sage held her breath and plugged them in. They were old and that meant if one was shot none of them would light up. Then the painstaking job of unscrewing one bulb after another began until they found the one that was the dirty culprit with the blown filament.

She stuck it in the socket and hurried outside.

"Well, shit!" she yelled and shook her fist at the lights around the barn.

Creed was busy twining the next roll around the top string of barbed wire on the fence.

"Problem?" he asked.

"We've got a blown bulb somewhere. I'll get a good one from the bin."

"Why?"

"Because these are those old lights and if one is blown none of them work. And you have to replace them one at a time to see which one is bad."

"Sage, there is no electricity."

She popped her palm against her forehead. "Duh!"

"Don't beat yourself up. I still turn the light on in the bathroom every time I go in there and the oil lamp is right there to remind me."

"Crazy, ain't it? If you are finished, let's go get two boxes of decorations and start on the tree."

They had barely shut the door to the bunkhouse when a rat came out of nowhere, ran across the toes of Creed's boots, kept moving until it hit Sage's leg, climbed up one side of her jeans, scooted across her butt, and hurried back down the other side.

Like a contortionist she tried to turn her upper body

around on the lower. She slapped at her butt without touching it, screamed, and did a fancy dance.

Creed's grin went to a chuckle which quickly turned into a belly laugh.

"It's not funny!" she said.

"That was one fast rat."

"I hate those things. They get in the barn and stare at me with their little beady eyes, and you can stop laughing at me."

"I'm not laughing at you, darlin'. I'm laughing at the way that crazy rat turned you into a pretzel. Your pretty long legs and cute little butt were pretty close to break dancing. I hadn't ever seen a real person do that kind of dance. Don't worry about them pesky rats. Angel will take care of them for you. We'll put her and the kittens out in the barn and believe me, there won't be a rat problem."

"We can't put them in the cold. Maybe when they are older."

Creed crossed the floor and hugged her tightly to his chest. "It startled me too when it dashed across my boots."

She looked up. A kiss would go a hell of a long way to settling her nerves.

If you think that, you've lost your mind. Every time that cowboy kisses you, every nerve in your body starts wiggling and whining for more than kisses.

His eyes closed and his mouth settled over hers. His hands were suddenly under her shirt and on her bare back. This time she felt the hooks of her bra coming undone and his fingertips massaging from bra level to her neck. The rat was completely forgotten.

"Hey, anybody home? Sage, where are you?" a voice singsonged between the house and the bunkhouse.

She stepped back, quickly redid her bra, and adjusted her breasts into the cups. "It's April," she said.

"Didn't sound like one of my brothers." Creed grinned.

The door burst open. "You in here?"

Another ten minutes and they would have damned the torpedoes and rats and it would have been full speed ahead right there on the old worn-out sofa in the bunkhouse. If it wasn't for bad luck, Creed wouldn't have a lick of luck at all.

April looked from one to the other. "Hey, I figured y'all were decorating when I saw the lights around the barn. Got electricity yet?"

"Not yet. Y'all got any over on the Canyon Rose?" Sage left Creed's side and hugged April.

The woman reminded him of Macy, his old flame. She was short, blond, and built on a small frame. Her face had those delicate features that took a man's breath away and made him want to protect her forever.

Creed looked from one to the other. How could he have ever been attracted to someone like April? It was Sage, with her dark hair, chocolate-colored eyes, and long legs that threw extra beats into his chest.

"Have you met Creed Riley?" Sage asked.

April removed her stocking hat and shook out her blond hair. "No, I haven't, but Daddy says that Grand said good things about him when he took her to the airport."

"Well, then Creed meet April Pierce. And April, meet Creed. Since you are here, you can carry a box of decorations to the house and have dinner with us," Sage said.

"I'll help carry, but then I have to go back home. Hilda is bakin' a ham and she'll skin me alive if I'm not there for dinner. I was going stir-crazy in the house with all this snow and no electricity. Daddy called the power company. They said they'd have ours up and going by Monday or Tuesday. Lord, I didn't realize how much I depended on a hair dryer and a curling iron until they weren't available. How y'all been handling it over here?"

Sage handed April a box and led the way outside. "Not too bad, but we need to do laundry, so we'll be glad to have the electricity back. It's been early bedtimes with nothing but lamps."

April giggled.

"Get your mind out of the gutter," Sage whispered.

"With that hunky cowboy, there's not a chance of that happening," April whispered back.

Even though they were whispered, Creed heard every word. He wouldn't have minded a trip to the gutter that morning. No, ma'am, not one bit!

Chapter 9

SAGE AND APRIL SET THEIR BOXES ON THE KITCHEN table. Noel didn't growl, but her tail didn't wag in acceptance of the new human either.

April pointed. "What is that?"

"That's my new dog. Her name is Noel and she going to have puppies."

"I don't believe it," April whispered. "You got a dog and a pregnant one at that. That is even more amazing that Grand selling the ranch. And it's ugly, Sage. Grand would have bought you any kind of dog out there on the market and you buy that thing?"

Creed kicked the door shut with his boot. "She didn't get the dog. The dog got her. Someone must have dumped her and the cat on the road just before the blizzard. They found their way here."

He put the box he'd carried in on the table, hung his coat on the back of a chair, and went straight to the pantry for a mop and bucket. "I'll get the water mopped up before it gets into Angel's basket and she moves the kittens."

April peeled out of her heavy coat and hung it on the coatrack before she slouched down into a chair. "You're kidding me."

Sage removed her work coveralls, set a pot of coffee to perking on a back burner, and joined Angel at the table. "No, Angel is the cat. We think she got tossed out at the same time Noel did. We found her and the newborn kittens in the barn the next morning and it was evident that Noel knew her. I'll make a small pot of coffee. You can take time for a warm-up before you go back home. It's not dinnertime yet."

"A dog. A cat. A hunky cowboy that mops the floor. What happened over here?" April whispered.

"Crazy, ain't it?"

Creed finished mopping up and emptied the water into the sink, used some dish soap to wash out the bucket and the mop, and carried them back to the pantry. "I'm going out after those next two boxes. Be back in a minute."

"And he has the sense to get out and let us talk," April said. "If you don't want him, kick him over the fence onto the Canyon Rose. I won't let him get away."

"I'm mixed up about this whole thing. He's a good man but…"

"Ain't no buts involved except the way he fills out those jeans. I can see where you'd be in a tizzy though, girl. It would break my heart if Daddy sold the Canyon Rose even if he did hand me a cowboy like that one on a silver platter," April said. "Is he good in bed?"

"April!"

"Well, that ought to have some bearing. And I can see the way he looks at you and he mops, for God's sake, Sage."

Sage pushed her chair back, poured two mugs full, set one in front of April, and shoved the sugar bowl across to her.

"Well we aren't going to solve my problems, so let's work on yours." Sage turned the subject around.

April flicked her wrist. "My problems aren't ever going to be solved. Momma wants me to finish college and go on to vet school, and I want to learn to run the ranch that I'll inherit. Momma says that Daddy is still young enough to produce another baby or two and that the new wife will insist that the new kids wind up with the ranch, especially if the new wife gives Daddy a son."

"If Lawton was going to remarry, he would have already done it," Sage said.

"That's what I think."

"He'll always love Eva."

April nodded. "She hasn't remarried either. She used to date a lot but lately she's married to her job."

"Think they'll ever come to their senses?"

"I didn't, but then I come over here and you've got the ugliest dog on the face of the earth and there's a cat and kittens. I think I believe in miracles again. Hell's bells, Sage. Santa Claus might even come down the chimney at Canyon Rose again!" April laughed.

"Want to see Angel and the babies while the coffee cools?"

April followed Sage into the living room.

The yellow cat looked up at the intruder with indifference and curled tightly around her kittens.

"Ahh, they are so cute. What are you naming them? Going to keep them all?" April asked. "That was one of my favorite parts of coming to the ranch in the summer. There were always baby kittens to play with."

"Haven't decided on names, but they'll be taking up permanent residence in the barn as soon as it gets warm. Creed assures me that Angel will kill her weight in rats at least three times a day."

"Well, they should have Christmas names since their momma is Angel and they were born in a manger. If there's a boy, name him Rudolph."

Sage picked up one of the fat little kittens and held it to her cheek. "This one looks like a Rudolph, doesn't it? Boy or girl, I christen you Rudolph today."

"Well, I've done my day's work. I named a kitten for Sage Presley. Call the Smithsonian or at least the Guinness people because it has to be recorded in someplace real special," April said. "I'm headed home now. I'll be back. Next time I'll knock before I rush in. I wasn't thinking about the cowboy and you being in the bunkhouse together."

"We were just getting Christmas decorations."

"Sage, honey, you don't lie worth a damn."

April took a couple of sips of the coffee, donned her coat, and closed the front door just as Creed opened the back one. He brought in another big container and carried it all the way to the living room. "Looks like the tree has dried out. Want to eat or start decorating? Where's April?"

"I'll put a frozen pizza in the oven and we can string the lights while it cooks. April went home," Sage answered.

"Cardboard pizza. My favorite," Creed said.

"Don't make fun of them. It's better than a bologna sandwich, and that's the alternative."

"I was serious. When I was a little kid, Grandpa Riley would make them for me. I don't know if it was really the pizza or spending time with my grandpa that I liked. The tape on this box says it's got the tree lights in it. I'll hold them on my arms and you can put them on the tree."

"This ain't your first rodeo, is it, Creed?"

"No, ma'am. And none of us want to suffer the wrath

of Momma if we don't put the lights away right when they come off either," he answered.

"She must be kin to Grand. Don't matter if it takes a whole week—the lights best be stored just right without any tangles."

He got the first strand ready and waited for her to slide the pizza in the oven. She kicked off her boots and giggled on her way across the living room floor.

"Do I look crazy standing here with lights around my arms like knitting yarn?"

"No, I was thinking that you are pretty vulnerable. If you drop those lights one might break and we'll have to test them all. And if you drop them they'll tangle all up and we'll have to spend hours getting them ready to go on the tree."

"So don't drop the lights, right?" he asked.

"So I could do whatever I wanted to you right now, including hanging those jingle bells on you somewhere," she teased.

"I'll stand very still."

"Creed Riley, you aren't any fun at all."

"Sounds like fun to me."

The air around them crackled with heat and suppressed desire. The back of Sage's neck tingled. If someone had told her the week before that she'd be flirting with a cowboy on the Rockin' C by the next Saturday, she would have had them declared insane.

She grabbed the end of the light string and deliberately brushed her breasts against his arm. His sharp intake of breath said that it affected him every bit as much as it did her. She bent over to start at the bottom tree limbs and his knee touched her fanny, setting it on fire.

She was flirting like a teenager, but it was so much fun that she didn't want to stop. When the lights were finally perfectly strung, she plugged them in to see if they worked.

"Still no electricity," he said.

"Shit! I knew that. Habits die hard."

Habits die hard. I hate change. But it happens and I'll have to deal with all of it when it does.

With the aroma of cedar and pizza combining and a Christmas tree right there in front of her, Sage decided that none of it was going to kill her.

She turned to find him so close that she threw up her hands to land on a chest full of hard muscles. His lips touched hers in a kiss that was a blend of sweet and hot. With a gentle probe his tongue asked permission to enter her mouth. She gave it by opening up and inviting him right inside.

And then the timer on the stove buzzed, telling them that the pizza was ready.

"God hates me," Creed moaned.

"No, He loves me," she laughed.

Creed followed her into the kitchen. "How do you figure that?"

"Twice today we've been interrupted. I think it's an omen. It's not time for the next step, Creed."

"That commitment word?"

She pulled the pizza from the oven. "No, that Creed word. We need to slow the buggy down and step back to think about what we're doing."

"That's not cardboard pizza. That is the real thing," he said.

"It's just a better frozen pizza than those little thin ones. I'll pour some sweet tea if you'll slice it up."

"Why?" he asked as he pulled up the lever and popped ice cubes from an old metal tray.

"Because it's hot."

"I make you hot?"

"I don't think we're on the same page. I was talking about pizza and needing tea because it is hot."

"Okay, why slow the buggy down?"

"Because. It's going too fast."

Creed understood, but like she had said earlier, he didn't have to like it. He wanted the ranch, but he didn't want there to ever be reason later in life for her to think he'd used her as a pawn to get it.

He set two glasses of iced tea on the table at the same time she put a big round pizza on a hot pad in the middle. He bowed his head and laid his hand on top of hers for grace.

"Amen," they said in unison when he finished.

"I'm starving."

"It takes a lot of energy to find a tree and put it up. Think we will survive all this?" he asked.

"What kind of question is that?"

"We managed to get through the blizzard without killing each other. I even decided you weren't such a bad person after all."

"Oh, you thought I was at one time?"

"Hey, put yourself in my shoes. Woman sells me the ranch but I have to sign a paper saying you can live on it until you die. Then she tells me that when you get home get ready for a shit storm because you don't want her to sell and you are going to pitch a fit like what ain't never seen in these parts. What would you think?"

Sage smiled. "Did she really say it like that?"

"She did and I was so damned glad to hear the news that the roads were closed that I almost danced a jig, woman. Truth is, I was about half-afraid of you. That morning when I found you in the kitchen I was stunned out of my mind. It's a wonder I could speak."

"So I wasn't what you thought I'd be?" she asked.

"I was expecting something way, way different, lady. Your picture doesn't do you justice. You are one beautiful woman."

"Thank you for that. But put yourself in my place."

"Are you going to be really angry when she sells me this ranch?"

Sage thought about the question while she chewed. "Not angry. Sad."

"That's what you were thinking about this morning, isn't it?"

She nodded.

"My momma was hoping I'd hate this place. All of her kids are within a thirty-minute drive but me. I'm the only one who won't be there for Christmas."

Sage looked up quickly. "But you can go home for the holidays if you want to. Grand will be back for those days. She and I can do the chores."

"This is my home. I knew it when I walked up on the porch that first day. Home is where the heart is, not where you hang your hat, and for the first time in my life I want to be here. Going to Ringgold now is going to Momma's house, not home. And I want to spend my first Christmas on my very own ranch, not at Momma's house."

"Okay then, let's eat and start decorating the tree. I bet we can get it done before time for chores," she said.

———w———

They looped the tinsel on the tree and then began hanging the ornaments. He removed each one from a bit of tissue paper and handed it to Sage, who told stories as she hung them.

She'd made the reindeer ornament from an old wooden clothespin with the glued on eyes and red felt nose in kindergarten. The long, skinny glass ones had belonged to Grand's mother, so she hung them in the middle of the tree to make sure Angel and later Rudolph and his siblings wouldn't bat them off.

"How do you remember all that?" Creed asked.

"I've been reminded every single Christmas that I can remember. I loved hearing the stories behind the ornaments and Grand loved telling them. Grandpa bought a new ornament for her every year. This is the last one he gave her."

She held up a gingerbread man made of cedar. "He made it himself."

"He was pretty good with a whittlin' knife, was he?"

"He was gone before I was born but he must have been because some of the ornaments are made of wood. Grand said that those were the lean years when he couldn't afford to buy her anything so he made one. It just dawned on me, Creed. Grand took over running the whole ranch all alone when she was in her early forties, after a bad year. And then in the next seven years she lost her son and her daughter-in-law and was left with me."

"She must've always been tough."

Sage nodded. "She ran this place and raised me with a steel hand, but she's also soft. I remember… we've got to make cookies."

He looked up at Sage and grinned. "Lord, girl, you can turn the course of conversation around on a dime."

Sage's lungs burned as if the air was hot and her mind really did plunge into the gutter. If he walked into a room full of women and looked out over the crowd and smiled, the women would flock to him like bees to a honey jar.

"People will be stopping by during the holidays. Grand always offers them a cup of coffee or hot chocolate and she puts a plate full of cookies and candy on the table."

"What kind of cookies?"

"All kinds, but especially sugar cookies with icing and gingerbread bars. We have to make gingerbread bars because Grand said her great-great-grandmother made them and it's a Christmas tradition."

"O… kay!" Creed dragged the word out to four syllables.

She hung the last ornament and stood back, adjusted a few, popped her hands on her hips, and declared it finished. "Now when the electricity comes back we'll light up the whole ranch. Well, we will when we get the lights on the house and that's the next job."

"You are a drill sergeant. What if I wanted to take a long nap, do chores, and read until my eyes get tired?"

She air-slapped him on the shoulder. "Really?"

He laughed. "No, Sage. I want to finish decorating and then make cookies. I can guarantee you that I'll eat them as fast as they can cool, so you'd better make a whole bunch."

She sat down in his lap. "You are a good sport, Creed Riley."

Chapter 10

CREED HELD A SINGLE STALK OF MISTLETOE TOWARD Sage. It was covered with white berries, but the leaves on it weren't as thick as the ones he'd either brought in on his shoulder or else tracked inside.

"You ever heard the legend of the mistletoe?" he asked.

She laid it on the window ledge. "No, I haven't. You can tell me about it in front of the fireplace. It's colder this morning. I turned on the oven and two burners on the stove to warm up this end of the house. Coffee?"

"Yes, please. According to the thermometer on the fence post out there it's eighteen degrees. Snow ain't meltin' at this temperature. Noel ran out long enough to make some yellow snow beside the porch and whined to get back inside. She didn't even go feed with me. The rooster didn't want to do much crowing and I didn't even hear a grunt coming from the hogs."

She carried two steaming mugs to the living room, set one on each end table, and pulled a quilt from the back of the sofa. She curled up on the sofa with a quilt wrapped snuggly around her legs. "It's a wonder the cow even gave milk."

"Well, it did look like ice cream," Creed teased as he hung his hat on the rack. "The refrigerator is full of milk, Sage. What are we going to do with all of it?"

"Grand gives it away or she skims it, uses the cream

for butter, and feeds the rest to the hogs. Now tell me about the legend thing. Listen to that wind."

"It's howling worse than when the blizzard was in full force. You'd think the sheer force of it would melt some of the snow, but it ain't happenin'. All it did was blow it around and drift it up against the house and barn. I'm not seeing much thawing. At least it puts nitrogen back into the soil and we'll have some pretty pasture grass come springtime."

Sage snuggled deeper under the patchwork quilt. She was glad for a small house that morning because it heated quickly. If the temperature kept falling they'd have to light the propane heater on the south wall of the living room. She and Grand saved that for the last resort in the winter. Propane was expensive and they had to use it for cooking and hot water. But they always used as much wood as possible to heat the house. Mesquite was cheap and using it was two-fold. It cleared the land and warmed the house.

What kind of setup would she have in a trailer? After the mother of all storms, she sure wouldn't have anything that was totally electric.

"You were going to tell me about the mistletoe," she said.

"Just getting my toes thawed out before I started talking."

Sage set her mug on the floor. "There's lots of quilts in the linen closet. I'll get another one."

She tossed the one she'd been using on Creed's lap, tucked it around his thighs, and made sure his feet were covered well. "Your toes are frozen, Creed. And you've only got one pair of socks on your feet."

"I didn't realize it was so cold until I got out there. It was thirty-two degrees yesterday and the sun made it feel even warmer. I bet the wind chill brings it down into the single digits tonight."

"It's a wonder you've got any digits after being out there more than an hour with only one pair of cotton socks. Are all your good wool boot socks dirty? We can do hand laundry and hang it in front of the fireplace to dry, or we could light the heater and dry things on chairs in front of it. Even if everything in the house is running, it won't use up all the propane in just a week."

She mumbled the whole way from the hall to the linen closet and back. Mainly, it was to cover the feelings brought on when she touched him. She'd hugged lots of men, danced up close and personal with men, and brushed against them in the grocery store or the pew after church. None of them turned up her hormones like tucking a quilt around Creed's toes did.

Creed raised his voice. "Do you know anything about the gas pump? Is there enough in the tank to keep the generator running? I haven't had to put any in the tractor or my truck since I got here, but the gauge is broken so I don't know how much is in reserve."

"Gauge has been broken for years. The gas company checks the pumps on the tenth of the month. The weather kept them from getting here but now that the plows have cleared the roads they should be here any day. Do y'all keep diesel and gas pumps on your property in Ringgold?" she asked.

"Yes, ma'am. Farmers and ranchers don't like to stop working and drive twenty miles to get a tank full of fuel for a tractor or a pickup. And thank you for the quilt. It's warming my toes right up. I don't think any of them are going to fall off from frostbite."

"Next time wear warm socks," she said. "You were going to tell me a story about the mistletoe, remember?"

"In the early days when folks hung up the kissing plant or a kissing ball, each time a feller kissed a girl he had to pick off a berry. When the berries were all gone then the kissing was finished for that season," he said.

"Us tall, gangly, cosmetically challenged girls had best claim a spot under it pretty early then because when the berries got scarce the good-lookin' cowboys would be more particular, right?"

"Sage Presley, there isn't one thing awkward or gangly about you. Cosmetically challenged, my ass. You are the most beautiful woman this old cowboy ever clapped his eyes upon. And believe me, if you ever got stuck under the mistletoe, cowboys would be pushing each other out of the way. Hell, there might even be pistols drawn and blood shed just trying to get to you."

She shook out a second quilt and covered herself with it when she sat down. "And where would you be in all that pushin' and shovin'?"

"I'm the one with one arm holdin' you close, the other one pickin' berries as fast as I can, and my lips on yours. When they're all gone then the other cowboys can go home," he teased.

Creed, with his hard muscles and his dreamy green eyes, had said she wasn't cosmetically challenged but that she was the most beautiful woman he'd ever seen. Had he not seen many women or was she really that special?

"Sounds like we'd best take advantage of the oven being hot and make a pan of biscuits to go with some sausage gravy for breakfast," he said. "And then you mentioned us making more cookies today?"

The man was so frustrating that she could have thrown him out into the cold to freeze his toes the rest of the way off. One minute they were discussing things that made her heart thump; the next minute his mind was on food. The vibes that were making her jumpy as a virgin bride couldn't have affected him at all or he wouldn't be talking about cookies.

She stood up too fast, got tangled up in the quilt, and fell headlong toward the fireplace. Strong arms caught her and whipped her around away from the fire.

Creed's deep voice said, "Whoa, darlin'. That ain't no way to get warmed up."

She hung on to him like he was a rock in the midst of a whirling tornado.

"That was scary," she panted.

When he didn't answer, she looked up. She barely had time to shut her eyes before his warm mouth wiped out any thought of food, cookies, or even Grand. Then he scooped her up and settled her back on the sofa.

She didn't care if he was carrying her outside to roll her in the snow. As long as he kept kissing her, she'd be warm and safe. Forget that idea about a quilt to snuggle under. With the heat his kisses generated they damn sure didn't need anything else to keep them warm.

"I've wanted to kiss you all morning. You are so damn sexy," he whispered between lingering kisses that grew hotter and hotter.

She unfastened three buttons on his soft red and black plaid flannel shirt and slipped her hands inside. He wasn't wearing the usual thermal undershirt so her hands landed on hard muscles, hot skin, and taut nipples; oh yeah, he had felt the vibes, all right.

"Your hands are like silk," he said.

"Touching your skin makes them hotter'n the devil's pitchfork," she mumbled.

His warm breath created scorching waves up and down her whole body when he said, "Oh, honey, you don't even know what hot is."

Her pulse quickened and her heart raced with pure old sexual desire.

He unzipped her coveralls, reached inside, and unfastened her bra. She shifted when his hand moved from her back to the front to give him easier access to her breast. His sudden intake of breath said that he liked the way it filled his hand as much as she did.

His lips strung a trail of slow steamy kisses down her long, slender neck and ended at the breast. She shouldn't be doing this. It would only lead to the point of no return and then she'd feel even guiltier after sex with Creed.

"You taste like heaven," he said.

"How many times have you tasted heaven?" she gasped.

"Darlin', a man only gets one taste of heaven in a lifetime."

She didn't care if she never found her way back. She wanted to be his one taste even if it meant a heartache when he drove away from the ranch. Her arms went around his neck and she grabbed a fist full of dark hair. She felt as if she were driving down into the canyon on ice with no brakes.

"I could die right here," he mumbled.

"Please don't. Not just yet."

She let go of his hair and found her way back inside his shirt.

He grabbed her hand and brought her fingers to his lips, tasting them one by one. She'd never known that the tips of her fingers were erogenous zones until he licked each one like he was eating an ice cream cone on a hot summer afternoon. If it meant living forever if he stopped or dying if he kept on, she would have still wanted him to keep touching her.

He'd stopped abruptly and the message was loud and clear. He was gentleman enough to stop right there and make cookies the rest of the morning.

Flirting was done. It was her call.

The choice came down to two options. It was either mount up and ride or else put the horse back into the pasture and never saddle him up again.

The phone didn't ring. April didn't knock on the door. God wasn't going to interfere. It was totally up to Sage, and she didn't have cold feet. She wanted more.

His heart matched hers for speed, and one thumb made slow lazy circles against her cheekbone while the other one did the same on the soft skin on her wrist. Lord, where did all those sex zones come from anyway? Or was it just Creed? He could probably kiss the callused soles of her feet and send her into a tailspin.

She could feel his erection pushing against his jeans and into her belly. The heat of it would leave something akin to sunburn right above her bikini panties, even though two layers of denim.

"My heart is racing," he said.

"I can feel it. It's keeping time with mine."

Creed tucked her hair behind her ears and cupped her

face in both of his hands. His lips found hers in a passionate kiss that had a voice. It promised that he wouldn't leave her. That the Rockin' C really was his home.

That's what she wanted to believe.

Sage wrapped her long legs firmly around his waist. Without breaking the kisses, he carried her across the living room floor and started down the hall toward his bedroom.

"Oh, no!"

"What?"

"Not in there. She would haunt me. Let's go to my bedroom."

He grinned and her heart pumped harder. He eased the door open with his toe and laid her on the unmade bed. He stretched out beside her, one arm around her tightly, the other one cupping her neck for better leverage.

Without breaking the kisses, she removed her shirt and bra and tossed them onto the floor and then closed the space between them, pressing tightly against his chest. She reached a hand between them to undo his belt and unzip his jeans.

He gasped when she wrapped a hand around his erection.

"Soft as silk and hard as steel," she whispered close enough to his ear that she could nibble on it.

"My God, Sage.'"

"Looks like you are ready," she said. It was a heady feeling, knowing that she affected him the same way he did her.

"Ready as hell." He unfastened her jeans and tugged them away from her hips.

"Take them all the way off," she whispered.

She'd never in her life had sex in the house before. Would lightning flash through the roof and strike her dead?

He propped up on an elbow. "Sage, this is it. If you are going to say no then do it right now and we'll walk away from this bedroom. Because if you are completely naked in this bed with me, I won't be able to control a damn thing."

She didn't even hesitate. "I can get mine off in thirty seconds. What about you?"

"Darlin', if you aren't going to say no, I can shuck out of these jeans in ten seconds."

She jumped out of bed and removed her jeans leaving only a pair of red silk bikinis, which soon joined the shirt in the corner. "Ten, nine, eight," she counted.

All of his clothing was lying in a pile on the floor and he'd pulled the covers up over them when she reached the final number. His hands were both tender and demanding. His hands and mouth searched out her body for new territory to build the fire hotter and hotter until she couldn't bear another minute.

She'd touched, tasted, and returned his moves until she could feel the aching desire in both of them. She arched high against him and wrapped her legs tightly around his body as he pushed inside her. She wanted him worse than she'd ever wanted anything in her life. She rocked with him, his mouth on hers, his tongue making love to her mouth and his hands gliding over her sides and down her thighs at the same time.

"You like this?" he asked.

"Yes, sir! Please don't stop."

"I couldn't if I wanted to," he said.

There were no words to describe what she felt. A taste of heaven wouldn't come close. She wanted to last all day, but her body screamed for release. He took her as high as possible without giving her the ultimate satisfaction, then slowed his rhythm to let her cool slightly before he increased the speed once again. Finally, she was so frenzied she could take no more. She had to have the whole thing or her ribs were going to crack from her heart's fast pace.

"Please," she said.

"Right now?"

She nodded.

He increased the rhythm.

"Oh. My. Sweet. Lord." She could force out one word at a time and panted hard between them.

She might not be a virgin, but she was damn sure in virgin territory because the minute he gave a hard thrust and settled his face into her neck, she realized that this was a whole new game. Her brain was totally numb. Her body was totally satisfied. Her hormones purred like a kitten. Her skin finally felt cool.

He shifted to one side and drew her close, pulled the covers that had gotten kicked away up over them, and kissed her on the forehead.

Was that it? Would he turn over and snore now?

"Sage, I'd tell you how that felt and what I feel right now, but I can't find the words," he said softly.

She had gone to places she'd never been. She'd hit highs she didn't even know existed. Her heart and soul were so full that they were about to explode. She understood what he was saying.

"Just hold me, Creed," she said hoarsely.

He pulled her even closer, nuzzling his face into her neck.

She shut her eyes and snuggled up, her body melting against his.

And the two shall become one.

She'd heard that at weddings but she'd never understood it until that moment. Bittersweet as they were because Creed could still leave her if he decided not to buy the ranch.

Chapter 11

IN THOSE MOMENTS JUST BEFORE SAGE OPENED HER EYES she smelled coffee and something sweet. Then her bed bounced and she couldn't hold on to the dream, but she was sure it had to do with Creed Riley. And there he was, holding a tray with toast, scrambled eggs, cookies, and coffee.

"Good morning, beautiful," Creed said.

"Good morning, cowboy." Sex had not taken away his deep Texas drawl, and it sounded even hotter than it had when he first barreled his way into the kitchen.

"Hungry?"

She sat up and he quickly propped pillows behind her and set the tray on her lap.

"It looks wonderful. Have you eaten?"

"Yes, ma'am. Did the chores. Milked the cow and cooked breakfast."

She put a fork full of eggs into her mouth. "Good!"

"Good that I got the chores done or good eggs?"

"Both."

"Temperature dropped another five degrees. It's down to thirteen, but I saw the trucks from the electric company making their way down the road this morning. We might get our electricity back soon."

Not a word about the day before. Nothing about staying in bed and making love until dinnertime and then all the sexual innuendos that went on while they made sugar cookies in the afternoon.

"Should we talk about it?" she asked.

"Nothing to talk about. Either we get electricity or we don't. We've managed to live without it a week now. Would be nice to have lights and if it's not on tomorrow, I'm definitely going to have underwear and socks hanging all over the living room."

"I'm talking about sex, not electricity," she said.

"Oh, nothing to talk about there either. It was out-of-this-world fantastic."

"Creed, I don't do this kind of thing. I don't jump into bed with a man I've only known a week. I'm not that kind of person."

"I know," he said softly, "and we were supposed to be slowing the wagon down, weren't we?"

Did that mean he was sorry they'd gone over the barbed wire fence into territory they had no business exploring?

"Yes, we were, and hell's bells, this is supposed to be awkward."

He grinned. "But it's not, is it?"

"No, it feels right."

"I thought so too."

She reached out and touched his cheek. "Now that we got that out of the way, what's on the agenda for today?"

He leaned over and kissed her on the forehead. "First of all, you have breakfast and then we're going out for a drive in the big tractor to see how things are on the rest of the ranch. Bundle up good or you'll freeze your cute little butt off."

"Heater only works part of the time," she said.

"Then put on two pair of socks."

———

Creed picked up a sugar cookie and nibbled on it while Sage finished her breakfast. She'd said that the powdered sugar in the recipe was what made it melt in his mouth. He didn't agree. It was her hands in the dough that made it so special.

When she'd finished with her breakfast, he dropped a kiss on her forehead and headed out of the room, tray in hand.

"I'll brush my teeth and get dressed. I'll be there in five minutes," she said.

"I want to check the pastures to see when we can turn the cattle out of that feedlot. They're getting bitchy."

She laughed. "Most of them are cows and they've been cooped up for a week. They've got reason to be bitchy."

"You aren't."

"You callin' me a heifer?" she teased.

He turned at the doorway. "No, ma'am. This cowboy wouldn't make a stupid mistake like that. I'm saying that you're female, the prettiest kind of female, and that you've been a real trouper during all this. I didn't hear you whining about your curling iron or hair dryer not working. You barely even mentioned not having a washing machine."

"Well, then, thank you, Mr. Riley. Now if you'll move, I'll get ready to go straighten out those bitchy cows."

He took a step out into the hall and watched her all the way to the bathroom. She looked adorable in his red and black plaid flannel shirt hanging halfway to her knees.

———

Sage spent an extra few minutes brushing her hair and gathering it into a ponytail at the nape of her neck. She liked it higher up on her head, but that got in the way of her knit hat. If it was only thirteen degrees she'd need something to warm her ears. If she hadn't put the skids on the wagon, she could have depended on Creed to heat her up. Of course, sitting beside him in the narrow confines of a tractor cab could do the trick without him doing a blessed thing except being the sexy cowboy he was by nature.

She pulled on her last clean pair of jeans, two pairs of socks, and then started to unbutton his shirt.

"No," she said aloud.

She pulled the shirt up over her head, dug around in her drawer for a bra and a thermal knit undershirt, and put them both on. Then she put his shirt back on over that. It was soft. It smelled like him and she liked that.

When she reached the living room, she drew a rocking chair up to the basket of squirming kittens and picked up the yellow one. "Good morning, Rudy."

"You better name the other two or they'll feel left out," Creed said.

She picked up the bigger of the two black ones. "These two should have reindeer names too. Look, Creed, there's a little white blaze on his hip that we didn't notice. He is definitely Comet. And the solid black one is Donner."

"What if they're all girl kittens?" he asked.

"Then we'll take them to cat therapists when they are teenagers and get help for the complexes they'll have because they have weird names," she laughed.

"You about ready?" he asked.

"Almost."

She went over to Noel's blanket and squatted down to pet her. "Did Creed run your legs off this morning doing chores, girl? You look like you could sleep all day long. You take a good nap and we'll be back in a little while. In a couple of days we'll go up to Claude and get you some of that fancy dog food in cans. Will you like that?"

Noel wagged her tail and licked Sage's fingers, but she didn't move from her blanket. Sage straightened up and went to the kitchen where she put on her old work boots. "Who would have thought I'd be attached to a dog and a bunch of cats or that I'd let them come into the house?"

"You have a good heart, Sage. You wouldn't deliberately let something stay out in the cold and freeze to death," Creed said.

"And besides, who'd take in something as cosmetically challenged as Noel?" she giggled.

"Beauty is in the eye of the beholder," he quipped.

"She does grow on you, don't she? I thought she was the ugliest mutt I'd ever seen when she got here, but she gets cuter by the day."

He settled his felt hat on his head and handed her a black knit stocking cap. "Yes, ma'am, she does."

The tractor didn't move fast, especially through snow. He turned on the radio and picked up a station out of Amarillo that played all country music.

"You like that kind of music?" Sage asked. She'd been to bed with him, kissed him until her knees were weak, and tried to accept the fact that he'd be living on the ranch, but she didn't even know what kind of music he liked.

"Yes, I do. What do you like?"

"Rap," she said seriously.

He jerked his head around so quick that his hat fell off and landed in her lap. She picked it up and handed it back to him.

"I'm teasing. I grew up on country because that's what Grand likes. So yes, I like that station. It does seem strange after a whole week of nothing but silence to have music again. I didn't realize how much I've missed it."

Brad Paisley began to sing a song called "Long Sermon." It talked about two boys sitting in church listening to a long sermon when they'd much rather be outside in the sunshine in a boat doing some serious fishing.

Creed kept time with his thumbs on the steering wheel and sang along with the chorus.

"Ever done that?" Sage asked.

"Oh, yeah, I have. How about you?"

"Don't tell God but I've painted dozens of pictures in my mind while the preacher sermonized," she said.

"Where do you go to church? Claude?"

She shook her head. "We go over to the chapel at Canyon Rose on Sunday afternoons."

"Afternoons?" Creed asked.

"The preacher comes from Amarillo. It's just a little missionary church so we have our Sunday service at two thirty on Sunday afternoons. Unless the canyon fills up with snow and the preacher can't get down the roads."

"Baptist?"

Another shake of the head. "Methodist. But everybody in the canyon comes to it. Catholic. Methodist. Holiness. We don't pay much attention to denomination."

An Alan Jackson song followed that song and then

there was a five-minute spread of news that talked mostly about the power outages and the snowstorm. That was followed by the weatherman telling them that there was another cold front coming across the plains that would hit that night. Temperatures would drop even further, but there wouldn't be any moisture with it.

"However," he said, "folks can begin to rest assured if they live in the Palo Duro Canyon that they are going to have a white Christmas. Don't put the sleighs up yet. You might need them and the horses to get around. And for the next hour we'll be taking requests for your favorite holiday songs by country artists. And our first request is from a listener in Claude who wants to hear 'Joy to the World.'"

"I love Christmas carols," Sage said.

"We used to go caroling in Ringgold. We'd gather up at the church and Daddy would hook up a trailer to the back of his pickup. He'd throw some little square hay bales on it for the O'Donnell crew to sit on as they played. Those folks can play anything that's got strings on it. And we'd go all over town, then we'd cross the Red River into Terral, Oklahoma, and serenade those folks too."

"That sounds like fun. We should do it here," she said.

"Maybe next year," he said. "We'll plan it early and get lots of folks to go with us."

"I'll be Home for Christmas" by John Berry started playing.

Grand would at least be home for Christmas. Why couldn't they all live on the ranch? Grand, Essie, Creed, and Sage?

You can't have it both ways, Sage. Grand's voice pestered her again.

"O Come All Ye Faithful" was the next song.

Faith! That meant trust. She wanted to have the faith to believe that everything would work out for the best in the end, but it wasn't easy for Sage. That old adage about changing what she could and accepting what she couldn't came to mind. The last few words that said she wanted the wisdom to know the difference played through her mind like a broken record.

Creed reached across and covered her hand with his. The heat was still there in all its radiant glory. Sparks still bounced off the windows of the tractor cab. She looked out across the snow-covered canyon, but it didn't take her mind from Creed and the way he'd controlled her body the day before.

Accept it. Stop fighting what is right in front of you and accept it.

"What's your favorite?" Creed asked.

"Favorite what?"

Part of your sexy body? Your eyes. No, your muscles. Hell, don't know.

"Christmas carol," he said when she didn't answer right away.

"'O Holy Night,'" she said. "Yours?"

"Well, I like 'Grandma Got Run Over by a Reindeer,' but my favorite is probably 'Mary, Did You Know?' That one brings tears to my eyes."

She reached across the cab and slapped him on the knee. "You had me going there for a while."

"So do you like the one about Mary?" he asked.

"Yes, I do. It's one of my top five Christmas favorites.

The preacher's wife usually sings it at the Hanging of the Green ceremony at church."

She was amazed when the DJ told time and temperature before he started the next five minutes of songs. It was sixteen degrees and it was after eleven o'clock. They'd been out for more than two hours and it was almost dinnertime already.

Sage didn't realize she was so cold until she started toward the house. Her nose felt as if it would fall off if she touched it, and her toes were numb. If Creed got cabin fever any more that day, he could take another tractor ride by himself. And her stomach had set up a growling noise. Every bit of her breakfast had gone to make energy to keep her from freezing plumb to death.

Once inside, she shrugged out of her coat and hung it up. Summers in the canyon might be hot as a barbed wire fence in hell, but by golly, she didn't have to keep putting on and taking off her coat or coveralls. Well, they could dry out completely because she was going to paint all afternoon and nothing or no one was going to get in her way.

Right after, she threw a couple more sticks of wood on the fire and warmed her fingers enough so that they could hold a brush. A whimper came from the living room and Sage rounded the end of the bar to see if Noel was waiting at the front door. Creed hurriedly hung up his coat, kicked off his boots, and beat her to the Christmas tree. Crazy cowboy! The dog wouldn't be whining at the Christmas tree if she wanted to go outside.

"Merry Christmas, Sage," Creed said.

Why in the world would he tell her that right then? It was the tenth of December, fifteen days before Christmas.

He pointed at Noel, who was lying on her blanket wagging her tail.

She'd had the dog more than a week now. How could that be her Christmas present? Creed stepped to one side and she saw the puppies inside the C that Noel made with her body. She squealed and ran across the room, fell down on her knees, and rubbed Noel's ears.

"Three of them? And they are beautiful," she whispered. "Look at the little spotted things, Creed. Not a single one looks like her."

Creed squatted beside her. "They all look just like bluetick hound dogs."

He picked up one and handed it to her.

She rubbed its head against her cheek. "I don't know why I fought Grand against a pet." She held it out from her and studied it: black ears, brown around where its eyes would be when they opened up, a splotchy blaze up across its square black nose. The rest of the white dog was covered with what looked like big blue ticks.

"Hello, Elvis," she said.

"Elvis?" Creed asked.

"He sang about a blue Christmas. And there ain't no doubt this little bluetick hound dog is Elvis. Besides, Elvis also sang about a hound dog. Put him back and let's look at the next one."

Creed put a second one in her hands and she kissed it on the nose. "It's a girl and her name is Blue."

Two big dark spots that looked like black paint had dripped on the pup's back. Her muzzle was white and covered with a black mask around her eyes. If she'd been a boy, Sage would have named her Zorro. She wiggled and whimpered so Sage held her close to her chest. She settled right down when she was next to the flannel shirt and Sage sang a few lines of "Blue Christmas" to her.

"She's sleeping now. Give her back to Noel and let's take a look at the next one," Sage said.

Creed handed the runt to Sage.

"Oh, look! It's so tiny and has hardly any color at all except for the dark-colored ticks all over her."

Sage held her out and looked at her carefully. "You are Lady Crosby. I bet you grow up to be a better singer than either Reba or Wynonna."

"Hey, now!" Creed said.

"She will. She'll make them look like they can't carry a tune."

"How did you come up with that name?"

"Bing sang 'White Christmas,' remember?"

"And we do have a white Christmas coming up." Creed nodded.

"That's right." Sage laid the puppy close to Noel, who wagged her tail even harder. "That's why you didn't want to go with us, isn't it?"

Then it dawned on Sage.

"You knew, didn't you? That's why you took me out to check on things, right?" she asked Creed.

"I did and you are right. You'd have fretted yourself sick about her if you'd known she was knottin' up with contractions."

The cowboy just flat-out amazed Sage.

~~~

The puppies were cute right then. But they'd grow up fast, and pretty soon there would be lots of problems and messes everywhere, so his next job would be building a

doghouse. He could set it on the front porch and as soon
as the cold snap was over, Noel and the puppies would
be nice and warm out there. He chuckled softly at his
next thought: a cathouse. There was no way Sage would
put Angel and the kittens in the barn, so he'd better start
designing a cathouse as well as a doghouse.

He visualized miniature log cabins. He could insulate
the inside and cover the walls with plywood, put a flap
door on the front, and run wire for a lightbulb through
the window. A nice worn blanket and a forty-watt in
the attic of each house would keep the animals cozy on
cold nights.

"What are you thinking about so hard?" Sage asked.

"Construction work. Let's eat and then you can paint
while I design."

"What kind of construction work?"

"A surprise," he said. "Listen. A norther just hit. We
barely got back to the house in time, Sage. That wind
sounds pretty ferocious out there."

She shivered. "We probably won't get electricity
today."

"Maybe not."

An hour later she was painting and he had a notebook and several sharpened pencils in front of him on
the kitchen table. Four of Sage's pictures were drying in
the pantry and she worked on the one with the mistletoe
and icicles in the top of the snow-dusted scrub oak tree.
He picked up a pencil and figured out a comfortable size
for the dog and then for the cat and calculated the pitch
of the roof. The lightbulb should be close to the babies,
but not so close that they could touch it.

Or it could be behind a piece of glass at the back of

the house instead of inside the attic. That would work like the lights inside the chicken house where Creed's mother hatched out peeps in the spring time. There were basic woodworking tools in the tack room in the barn and some spare lumber pieces stacked in the corner. Some split fire logs would make a real log cabin exterior and look pretty fancy sitting on the front porch.

Sage laid her brushes down and sat down across from him. "What are you working on, Creed?"

"Building a couple of houses."

"Why? There is this house and then the bunkhouse. Why would you want to build two more?"

"For Noel and Angel. We're getting a little crowded in here, Sage."

"It's too cold to put them outside."

"Come look at this," he said.

She leaned forward and he told her his idea of putting the cathouse and the doghouse on the porch and how they'd heat the houses with lightbulbs. He drew a crude picture of what the houses would look like and then waited. She didn't say a word for a long time.

"It would keep the smell down in here, wouldn't it? We wouldn't have to have a litter pan and they'd just be right there on the porch where I could go out and play with them, right? And they could come inside for a little while each day?"

"Yes, you could, and yes, they could. But rest assured, eventually Angel and the kittens will wind up in the barn because that's where the rats are, and believe me, that's like round steak to them." He chuckled.

"And my puppies?"

"Will probably claim the porch, bark at any

newcomers, and trip you up when you try to bring in groceries," he told her.

She laughed. "Kiss me, Creed."

His expression made her laugh harder.

"Wasn't expecting that, were you?" she asked.

He shook his head.

"I can accept all that you just said if you kiss me."

She walked around the table and sat down in his lap so that she was facing him. She put a hand on each side of his face and leaned in for the kiss. When her mouth touched his, strong arms encircled her body.

When the string of hot, heavy kisses ended, he asked, "What does a kiss have to do with doghouses?"

"Not a damn thing. I heard you. I agree with you. But all I could think about when you were talking is how much I wanted to kiss the lips that were moving."

"I thought we were slowing this wagon down."

"We are slowing it down, but we aren't unhitchin' it."

—◆◆◆—

He kissed her again, this time controlling the pressure with his hand on the back of her head and teasing her lips with soft nips and his tongue. So she wasn't ready to unhitch the wagon and put it in the barn forever. Well, neither was he and if kisses were all he could have until after the sale, then he'd enjoy them to the fullest.

"I like the way you feel in my arms," he said.

"I like the way I feel in your arms too."

"But…"

"No buts; just kiss me again."

He held her chin in his hand. "But I can't do this all evening, Sage. Just sitting in the same room with you makes me crazy with want. Kissing you one time jacks up the heat in my body. A dozen times and I'm throbbing."

She moved back to her original chair. "Do you think Noel was in love with her old bluetick hound boyfriend?"

Creed wasn't sure how to answer that. Were they talking about dogs or dancing around their own relationship?

"I hope so. She's got three babies to raise… oh my God! Sage, I just thought of something. We didn't use a bit of protection yesterday. I didn't even think of that when we…" He let the sentence trail off.

"I'm on the pill. I've always had problems with regularity so I've been on it for years."

He wiped a hand across his forehead.

"You tellin' me you wouldn't want me to have three little dark-haired cowboys or cowgirls to run around in this canyon?"

"I wouldn't mind that at all, but I'd damn sure like for them to be legitimate. I got a feeling the wrath of your Grand would not be a pretty sight."

Chapter 12

CREED'S COMMENT ABOUT KIDS HAUNTED SAGE. IT hadn't been a drop-down-on-one-knee proposal, but it had rattled her nerves. If she had kids they'd grow up and leave her. She could barely think about putting Noel and Angel and their broods out on the front porch.

A child would be so much harder to lose. Her very own father was proof of that. He'd left the canyon to serve his country. Oh, he'd come home all right. The grave in the cemetery on the other side of the grandfather rock was proof of that. Sage laced her hands behind her head and stared out the window at the stars twinkling in the black sky. Grand was a strong-willed woman to survive losing her only child. And then she took in her daughter-in-law and granddaughter only for the daughter to die two years later. Sage wasn't sure she could live with that much pain.

She closed her eyes and sleep came easily, but the dreams haunted her all night. Dreams of little boys and girls chasing puppies around the yard and of Creed swinging them up into his arms when he came in for dinner. She watched the scenario as if it were a movie and felt the joy of the love surrounding them. When she awoke she wasn't sure if she'd been a character or someone viewing it from a padded seat with a bag of popcorn in her hands.

A pang of pure old jealousy stabbed her in the heart

when she thought of some other woman living on her ranch, raising Creed's children, and playing with her puppies and kittens. It was still pitch-black dark outside and the clock on her nightstand said that it was three thirty. She snuggled back into the covers, wished Creed was holding her so she wouldn't feel so alone, and went back to sleep.

The next time she awoke she was floating through the air. Afraid that she'd gotten too close to the bed and was falling off, she jumped and grabbed at the air. Only it wasn't air that she latched onto. It was Creed's big strong biceps.

"I've got you, darlin'," he whispered.

His heartbeat against her cheek convinced her that it wasn't another dream. He really had picked her up out of her bed and was carrying her off somewhere. Had she moaned in her sleep? Was he carrying her to a rocking chair to soothe her?

"Don't open your eyes until I tell you," he said.

She clamped her eyes so tight that her face hurt. He took a few more steps and sat down in a rocking chair but was careful not to set it in motion. Something sounded strange in the background. The smell of coffee filled the room but the percolator didn't sound right. He brushed a kiss across her lips and then planted one on the end of her nose and she forgot all about coffeepots.

"Merry Christmas, Sage," he said.

Her eyes flew open and there it was, not three feet from her, in all its glory. The Christmas tree was lit up with multicolored lights. The electricity was back on!

She threw her arms around his neck and kissed him hard and passionately.

"Hey, I didn't do it but I like getting the rewards.

When I came out of the barn the lights around it were all lit and when I got to the house, this is what I found."

"It's a Christmas miracle," she said.

"I'd say more like overtime for a lot of hard workers to buy Christmas miracles for their kids," he chuckled.

"Washing! We can do laundry!"

"Magic has gone. Mundane landed safely," he said in a monotone.

She gave him a big hug. "Mundane is magic today."

"Oh, and the news on the tractor radio says that the roads are being cleared but they're still icy so to use caution."

"Only thing we need from town is dog and cat food and they're not complainin'."

She hopped up off his lap and turned on the living room light, both lamps at the ends of the sofa and a floor light that usually sat between the rockers but had been relegated to a corner when her easel came into the house.

"Isn't it beautiful? That means television and I can paint until midnight if I want to."

He smiled at her and headed toward the kitchen to start making breakfast. Then he leaned over the counter and asked, "Television?"

She slung open two doors of a cabinet on the opposite side of the fireplace and there was a small television. "Works beautifully and we've even got cable. Grand loves her old Western movies."

"So do I," Creed said. "Since we have electricity, do you want toast with your ham and eggs?"

"I'm partial to skillet toast like you made when you brought me breakfast in bed. I usually use that toaster for Pop Tarts."

"Then fried toast it is. It's my favorite too. Grandpa hated the toaster and tossed it into the trash when Granny died. He said the thing only dried out the bread and it crumbled when you tried to put butter on it. When you took the toast out of a skillet, it was buttered, browned on the outside, and still soft on the inside."

"Smart man!"

Even the floor felt warmer with the lights all on as she padded across the room to pet her animals. Noel was curled around her puppies that were slurping noisily and kneading her stomach as they ate.

"She went out with me this morning. I flipped her blanket over to the clean side but it needs to be washed. You got another one somewhere that she could have while that one is getting cleaned up?"

"Sure, and I'll put a fresh one in Angel's basket too. We should do that first. They'll be done by the time we get our beds stripped down and our stuff all sorted out."

Creed would have never believed that talking about laundry and dog beds could be sexy, but it was. Listening to her talk about stripping down the beds sent his thoughts back to what had gone on in her bed and a stirring started in his jeans.

The phone put an abrupt halt to his visions and he picked it up on the second ring.

"You still frozen in?" his brother, Ace, asked.

"We got electricity just this morning and the snow-plows are still working on clearing the roads. Sage tells me that we are always the last to get dug out because our roads are the least traveled, especially this time of the year. We still haven't even plugged in our phones and computers to recharge them."

"Then you're on your way back to civilization. It hit us last night but we only got the tail end of it. A couple of inches on the ground and the sun is out so it'll melt soon. Jasmine and Lucy are outside building a snowman about waist high. They plan to take pictures of it with Jazzy. She says this is the baby's first snowman even if she can't see it. I told her to pull up her shirt. Maybe the baby can see it through her belly button, kind of like a camera lens."

Creed laughed. "I bet that got you a slap on the arm. How is Jasmine? Things going all right?"

"Oh, yeah. We can't wait until spring for her to be born. I swear, Creed, there is nothing like the feeling or the fear of being a father. I don't know how Dad did it seven times. I hear you got holed up with the granddaughter of the ranch owner. How'd that work?"

"Not so bad. Could have been worse."

"Good-lookin'?" Ace asked.

"Oh, yeah!"

"Do I hear something in your voice?"

"I couldn't answer that, brother."

Creed heard a commotion in the background.

"I miss Lucy's giggles. Tell Jasmine I'll send her a picture of a whole snow family as soon as I get my phone and laptop charged."

He put the receiver back into the base and it rang again before he could turn around.

Sage reached over his shoulder and grabbed it.

"Hello."

No more than two seconds clicked off the clock.

"Oh, Grand, I'm so glad you called. The electricity is back on. We have puppies and I named the girls Blue and Crosby and the boy Elvis, and Creed says their poppa is a bluetick hound. And the kittens are named after Santa's reindeer. I can't wait for you to see them. Creed says they'll all have their eyes open by Christmas and he's going to build a doghouse and a cathouse…"

A short pause and some laughter. "I know it's funny, but what else would you call it? Bet you never thought you'd have a cathouse on the Rockin' C, did you? Anyway, he's going to run an electric cord out into their little houses on the front porch and we'll keep them warm with a lightbulb. Kind of like you do in the spring to hatch out the chickens."

There was silence for a while and Sage wiped a tear from her eye. "I miss you. My cell phone will be charged up by noon and I'll have it with me all the time."

Creed's heart went out to her. Should he back out of the sale? She'd never be happy without her Grand close by, and her happiness was more important than anything.

———※———

"You miss her bad, don't you?" Essie asked.

Ada nodded. "But she needs to cut the apron strings and realize that just because someone leaves her doesn't mean they are gone forever. I'll go back and visit the ranch often and you're going with me."

"Not in the summer. I'd die in that godforsaken place in the summer. My poor little fat cells would all melt and there'd be nothing left of me but wrinkled skin and brittle bones."

"We've got an air conditioner. You can take your

knitting and sit in the living room all day, but we're going back every three months. After the first year, you can play with the great-grandbabies. Until then you'll have to make do with puppies and kittens."

Essie shook her head. "Don't like cats and barely tolerate dogs. When the boys were grown, I said no more pets in this place."

Ada slapped the kitchen table. "Looks like you'd best learn to tolerate them because the choice you got is a week out of every three months in Texas with me or a nursing home with a whole new set of friends."

"You are a hard woman, Ada Presley," Essie pouted.

"I learned it from you."

Essie stuck out a hand. "Deal."

Two hardworking, veined hands clasped together in an unwritten agreement that was as binding as ink on paper.

When the hand shaking was over, Essie laughed. "I would have gone for two weeks four times a year."

Ada smiled. "I would have settled for three times a year."

"You know she's enough like you that you can't force her into doing what you want, right?" Essie said.

Ada threw an arm around her sister. "She gets that from you."

———※———

Noel and Angel both had clean beds and two sets of sheets were in the washing machine. Sage and Creed carried their overflowing laundry baskets to the kitchen and set them on the floor.

She dumped hers. "Might as well combine the loads. It'll take less time."

He dumped his on top of hers. "I agree."

Putting her underwear in with his was the hardest thing she'd ever done in her life. It seemed so personal, so symbolic. Not even a long morning of sex had made her blush scarlet. But she did as she sorted clothing and visualized their personal things tangled up in the washing machine together.

When the kitchen floor looked like an explosion in a Goodwill Store, she poured a cup of coffee and carried it to her easel. The canvas looked different with overhead lights, and lamps added to the sunshine pouring in from the window.

"That sun promises warmth, but if you poke your head out the door that cold wind will freeze your nose off," Creed said.

"It's better than snow falling so hard that you can't see your hand in front of your face. Aha! I can turn on the radio. Six days and I'd already forgotten what all electricity does bring in the house."

She picked up the remote, hit a button, and music instantly filled the room.

Creed exhaled loudly.

"What?" she asked as she poked a button on the stereo unit inside the cabinet with the television.

"I liked the feeling of no technology. It's crazy, but I did. It's the same feeling I got when I first came out here."

"Want me to turn it off?"

"No, I'd like to hear the news before I go out in the barn and start building the dog and cathouses," he answered.

Toby Keith sang his newest song and then there was five minutes of news, most of it still covering the snow and all the damage it had caused. When that was done, Creed pulled on his coveralls, gloves, and boots and settled his hat just right on his head.

"See you at dinnertime," he said.

"I'm making tortilla soup."

He made his way around the piles of clothing and kissed her on the cheek. "That sounds great."

The house felt empty with him gone. Even the DJ and the constant noise of Christmas songs from country artists didn't fill the void. The dryer buzzed telling her that the dog and cat bedding was ready to fold. She laid her brushes to the side and went to the back side of the huge walk-in pantry.

It needs to be as big as the kitchen. It has to house the freezer, the washer and dryer, and enough food to last a month, my child. It's our grocery store and our laundry all rolled into one. Grand's answer to her question when she was a little girl flitted through her memories.

Would she ever tell her daughter the same thing when she asked why the pantry was the biggest room in the house?

She pulled the old blankets from the dryer, cleaned enough lint from the filter to make a bonfire, and switched the sheets over from the washing machine. Then she gathered up a load of towels, put them in the washer, and added detergent.

Noel cold-nosed her hand when she started back out and Sage yelped.

"You scared me, girl."

The dog went to the door and put a paw on the doorknob.

"It's cold out there," Sage said.

The dog barked and she opened the door. Noel meandered out and headed straight for the barn. Other than
her floppy ears blown back against her head, she didn't
act like she even felt the cold. But Sage shivered when
the icy wind shot up under her shirt. She quickly shut
the door.

"Creed is tough as nails to work outside in this kind
of weather," she said aloud.

She carried the laundry basket to the table and folded
the two ratty blankets. Grand saved everything until
she'd gotten the last drop of good out of it. Sage would
have tossed those two blankets years ago, but not Grand.
And now they'd come in almighty handy.

She put them back in the linen closet and worked on
her painting again. In the thirty minutes before it was time
to switch clothing to the dryer, she could get part of the
mistletoe painted.

When she painted the world disappeared. But that
morning was different. She painted the waxy green leaves
and white berries, but Creed would not leave her mind.

Grand had been right about him. He was the perfect
cowboy to take over the ranch and Sage was coming
to grips with the idea. Still, she felt guilty. She should
be fighting harder to get her grandmother to stay and
not leave for that godforsaken place in the mountains
of Pennsylvania.

—◆—

Creed measured the boards for the floor of the doghouse
and added four inches all the way around. When they
went into town he'd buy a roll of insulation. That would
keep the cold from sneaking in between the boards.

"I could just buy a couple of decent doghouses, but what's the fun in that?"

Besides, you had to get out of the house. One more lonesome tear from Sage's eye and you'd be calling Ada Presley and telling her to come home on the next flight. You'd declare that you couldn't live in this desolate hole in the ground, but it wouldn't be that at all, would it?

"Shut up," he demanded out loud.

He finished nailing the floorboards to the base and fixed the studs to the sides. Noel meandered in, her ears drawn back against the cold wind. She curled up in a pile of loose hay with her head on her paws and watched him.

"It's for you and the puppies. I'll build one for Angel too, so get that sad look off your face. She won't be taking up permanent abode in the house either."

Noel's tail wagged, scattering loose hay all around her.

"How'd you talk Sage into letting you out?"

Noel raised her head and barked her answer.

"Lied about having to go, did you?"

He discussed everything with Noel as he worked. He told her how big her house was, how much insulation he planned to put inside, how he'd put the bulb in the attic with a piece of glass between it and the ceiling so the puppies wouldn't slap at it and get their paws burned. He told her about his new feelings for Sage and how he couldn't stand to see her cry or know that he was the cause of her unhappiness.

"I'd planned on fighting with her to the bitter end, but I'm a sucker for tears." He sighed.

Noel growled.

"You don't think so? Well, that's comforting that you

don't think I'm a sucker. So what do you think, girl? Will you like your new log cabin or did you want it to look like a white mansion?"

Noel shut her eyes and went to sleep.

"Log cabin it is. I'm glad we agree. I'll get the outside covered and then put the insulation in the walls and cover the inside with quarter-inch plywood. It'll be a nice home for you and your bluetick hounds."

Noel got up and meandered out of the barn as slowly as she'd come in. She looked over her shoulder and gave one more bark but didn't slow down.

When she was gone, Creed realized that he couldn't feel his nose and his fingers had begun to tingle in the bitter cold. He unplugged the circular saw, put it back in the tack room, and left the beginnings of a doghouse sitting right in the middle of the floor.

———∿∿∿———

The dryer beeped and Sage laid aside her brushes again. She'd barely made it to the kitchen when she heard scratching on the back door. Noel ambled inside when she opened it and went straight for her bed without stopping to have her ears rubbed.

"Got cold out there, did it?" Sage asked. "Your babies didn't even miss you. They slept the whole time you were out."

She followed Noel. "See, I told you. I'm a good babysitter. If they would have whined, I would have rocked them back to sleep."

The back door opened with force and Creed came in stomping his feet and clapping his hands. "Damn, it's cold out there."

"Weatherman says it's going down to single digits by night and for us to brace up for another norther. Did you bring all this with you from Ringgold, Texas? We haven't had a storm like this since I was born and when you arrive, boom! Look what you caused."

"No, ma'am. Where I come from, we get excited about two inches of snow. It gets cold but it don't last forever. And please keep that idea to yourself about me causing this. The other farmers will take me out behind a mesquite thicket and stone me to death if I'm the culprit who caused a blizzard."

The dryer beeped again and she started toward the kitchen.

Creed held up his palms. "Let me. Whatever it is, I'll get it out and fold it just to get something warm in my hands."

She wiggled her eyebrows.

"Honey, I'd put frostbite on your pretty skin if I touched you right now. You ever lick an old metal ice tray?"

She nodded.

"Well, that's what would happen if I kissed you. We'd be joined at the lips until the spring thaw. Go on back to your painting. I like the way the mistletoe came out. Looks like I could reach right in there and pick it out of the picture."

Sage picked up her brushes. It wouldn't be so bad to be joined at the lips until the spring thaw. If his kisses could set her ablaze in the middle of a Texas norther, what would they create in July or August? Her heart wasn't in painting, so she cleaned her brush and put her palette in a plastic container with an airtight lid to keep the paints from drying out.

When he brought the load of towels to the table, she picked up an armful of white clothes—T-shirts, thermal undershirts, and underwear—and carried them into the pantry. She switched a second bunch of towels to the dryer and stuffed the washer full one more time. He had almost finished folding the towels when she got back.

"You can keep on painting, Sage. I know how to do laundry. I promise I won't put red socks in with the white clothes," he said.

"I need to think about it for a while, and besides, it's time to start the tortilla soup. How much did you get done on the doghouse?"

"Floor is in. Studs are up and the siding is going on. It'll be a fine log cabin. Noel says she likes it," Creed said.

"Is the door going to be a gaping hole?"

"I'm a better carpenter than that," Creed answered. "It'll have one of those doggy doors that they can push in from the outside or out from the inside."

"Why are you building it so well? It's just a doghouse," she said.

"Shhh... you'll hurt her feelings. If she's going to be thrown out of the big house, she needs to feel like she's getting a good deal. And besides, we haven't had an argument yet."

"What does us arguing have to do with her house?"

His eyes twinkled in mischief. "Not a thing."

Sage racked her brain for what could be so funny, but not a single thing surfaced.

"Explain please," she said.

"For a kiss. My lips are warmed up and yours look hot."

She wrapped her arms around his neck, pressed up close to him, and kissed him right there in the brightly lit kitchen. She nipped at his lower lip and slid her tongue into his mouth. When she could feel the effects pressing against her belly she stepped back.

"Now explain, please," she said.

"When we have our first big argument and I'm relegated to the doghouse I intend to make sure it's cozy and big enough for me," he teased without taking his hands from her waist.

She took a step forward and leaned in for a second kiss. "You are a very smart man, Creed Riley."

The kiss sent shock waves down to their toes and warmed the very floor where they stood.

"Does that mean you'd put me in the doghouse if you got mad?"

She looked up into his sexy green eyes and said, "And nail the door shut."

He led her to the sofa and pulled her down onto his lap. "Maybe we'd better talk about what could bring on such a thing."

Her cell phone rang before she could list all the things that would put him in the doghouse. She picked it up from the end table and answered it without leaving his lap.

"Sure. Can you stay for dinner?"

Creed shook his head.

"Tortilla soup. Hey, for Aunt Bill's Candy, I'll gladly go Internet shopping with you, kiddo."

"April?" he asked when she laid the phone back down.

"Yes, it was. She's coming over right after lunch and bringing some of Hilda's famous Aunt Bill's Candy. We are going Internet shopping for dresses for the Christmas party."

"You're not wearing my red and black flannel shirt to the party? I'm hurt and so is it. It thought it was your favorite item of clothing."

She kissed him on the cheek. "I save that for things more important than parties."

She didn't tell him that she'd hated to put it in the pile with his other dirty shirts because washing it would erase the smell of his shaving lotion. Or that she'd slept in it again the night before.

Chapter 13

THE ENORMOUS GRANDFATHER ROCK FORMATION HID the small family cemetery. The only way to get to it was by four-wheeler, by foot, or that afternoon, by tractor. It was surrounded by a picket fence that could not protect it from the snowstorm and shaded by the big rock so the sun couldn't melt away any of the drifts.

Sage found the top of the gate and shoved, but she couldn't budge it with the drift against the back side.

"Shovel time," Creed said behind her. "Which way does it open?"

"Outward," she answered.

It didn't take long for him to throw the snow to one side, break the ice on the hinge, and open it for her. But it did little good when there was still a drift on the other side.

"I'll get the second one. The graves are all the way to the back side of the cemetery and it'll go faster if we work together," she said.

He didn't even look up and kept slinging snow to one side and then to the other. By the time they had shoveled it away they were both leaning on their shovels and trying to catch their breath.

"Tell me again why we're doing this today?" Creed asked.

"Blame it on the weatherman," she panted.

The rock protected them somewhat from the bitter

wind but it couldn't make it warmer. Shoveling dirt or snow was hard work and used a lot of energy as well as plain old elbow grease. Under the coveralls she was warm as toast, but her nose was numb, and even with two pair of socks, her toes were beginning to feel the chill.

Creed went back to work. "Why is it his fault?"

"Because he won't tell us that the temperature is going to rise and melt this off by Monday. I think his wife is going through menopause and has hot flashes all night. He can't sleep because she's constantly kicking the covers off or else putting more on, so he is grumpy and takes it out on the whole world. That makes it his fault. And we have to get the snow cleared away so we can put flowers on the graves when we come back from the shopping trip the first of the week."

Creed chuckled. "You've got an imagination, darlin'. Maybe you should write books rather than paint pictures."

She dug the square-nosed shovel into the snow and tossed it to her left. "No thank you. I'll stick to my pictures."

"Do you see another picture out here this morning?" he asked.

Tombstones of various sizes created different heights and widths of miniature mountains all around her. No one would be interested in buying a picture of a snow-covered cemetery, not even with mistletoe clinging to the tops of the scrub oak trees surrounding it.

"Well?" he asked.

She shook her head. "Not a thing."

They stuck their shovels into the snow and started walking through the shallow places and the idea started to nag at her. She'd never painted the big rock from the back side. The front of it had given her many paintings, all with life in them. Her grandfather when he was still living, an Indian surveying the land, eagles, and even a howling coyote. Should she paint the other side from the land of those who'd already gone on?

"Whoa!" she said.

He stopped. "See something?"

"No, this is it." She brushed the top of his tombstone clean. "This is Grandpa's grave. The valley there is where… well…" she stammered. "Next to the valley is my father's and then my mother's."

She tried to keep the tears at bay but the dam broke. Thinking about a tombstone sitting there someday with Grand's full name, date of birth, and death engraved on it was more than she could handle that morning. The tears were scalding hot as they ran down her cold cheeks. She wished that she would have worn her face mask to soak them up and so that Creed wouldn't see her crying like a baby.

He pulled her to him, letting her cry on his shoulders. Layers of clothing plus heavy coveralls didn't keep her from hearing his steady heartbeat. Creed was a good man. He'd do well with the Rockin' C. And even if he wasn't a Presley, someday he would claim a spot in the family cemetery.

The idea of a stone with his name on it brought on more tears. Sobs racked her shoulders and he hugged her even tighter against his body.

"It's all right, Sage. It'll be a long, long time before Miz Ada is in this place. She's still got too much spit and vinegar in her for God to want her just yet," he said.

He's got that right. Listen to him, Sage. And remember, there will be a Presley on the ranch as long as you don't leave it. It's not like I'm forsaking the whole heritage. That's why I sold it to him so cheap. He's responsible to keep it running, but it's your responsibility to make sure there's Presley blood on the Rockin' C.

Grand's voice was as clear as if she was sitting on Grandpa's tombstone right beside her, but Sage didn't open her eyes and look because she knew she would be disappointed.

A soft cloth wiped the tears away from her cheeks. His handkerchief was cold but his touch was light. His fingertips grazing her frozen cheeks weren't blistering hot like usual but comforting.

"Thank you," she whispered.

"You are very welcome, darlin'. Let's go to the house. You are shivering and it won't take any time at all to take care of the rest of the job when we bring the flowers out here," he said.

Sage didn't disagree. She wanted to be surrounded by the warmth of a glowing fire, the Christmas tree, and her dogs and cats. She wanted to laugh with Creed and make more cookies. She didn't want to think about the future or the past.

Going back to the tractor, she looked up at the big rock and saw her next picture as clear as if it were already completed. She'd never painted the formation using only the wide, furrowed base, but that's where her next picture started. Not at the top but at the bottom with a tiny little cedar tree that would barely reach her waist and a gray dove sitting in its branches.

But where is the mistletoe?

She looked up and a scrub oak had sprouted above the cedar, its branches bending out like naked arms over the cedar tree, and sure enough, there was a single bit of mistletoe nestled in the fork of the branches.

Creed's arm was thrown around her shoulders and he stopped so quickly that she felt a small jerk. "Would you look at that? I swear the stuff is everywhere."

Her eyes followed his pointing finger and there it was, blown no doubt by the hard wind and stuck in the gate. One little twig of mistletoe. The scene branded itself into her brain, warming her from the inside out. It was symbolic of leaving the past behind and looking forward to the future.

"Hold up. I've got to take a picture to send to my folks. They can't fathom this much snow. Reckon I should tell them that gate is six feet tall?" he asked.

Her smile was weak. "It's bad enough. Don't exaggerate."

The tractor cab wasn't cozy, but it was a lot warmer than the temperature outside. Her face tingled as the nerve endings thawed, but it still felt stiff where the tears had dried. She couldn't remember the last time she'd cried like that. Certainly not when either of her previous relationships had ended, and not when she'd gotten Grand's phone call saying that she'd sold the ranch.

Those times she'd been angry, not sad.

"Look, the wind has blown most of the snow off the pond and it's frozen. Want to go ice skating?"

He stopped the tractor. "I don't have skates. Do you?"

"No, but a pair of old socks pulled over your boots makes a pretty good substitute. Let's go have some dinner and then come back this afternoon. I was in junior high the last time the cold lasted long enough to freeze up the pond."

———

Creed would have moved heaven and earth to make her happy right then. Her tears had practically brought him to his knees. He'd felt a loss when his grandmother died and again when they lost his grandfather. But he'd still had six brothers, sisters-in-law, his mother and father, and a whole support team to comfort him. When her Grand went, April would be there and the neighbors. But they weren't real kinfolks.

"Only if you promise not to laugh at me. I'm not real graceful on the dance floor."

"What's that got to do with ice skating?"

"Honey, a dance floor is not as slippery as a greased pig. If I can't master the dance floor, it'll be tough to master an icy pond."

Her laughter was music to his ears.

He went on, "If you could shake a little cornmeal or saw dust on the pond, it might help me stay upright. Or maybe I could rig up a pillow to my ass."

Her eyes twinkled. "That visual is beyond funny. We could just get Grandpa's old sled out of the hayloft and play with it. It's wide enough for both of us. We could drag it up the hill."

"What hill?"

"The roads are still icy so they aren't open yet," she said.

"Are you serious?"

"It's that or skating."

He weighed the options.

"Neither. Let's make popcorn and hot chocolate and watch an old Western movie on television. We can cuddle up together under a nice warm quilt on the sofa and Noel and Angel can check on us if we fall asleep."

"Right now that sounds like a wonderful plan. You ever seen *McLintock!* with John Wayne?"

"Only about twenty times. It's one of my favorites."

"It always reminds me of Lawton and Eva. We've got it on DVD so we could watch it this afternoon."

"Sounds a lot better than bustin' my butt on the pond or breaking my neck with your grandpa's sled. Why does it remind you of Lawton and Eva?"

"Well, Lawton is kind of like a young John Wayne. He doesn't look like him. Lawton is a whole lot more handsome. But he's got that bigger than life force about him. And Eva, well, she's this fiery redhead with a flaming hot temper to go with her hair. They're clashing all the time over April."

"Think they'll ever get back together?"

"Oh, no! She's settled into her real estate business and he's a cowboy. And she hates the canyon. I mean she really hates it. It would never work, but still the movie kind of reminds me of them."

Creed would watch a musical chick flick that afternoon if it would take Sage's mind off the cemetery and the empty space between the mound of snow where her grandfather was buried and the next one over where her dad's remains had been put to rest. And Creed did not like musicals or chick flicks.

For their noon meal they had grilled cheese sandwiches and hot tomato soup that she'd spiced up with some garlic powder and a dash of Worcestershire sauce. Afterwards she arranged a dozen cookies on a platter and set them in the middle of the table.

"Toes about thawed out?" he asked.

"They're tingling," she answered.

"Won't be long then. Let's take a cup of hot chocolate to the living room and watch Lawton and Eva."

"Wait until you meet them both. I swear this could be their story, only theirs doesn't have a happy ever after ending."

"You believe in happy ever after?"

"Only in books and movies."

She pulled the quilt from the back of the sofa over them. He put an arm around her and pushed a strand of electrified hair out of her face. She pushed a button on the remote and the music at the start of the movie began. Until that moment, Creed had never realized that the movie was a chick flick before chick flicks were even popular. The first song talked about birds and bees, flowers and trees, until they were up to their knees in love.

The first scene showed a hat on the weather vane and two cowboys arguing about whether it was the sixth or seventh time that week that the boss had arrived home snockered and thrown his hat up there.

Women could drive a cowboy to drinking for sure, but Creed wasn't sure in his drunkest state that he could have landed his hat on the weather vane on the top of his folks' house.

The second scene was the sound of cattle bawling as John Wayne's character rode his horse into the middle of the herd. Cowboys rode horses and drove bawling cows down a mountainside. The terrain in the movie reminded him of the canyon. The mountains weren't as steep, but the Palo Duro had ridges and backbones just like the scene in the movie.

Her hand snuck inside his flannel shirt and rested on his chest. He covered it with his and kissed the top of her head. She raised her head and their lips met in a clash.

"This is not slowing down a wagon, Sage. It's letting it go full blast down the sides of the canyon walls."

———∿∿∿———

"I want you," she said simply. Visiting the cemetery that day reminded her that the past was gone. The future was just a dot on the horizon. Today was all she had and she wanted Creed.

His arms tightened around her. Today, she reminded herself again, was all she had and she wanted Creed to make love to her. She wanted to feel the excitement of sex. She wanted to see if the afterglow she'd read about could be a reality with the right man. She wanted to make memories that would keep her warm when he was gone. And she didn't want to think about him not being there.

His arm moved from her shoulders to her butt, cupping it gently.

"Lie beside me," she said.

He stretched out beside her on a sofa that was barely big enough for them.

She smiled and straddled him, kicking the cover off to one side and lying on top of him. There was noise in the background from the movie going, but it was a blur when she deftly removed her shirt and bra and unbuttoned his shirt.

"I love the way your chest feels on my boobs," she said.

"Do you have any idea what you do to me?"

"You do the same thing to me," she told him. "Every nerve in my whole body is tingling."

"Well, my body is hot as hell. It wants you too, Sage."

"Then let's give it what it wants." She undid his belt buckle and unzipped his jeans. "Time to come out of the clothes. We'll cover up with the quilt."

"I don't need any covers. I'm really hot," he said.

She pointed across the room. "Yes you are, darlin', but we can't have sex in front of the children."

"Then we'll cover up with the quilt," he said.

They quickly undressed and she gave a hop and wrapped her legs around him. He caught her with one hand firmly on her naked butt and the other around her waist.

He backed up and sat down and she wiggled until he had slid inside her. Then she tasted his lips. She didn't kiss him with a passionate force but tasted gently, feeling the heat rising and meeting throbbing desire as she began a steady rhythm.

The quilt was around them. She wasn't sure when he'd wrapped them into a cocoon, but only their heads were visible. They'd gone from kissing to truly exciting sex during the first ten minutes of the movie. She wondered if the credits would roll before they finished.

He flipped her over on the sofa and took control of the rhythm, speeding up until she thought she'd fly right off the top of the mountain, and making love to her with his fingertips and his tongue. And then he would slow down and gently kiss her eyelids, her ears, and the tip of her nose.

"Tell me what you want, Sage," he said hoarsely.

"I want you to never stop. You are doing everything I want right now," she said.

He grinned and she reached up to touch the corner of his mouth.

"You have a sexy mouth, Creed. But your eyes are your... oh my God, don't stop doing that with your fingers."

His fingertips teased the soft skin below her ear. "Like this?"

"Dear God."

"Don't tell Him. Tell me."

"Yes, yes," she said.

His mouth covered hers in a blistering hot kiss. "And this."

In her other relationships there had been no sweet talk—just a few kisses, shed the clothes, get it done with a couple of *oh, babies* muttered, and then he would collapse on top of her. Afterwards there was very little cuddling because he fell asleep or wanted to get right up and make sandwiches or order pizza.

She loved the sweet-talking. She even loved the loud music playing on the television as the movie kept running.

"I feel like I'm making out in a movie theater," she gasped.

"Darlin', they don't have sofas in the theaters I went to."

She smiled and bucked against him.

"Now?" he asked.

She raked her nails across his back and wrapped her legs more firmly around his waist.

"Please, now!" she whispered.

"I'm not ready for it to be over," he said.

"It doesn't have to be over for good, just this time!" Her voice sounded squeaky in her ears.

One firm thrust and she felt herself floating, then the afterglow settled around them like warm sunlight. He shifted his weight until they were face to face on the narrow sofa and he pulled the quilt more firmly around them.

"Sleepy?" she asked.

"Too fired up to sleep, darlin'. I just want to hold you and whisper sweet things in your ear the rest of the day."

She cuddled even closer to him on the narrow sofa. "I could stay right here forever. I *am* so sleepy."

It was there. It wasn't a myth that writers talked about. There was really afterglow and it really did wrap around them like golden sunshine.

He picked up her hand and kissed her fingertips. "Then nap, sweetheart. I'll be here when you wake up."

"Promise?" she asked.

"I'm not going anywhere, Sage."

She awoke to G. W. McLintock's buddy saying something about him knowing what Katy's temper was. She opened her eyes to see a dark-haired woman sitting on McLintock's lap and he had a whiskey bottle in his hand.

Creed would be dead if he ever cheated on her. Her predominant genes had gotten the upper hand with her body, but the hot-tempered Irish genes ruled her heart. Creed's chest shook with laughter. She watched him for a long time, being very still and studying his cheekbones, his full sexy mouth, his heavy dark lashes. How could she ever let him go?

The movie was near the end and McLintock was chasing the flaming redhead, Maureen O'Hara, through the streets when Creed looked down and realized she was awake.

"Well, hello, sleepyhead. The movie is about over

and it's even better than the last time I watched it. Would you get that mad at me over lipstick on my collar?"

"Number one, we are not married. Number two, you don't want to test my mettle."

"You've seemed pretty tame to me," he said.

"Honey, cowgirls can't be tamed and this cowgirl has some pretty hot Irish blood in her."

"But you are a painter, not a cowgirl."

She reached up and patted him on the cheek. "You can take the cowgirl out of the canyon. You can put paintbrushes and sketch pencils in her hands. You can even put a dress on her. But you can't take the canyon out of the cowgirl and all this old canyon knows how to produce is cowgirls. A mealymouthed, sissified woman wouldn't last two weeks in this place."

"That what happened to Mrs. Lawton?"

"Eva? No, she was a cowgirl from Claude, Texas. You ever seen a baby chicken right out of the egg?"

He grinned and kissed her on the nose. "Of course. Baby chickens, baby geese, and baby ducks."

"They don't have much in the way of wings until they're a few weeks old. Eva was just getting her wings when she got pregnant and had to marry Lawton. When they came in full strength she wanted to fly but she had a husband, a ranch, a mother-in-law from hell, and a new baby all tied around her neck."

"So she flew away?"

"That's right. She did."

"What happens if I test your mettle?" he teased.

"You'd better make that doghouse real comfortable."

—⁓—

There had been no doubt in Creed's mind that he was going to buy the ranch when Ada Presley came back. He liked it. The price was more than right. And he'd fight Sage to the last breath to have it.

And then he lost his heart to her.

And then she cried.

He laid aside his book and turned out the lamp on his nightstand. He'd rather be curved around her body in her bed, but she hadn't asked him to spend the night with her. They'd had glorious daytime sex twice, but when it was over they'd gone on about the business of running a ranch or in her case, painting a picture.

He wanted to wake up with Sage in his arms. The time between that Wednesday night and the day Ada would come home was so short. In two weeks it would be over and he'd be driving up the road out of the canyon.

Sage deserved happiness and he loved her enough to give it to her.

He laced his fingers behind his neck. With the curtains opened, he could see the Christmas lights burning brightly on the barn and barbed wire fence. He imagined Sage as a child running down the short hallway, slinging open the door and jumping on the bed on Christmas morning.

The room went from semidarkness to instant light. He threw a hand over his eyes and sat straight up in bed. Electricity could plunge the house into darkness but he'd never heard of it flashing on when the switch was off.

The bed bounced when Sage jumped in the middle of it.

"Creed, wake up, you've got to see!"

Things came into focus slowly when he uncovered his eyes. She was sitting in the middle of the bed in his red and black plaid shirt. It had been in the laundry and he'd hung up all his shirts after they'd dried, so why was she wearing it?

"Look!" She was fairly well bouncing. "Wake up, Creed."

He looked where she was pointing. She'd made a hollow in the bedspread and there were three wiggling kittens. Where had she gotten more kittens? Was she going to be one of those old eccentric women who took in cats by the dozens now that she'd found how much she liked them?

He rubbed his eyes. "Where did you get those?"

"In the barn," she said happily.

"Why were you in the barn this time of night?"

She touched his forearm. "Creed! These are Angel's babies."

Angel landed in the middle of the bed, made sure her kittens were all right, turned around a couple of times on the spare pillow, and then lay down.

She held Rudy. "And their eyes are open. Look, they can see!"

Sure enough the kitten's eyes were wide open but it wasn't Rudy's eyes that made him smile; it was Sage's. If she got that excited about kittens, what would she do the first time her child did something fantastic—like clasp her finger or make goo-goo noises?

"Well, I'll be damned. They're some really smart kittens to open their eyes this early."

"You think so? I thought he looked a little slow," Sage said.

Creed's laughter bounced off the bedroom walls and the cows out in the feedlot probably heard the commotion. "He's got to get adjusted to the world. Right now everything is probably one big blur, even his momma. By Christmas, they'll be playing and biting each other's ears."

"They'll fight?" she asked.

"Yes, ma'am. That's what siblings do."

"Did you bite your brothers' ears?"

Creed threw back his head and laughed again. "Not exactly, but that didn't mean we didn't spit on our knuckles and have it out."

He took Rudy from her and held the cat close to his chest. "You aren't going to have to take special classes at the kitty school, are you, Rudy? You'll learn how to catch barn rats and climb trees and get As on all your report cards. Yes, sir, you're going to be a smart kitten when you go to school."

Sage shivered.

"I promise," Creed said.

"It's not that. My feet are cold."

"Then get under the covers and sit beside me."

She handed the other two kittens to him and repositioned herself so that she was covered from the waist down. He laid the kittens back in her lap and kissed her on the cheek.

"You're going to make a great mother, Sage."

"I'm not so sure about that. I've never been around babies in my life except at church, and then there was April, but I was just a little girl back then," she rambled. "I'm going to put them back in their bed now."

"And then you'll come back to bed with me?"

She shook her head. "Not in Grand's bed. You can come over to my room but Grand would haunt me if I…"

˙   "I'm not asking you to have sex with me. I just want you to feel your body next to mine," he said.

She looked at the four bedposts as if hunting for something.

Creed laid a hand over hers. "She hasn't haunted me one single night, but I'll gladly come to your room."

"Thank you," she whispered.

Chapter 14

Sage was always glad to see April. They talked weekly when she wasn't at the ranch and when she was they saw each other often. But on Friday morning when she showed up with a big flat box and an even bigger smile, Sage wanted to kick her off the front porch.

Tradition.

It was a bitch.

On the day before the Canyon Rose Christmas party, April always brought her new dress to model. Afterwards, she and Sage would talk shoes, hairstyles, and cowboys. That Thursday morning, Sage didn't want to talk about any of those things and she sure didn't want Creed to see the petite April strutting around in a deep blue velvet dress that hugged every one of her tiny curves.

One look at her using the living room floor like a model's runway and Creed wouldn't want to be seen with the tall gangly giant called Sage. Even April's name brought up visions of minty green leaves and new life, whereas the name Sage would remind Creed of a pungent aroma coming from an ugly green powder.

April plopped the box down on the kitchen table and pulled out a dark brown satin dress trimmed in ecru velvet. "Isn't it gorgeous? We should give all the cowboys a drooling bib at the door because they're going to need it when they see you in this."

The back door swung open and cold wind came inside with Creed. He hung his coat on the rack and kicked off his boots.

"Couldn't feel my fingers, and besides, the houses are ready for the insulation, so I couldn't go any further. What's that about drooling bibs? There going to be a bunch of babies at the party?"

April flashed him her best smile. "No, they're for the cowboys when they see Sage in this dress. She's going to be the queen."

Jealousy settled around Sage's heart followed by instant guilt. April wasn't making a play for Creed. And he didn't belong to Sage, so if she wanted to flirt with him, she had every right.

"I see," Creed said shortly. "I need something hot."

April giggled.

Sage shot him a dirty look.

"Guess that came out wrong, didn't it? And it sure didn't fit the conversation. I was thinking out loud. My hands are frozen. I need a cup of coffee or hot chocolate to wrap them around," he explained.

Sage's self-esteem plunged even lower.

He looked right at Sage and one eyelid slid shut in a sexy wink. "However, I do believe that Sage is going to be beautiful in that dress. When are you going to model it?"

"You don't get to see her in it until tomorrow night," April said quickly. "But I'll model mine."

"I'll look forward to it, ma'am." Creed poured a cup of coffee and carried it to the living room. He sat down in a rocking chair and listened to the music on the radio. "Waiting on a Woman" by Brad Paisley started playing.

Creed could relate to every word of the song where an older gentleman was telling a younger man about the art of waiting on a woman.

April tucked the dress back into the box and headed toward Sage's bedroom with it under her arm. Sage was right behind her and when she passed by Creed's chair he reached out and touched her arm.

She stopped and looked down at him quizzically.

"You sure look pretty this morning," he said.

His eyes had gone soft like they did just before he kissed her. All doubts about her size and her crazy name washed away. She bent and kissed him on the cheek.

"Thank you," she whispered.

"Run her off and let's go to bed."

Sage patted him on the shoulder.

"Or lock her in your bedroom and we'll grab that quilt and go to the barn."

She gave him a long, hard kiss that had both of them panting when she broke away and headed toward the bedroom. She held the handle for a full minute before opening it to catch her breath. She pasted a smile on her face, slung open the door, and found April standing in front of the cheval mirror in the corner. The blue velvet dress laid against her flawless, pale skin like it had been tailor-made for her. The hem stopped at midthigh and the neckline plunged low.

"Finish zipping me, please, so I can see if Hilda has to do any altering. I'm not letting Daddy see it until the party starts or he'll pitch a bitch fit about the neckline."

Sage pulled the zipper up the back and sat down on the end of her bed to admire April. "You are a perfect size three, girl. Hilda won't have to do a thing to it except put a collar on it or maybe some lace to fill in the neckline."

April turned every which way, checking out every angle in the mirror. "Daddy would make her do that if he saw it. Oh!" April gasped.

"What? Did you see a spider?"

April was terrified of spiders and they multiplied like rabbits in the canyon. Those and stinging scorpions were part of the terrain, along with lizards and coyotes.

"Two people slept in that bed. Both pillows have hollows and the sheets are rumpled and you are sleeping with Creed Riley."

"Sleeping, yes. But that's all that went on," Sage said.

It wasn't a lie. They had only slept in the bed the night before and she didn't have to explain the other times when they'd done things to melt all the snow in the canyon. She sure wasn't going to go into the story of what had happened on the sofa while John Wayne and Maureen O'Hara fought their way through an old Western movie.

"Are you freakin' crazy?" April hissed.

"Probably. It won't be easy to see him leave," Sage admitted.

"Not that! You got him into your bed and you didn't have sex? Are you blind?"

"Not last time I checked," Sage said.

"You have seen him, haven't you? I mean, you don't look at him and just see a cowboy trying to buy the Rockin' C. You do see those big old arms, that cute little butt, and those dreamy green eyes, don't you?"

"I see Creed," Sage said.

"Are you gay?"

Sage sputtered and almost choked on her own spit. "Why would you ask a fool question like that?"

"You haven't had a boyfriend in years. You've been shut up with that hunky man for almost two weeks and you sleep as in shut your eyes and snore? God, Sage, you just fell off your pedestal I've had you on all these years. You must be gay. Admit it. Come on out of the closet."

"I am not gay. I like men."

I love Creed. Now where in the hell did that come from?

April sat down on the end of the bed beside Sage.

"Well, thank God. Do you need me to give you some lessons in what to do with a sexy cowboy when he gets into your bed?"

"I think I can handle it." Sage grinned.

April slapped her on the arm. "You rat! You had me going. He didn't sleep with you at all, did he? You wouldn't do that when you're trying to run him off. We both know Grand would never sell the Rockin' C. She's just giving you a taste of what could happen so you will get on the ball and find a husband."

"You are smarter than the average rich kid," Sage said.

"Not much or I would have figured it all out before I blew a gasket."

—※—

Ada had been antsy since she awoke that morning. She had married when she was eighteen and had gone to live on the Rockin' C the day after her wedding.

Those were the days when Lawton's father had just taken over the Canyon Rose and the Christmas party had been an institution long before then. She'd attended ten or more parties before Lawton was even born. Fifty-plus years she'd looked forward to that party every year, and this year, she was sitting in Shade damn Gap, Pennsyl-shittin'-vania.

Listening to Sage describe April's dress just made her more homesick. Seeing the picture on her cell phone of Sage and April posing together in their new sexy dresses in front of the cheval mirror made her want to throw herself down and cry like a jilted bride.

Missing the party where Lawton threw his daughter over his shoulder like a sack of chicken feed, hauled her upstairs kicking and screaming, and then brought her back to the party with a buttoned up flannel shirt over that dress—well, hell, that was the toughest thing she'd ever done or would do in her lifetime.

And he would do that when she appeared at the top of the staircase and started down into the ballroom. Hell, she wouldn't make it to the fifth step before his boot heels sounded like drums on those oak steps and he had her over his shoulder. No way would Lawton let April wear something that revealing to the party, and Ada was going to miss the fun.

Essie peered over her sister's shoulder at the dress with the deep plunging neckline. "I'm durn sure glad I never had a daughter."

"One dress sure changed your mind in a hurry," Ada said.

"That ain't a dress. It's two Band-Aids stuck to a hanky. Lord, do girls really wear such things out in pub-lic? I wouldn't have worn something like that to bed with my husband."

"Times is different," Ada said.

"Must be. Wonder what her momma is going to say about it."

"Her momma won't be the problem. It's Lawton that'll throw a shit fit."

"He needs to. Why, if she got to dancing her boobs would fall out of the thing. That thing that Sage has got on is too tight and it's wintertime and there's a durn blizzard out there so it's got to be cold. It's above her knee and ain't got the first sign of a sleeve in it. She'll catch a cold and that cowboy you was crazy enough to trust will have to take care of her. He'll be going in her room with a hot toddy and her laying up in her bed in nothing but a nightgown."

Ada studied the picture. "You think so?"

"I swear it ain't got enough material in it to sag a clothesline, Sister."

"A person can always hope, can't they?"

Essie slapped her on the shoulder. "Ada Presley!"

"Or we could pray."

Essie giggled. "God would be so shocked if He heard you praying for anything that He'd faint dead away."

"I go to church every Sunday except when I've got hay to haul."

"Going to church and praying are two different things."

"And I suppose you know all about the fine arts of praying?"

Essie sighed. "If you'd had to put up with what I have you'd learn the fine arts."

Ada pushed her chair back. "I'm going to Chambersburg to the Walmart store. You want to go with me? We could have dinner at the Cracker Barrel and go to the Hobby Lobby store to buy a Christmas tree."

"I told you, I ain't put up a tree in twenty years."

"And I'm tellin' you, Essie, we will have a Christmas tree and we're makin' a big Christmas dinner for all your family this year."

She exhaled loudly. "Sounds like you're going to a lot of trouble for nothing."

Ada started toward the door. "I'll warm up the truck. You get your walkin' shoes on and your coat. I'm leavin' in five minutes."

Essie was sitting in the passenger's seat with her big black plastic purse in her lap in exactly three minutes.

—◇◇◇—

Creed could hardly believe his eyes when April appeared in the living room in her party dress. He had equated the Christmas party with the sale party held at his folks' ranch every fall. The girls all showed up in their tight-fitting jeans, fancy shirts, and best boots. A few came in a skirt, but it was usually something all decorated up Western style. April looked like she was headed to a party in a Dallas bar or for a walk down a model's runway, not in a sale barn.

"Just exactly where is this party going to be?" he asked.

April did a couple of runway spins for him. "At the Canyon Rose."

"In the barn?"

"No, silly, in our house. We'd all freeze in the barn."

Creed wanted to say, "You definitely would," but he held his tongue. "How many people will be there?"

"A bunch. You are supposed to tell me I'm beautiful in this dress, not ask a dozen questions," April said.

"Sorry, ma'am. You stunned me when you appeared in your dress and it is a lovely dress."

She turned one more time and headed back to the bedroom. "Thank you."

He looked up at Sage.

She shrugged. "The end."

"Does yours show your belly button?" he whispered.

She put a hand on each of his shoulders, leaned forward, and said, "I've ordered a brand new belly button ring."

She giggled when his eyes bulged. "Honey, there is too much woman in me to wear a dress like that."

"I rather like how much woman there is in you, ma'am."

"Sage, help me, please!" A plaintive cry came from the bedroom.

The rocking chair was set in motion when she pushed away from his shoulders and hurried back to her bedroom to help April get out of the revealing dress.

Creed imagined Sage in a dress like that. If it was for his eyes only, it would be fantastic. He could flip a breast out with nothing but his thumb. But if it was to be worn in front of a whole passel of other cowboys, well, now that was a different matter altogether. That set him to pondering the idea of going to a party where every cowboy in the canyon would know Sage and be angling for a dance.

Jealousy had reared its head right high by the time April breezed out of the bedroom with the dress box under her arm.

"See y'all tomorrow night," she said.

Sage followed in her wake and sat down on the floor to pet the puppies. "So now what did you really think? You sidestepped the compliment very well, but you did not say that you liked the dress."

"Is Lawton going to like it?" he asked.

"He won't even see it until she makes her grand entrance down the staircase into the ballroom."

"And what will happen?"

"What do you *think* will happen?" Sage asked.

"I don't know Lawton. I've never met him but I know what I'd do if she was my daughter. I wouldn't care if she was fifteen or twenty. She wouldn't be wearing that thing in public."

"It didn't look that low in the picture on the Internet. I swear it didn't or I would have talked her out of buying it."

The big yellow cat left her squirming babies and made a bed in Sage's lap.

"And the lion shall lay down with the lamb," Sage said.

"What's that got to do with a floozy dress?"

"Nothing," Sage answered. "But cats and dogs, especially those with babies, don't usually trust each other, do they?"

"I still think they were raised together and then dumped out together. And if I was Lawton, I'd send her back to put something decent on her body."

"Lawton will most likely take her back and put it on her himself. And then the fight will be on because she inherited her mother's flaming temper."

"She needs a mother," Creed said.

Sage put Blue back into the bed and picked up Elvis. "She has a mother."

"My daughter wouldn't wear something that revealing," Creed said.

Sage shot a mean look his way. "And you have how many daughters?"

Creed should drop the subject or change it abruptly. She was playing with cats and dogs and she'd tried to change it when she said that about lambs and lions lying down together. He wanted to, he really did, but he couldn't.

"Riley men don't often throw girl babies, but when and if I ever did, she wouldn't be wearing something like that to a party where a bunch of rowdy cowboys would be."

"Well, my daughter can wear whatever she wants when she's twenty years old."

Creed clamped his mouth shut.

Sage glared at him.

The silence created a tension so thick that a chain saw couldn't cut through it.

Finally, she laid Elvis close to Noel and went to the kitchen. The way she was banging things around left no doubt that she was still mad and that she wasn't going to talk about it. Well, that cleared up things for Creed. He wasn't going to entertain another moment of sharing his whole life with Sage. No, sir! A woman who couldn't rationally discuss important issues without clamming up wasn't worth wasting his time on and she sure wasn't worth giving up a ranch for.

He brought the chair to a standstill, stood up, and headed to the back door. She didn't even turn around when he put on his heavy coat and boots and went outside.

Sage attacked the butter and sugar instead of creaming them together for a batch of chocolate chip cookies. Creed was a pompous, egotistical male who should never have a daughter. He'd keep her wings clipped so close that she'd never be able to fly.

You are just mad because you pictured him with a daughter that wasn't yours, the voice inside her head said. It sounded so much like Grand that she whined out loud.

"I'm not fighting with you. Matter-of-fact, I'll prove my point."

She left the well-creamed butter and sugar and dialed Grand's cell phone number. When her grandmother answered she asked, "Did you get the picture?"

"Yes, I did."

"Where are you? It sounds like you are driving."

"I am but I've got it on speakerphone so don't say a word you don't want Essie to hear. And don't get her started about April's dress."

Essie's voice came through loud and clear. "That ain't no dress; that's two Band-Aids holding up a hanky. Her daddy should whip her fanny for even thinking about going out in public in such a thing."

"She's a little old to be getting a whipping," Sage said.

"Okay," Grand said. "If I'd been there I would have told her to hang that dress back for some other affair and wear one of her other party dresses. Change up the jewelry and the shoes and no one would even realize she'd worn it before. There will be a scene if she comes down the stairs in that thing. Lawton will have a fit."

"Creed and I just had a big argument about that. He said that his daughter wouldn't wear a dress like that."

"You are pregnant?" Grand asked bluntly.

"No, I am not," Sage sputtered.

Essie's voice was so loud that it hurt Sage's ears. "Well, I'd hope not. You've only known that cowboy for two weeks. For God's sake, Ada! Why'd you ask a dumb fool question like that anyway? Sage has enough sense not to go to bed with a man she's only known two weeks."

"Well, shit!" Grand said. "Then why'd you fight? You haven't even got the possibility of a daughter and April is Lawton's problem. Y'all ain't got no say-so in what she wears. And the fight will be between them and none of your business."

Sage couldn't think of an answer so she changed the subject. "Where are you going?"

"To Walmart, dinner at the Cracker Barrel, and then to Hobby Lobby," Essie said.

"You got all that in Shade Gap? I always thought it was just a little place."

"It is," Grand's voice came through again. "We're going over to Chambersburg to shop."

"What for?"

"Just stuff at Walmart, but a flier came with the newspaper today and Hobby Lobby has Christmas trees already on sale so I'm going to buy one. That ugly white thing that Essie had the last ten years is in the attic and I bet the rats have built nests in it so long that you'd never get the smell out."

"I don't have rats in my attic, I'll have you to know," Essie fussed.

"Well, I'm not putting up a damned old white tree. I'm buying one that will last until we're both dead and gone and it's going to be green. Our reception is about to go, Sage. These mountains are hell on phone reception. Tell everyone at the party tomorrow night hello for me and I'll send you a picture of our tree when we get it all decorated. When are you and Creed putting up one?"

"We already did," Sage said around the lump in her throat.

"It's getting crackly. I'm hanging up now," Grand said.

The last two words faded out and the phone went dead. She held it until the tinny recorded sound of an operator said if she wanted to make a call to hang up and try again.

She crammed her feet down into her work boots, didn't bother with a coat, and ran to the barn, the cold wind almost freezing the dripping tears into icicles as they fell off her jaw.

Creed was busy splitting a log when she burst into the barn. He laid down the ax just in time to catch her when she threw herself into his arms, sobbing uncontrollably against his chest.

"It's okay. Your daughter can wear whatever she wants," he whispered.

"She's not going to wear a dress like that, not if she's forty, and that's not why I'm crying. I just talked to Grand."

"Is she dying? Is that why she's selling the ranch?"

"Nooo," she wailed. "She's putting up a Christmas tree."

———— ⌇⌇⌇ ————

Creed patted her on the back and let her weep.

Why would a Christmas tree bring on tears? She hadn't cried when they'd put up their tree. She'd actually been quite giddy about it.

She swallowed a couple of times and said, "And she said that she was buying a green one that would last them until they were both dead."

"Is that the problem? Are you worrying about your Grand dying? Honey, she's as full of spit and vinegar as a twenty-year-old. She'll still be putting up that tree when she's a hundred."

That brought on another batch of tears and weeping so hard that it came nigh unto breaking Creed's heart.

"That's just it. If she's buying a Christmas tree out there, then she's serious and I won't ever be able to talk her into staying on the Rockin' C when you buy it. Creed, it's going to happen. She's not coming home to stay."

He picked her up and carried her back to the house. He took her all the way to her bedroom where he laid her on her bed. He stripped out of his coat, reached up to remove his hat, and realized he'd left it beside the ax, kicked off his boots, and stretched out beside her.

She instantly rolled toward him, cuddled against his side, and used his arm for a pillow. Creed held her close and let her cry it out. Finally, the weeping stopped and after a long sigh, she slept.

Half an hour later her eyes slowly slid open. "You still here?"

"Yes, I'm still here."

"Most men run from crying women."

"I told you in the beginning, I'm not going anywhere."

Chapter 15

CREED HAD SHAVED FOR THE SECOND TIME THAT DAY, combed his hair straight back, and dressed in his best Sunday outfit. Black starched and creased jeans, white shirt, black leather bolo tie with a silver and turquoise slide, and eel boots so shiny he could see his reflection in them. He hadn't brought his best Western-cut jacket so he'd have to wear a leather bomber, but with the party held in a house, jackets wouldn't stay on the cowboys long anyway.

He could hear Sage in her bedroom. Closet doors opened and closed. Mumblings went on. The whole time he had a visual of April in that skimpy dress and hoped that Sage didn't come out in something that revealing.

Finally, the door opened and there she was in classic elegance. His mouth went dry at Sage all dressed up. She'd been cute in her coveralls, hot in her tight-fitting jeans, and words didn't describe her without clothes. But when she stopped in the middle of the living room and turned around, his mouth went as dry as if he'd just drunk watered-down alum.

Her perfume reached his nose and he inhaled deeply. It was so exotic, as if it had been formulated especially for Sage, especially for that very night. His hands itched to touch her bare arms, to run his fingertips up her long legs going from simple high heel shoes all the way to the hemline of the snug-fitting shiny dress.

His heart skipped a beat and then lurched ahead so loudly that he could hear it pounding in his ears.

"Ready?" she finally asked.

"No."

"Well, get your coat. I don't want to miss any part of the party."

"It's not that."

"Dammit! Don't tell me you aren't going."

"I intended to until you walked out of your bedroom."

"Then what is the matter? This dress isn't like April's. I don't often even wear a dress, but when I do I don't want to have to worry about my boobs falling out or that the hem will ride up to my butt."

He couldn't wipe the shit-eating grin from his face. "Sage, you are so beautiful, so elegant all dressed up that my feet are glued tight to the floor and I'm tongue-tied. I don't want your friends to think you brought a stuttering idiot with you to the biggest party in the canyon."

Creed had seen big houses in his life. He lived in one that wasn't too shabby, but when they drove up to the Canyon Rose house, there was a hitch in his breath. It stood against the dark sky like a child's rendering of a house. A line across the middle of the page with grass on the bottom, sky on the top, and a house that sat on the line. Only this house wasn't two straight lines with two angles to make a roof. Massive white pillars held up a sun porch with white banisters around the top. The house itself was gray stone, and light flowed from an enormous room attached to the end that extended all the way to the second story. It was almost totally glass with a little bit of weathered gray wood holding the huge panes in place.

"Quite a place," Creed said.

"It is, isn't it, but I wouldn't want to have to clean the place," Sage whispered.

"I reckon they don't have to worry about their Christmas tree touching the ceiling." He nodded toward a huge tree with twinkling lights, and lots of brightly colored decorations sat against the window in the ballroom.

"I guess not."

"This reminds me of that house in that old James Dean movie," he said.

"*Giant*?"

"That's the one."

Sage laughed. "I always thought so too. I watched it when I was a teenager just to see what the big thing was about James Dean. And after that I told Grand that Canyon Rose reminded me of it. It is more intimidating at night all decorated than it is in the daylight. Is your house in Ringgold like this?"

"No, ma'am. It's big enough to house seven boys but it's a ranch house. One floor and a big front porch that wraps around the sides."

Sage did not think she had a stuttering idiot with her when she walked into the party. The buzz of conversation stopped for a few seconds as the women took in the cowboy beside Sage, and the men stared at the woman beside the cowboy.

Creed and Sage removed their coats and handed them

off to a lady in black pants and a white shirt. Quiet ended and the noise started again.

April left a group of young women and hurried to their side. She looped an arm in Sage's and one in Creed's and marched them across the room to the Christmas tree where her father was standing with a drink in his hand.

Sage felt like an overgrown giant beside the petite woman with her hair all done up in a mass of blond curls. Her gorgeous red velvet sleeveless gown with jewels around the scooped neckline dipped in drastically at her tiny waist and set off her creamy white skin. A tiny bit of train trailed behind her and a front slit stopped at her knee.

Creed would surely wish that he was with a woman like that rather than one who'd been called Mrs. Jolly Green Giant in high school.

"Nice dress," Creed said.

"Yes, it is." Lawton stuck out his hand. "I'm Lawton Pierce. I would've been over to make your acquaintance before now but the blizzard has wreaked havoc. It's taking every man I've got to get the feeding done and make sure I don't lose cattle."

"Creed Riley. Pleased to meet you. Come around anytime and if you need an extra hand, I'll be glad to help out."

"Thank you." Lawton turned to Sage. "You're looking awful pretty tonight, as usual."

Sage smiled. "And you guys clean up right good too."

"Well, we did take our monthly bath for this shindig, didn't we, Creed?" Lawton clapped a hand on Creed's shoulder. "Come with me and I'll make you acquainted with the rest of the canyon ranchers and with a lot of the cowboys who help run the Canyon Rose."

Sage waited until they were well out of earshot before she asked, "What happened to the blue dress? And I didn't even get to see your entrance. I feel cheated."

April's mouth firmed into a hard line. "I don't know how Daddy found out about the dress but he did. You didn't tell on me, did you?"

"Hell, no!" Sage said.

"Well, I opened my bedroom door and there he was, all John Wayne–like, sitting in a chair right in front of the door. Liked to have scared the shit right out of me. Just sittin' there, his arms folded over his chest and his hat cocked back."

"What did he say?"

"Not a word. He just pointed, Sage. I slammed the door and stomped around for five whole minutes. When I opened it again, he was still sitting there, just waiting."

A group of women waved from across the room and started toward them.

Sage said, "Hurry up and tell me what happened."

"I went back in the room and put on this dress. I wore it to a party at college before I left so no one has seen it here. I came out and he escorted me down the stairs. No big entrance for me this year. Oh, hello, Willa Sue! Darlin', you look fabulous in green. It matches your eyes so well."

Willa Sue was a small Hispanic woman with jet-black hair, lightly toasted skin, and full lips, but her eyes were light green instead of dark brown. Her dress was the same shade, reminding Sage of mistletoe leaves, which in turn made her think of Creed. She scanned the room and there he was, laughing and talking with a group of ranch owners. He took a sip of bourbon and his eye caught hers. Their gaze met somewhere in the middle of the room and he gave her a sly sexy wink.

"Tell us the truth, Sage?" Willa Sue asked.

"What? I'm sorry, I was looking around the room to see if Hilda decided to join us tonight," Sage answered.

"I was saying that cowboy that's buying the Rockin' C better get on his runnin' shoes because soon as this snow melts all us single girls are going to start cookin'."

Sage kept the moan at bay but it wasn't easy. She understood exactly what Willa Sue said. When the weather cleared up, there would be a stampede of women bringing cakes, pies, and casseroles to the new bachelor at the Rockin' C.

"And I was askin' if you thought it was a good idea or if that handsome hunk had already got branded since y'all are holed up together over there."

Maria, another young woman, spoke up. "And I told her that he's not your type. You'll go for a serious professor arty-farty type, won't you?"

Maria had strawberry blond hair, wore a short emerald green dress, and four-inch spike heels. Still, she barely came up to Sage's shoulder.

"The truth?" Willa Sue asked.

"To cook or not to cook? Is that the question that you need me to answer?" Sage asked.

Willa Sue and Maria both nodded.

"He knows how to cook, how to iron his own jeans, and how to use a mop. He can cut down a Christmas tree, run a ranch like he's been there forever, and he's easy to live with."

Maria groaned. "That's not fair."

"Something that looks like that cooks? I don't believe you," Willa Sue said. "You just don't want us over at your place chasin' him. I heard that Grand put a deal in the will that said you get to live there forever."

"She did," Sage said.

"Y'all might as well look on past him at the two new cowboys Daddy hired this week. They're standing over there in the corner. They're brothers and they're both blond-haired like you said you were going to hitch up with before Sage and Creed got here," April said.

All the eyes in the group went to the corner where April was looking. Sure enough, two tall cowboys were talking in a group of five other men. It was evident that they shared the same genes but one was slightly shorter than the other. The tall one had brown eyes and the short one had green eyes.

The one with brown eyes smiled at Sage and started across the floor.

Willa Sue tossed her long black hair over her shoulder. "Looks like we done attracted one."

The cowboy stopped right in front of Sage and extended a hand. "Hello, ma'am, I'm Rocky, newly hired on the Canyon Rose. The band is just gearing up for the first dance. You'd make this old cowboy real happy if you'd dance with me."

Sage shook it firmly and businesslike then let it drop. "I'd love to but I've already promised the first dance to someone else."

His head barely bobbed and he turned his attention to April. "I see. Well, how about you, darlin'?"

"Daddy always gets the first one. Tradition, but I'll save you one for later."

His brother had joined the group by then and he was cozying right up to Willa Sue. When the band broke into the first Christmas song of the season the dance floor cleared out and Lawton left his group to claim his daughter's hand for the first dance.

Lawton knew his business. If there was a stranger in the mix, he'd learn real quick that she was the owner's daughter and to tread lightly. Sage wondered if the protective father instinct came the day a man held his child or if it grew along with them. She remembered Creed talking about what his daughter would or would not do after he'd seen April in her revealing dress.

Evidently some men just had the instinct to take care of their womenfolk.

Rocky held out his hand to Willa Sue and she graced him with a brilliant smile. His brother was already on the dance floor with Maria.

Sage was so deep in thought that she didn't even see Creed making his way around the perimeter of the enormous room until he slipped an arm around her waist.

"Can I have this dance, ma'am?" Creed asked.

She slung both arms around his neck and he looped his arms around her waist. Creed Riley didn't just two-step to the country beat. His feet floated six inches above the floor and she felt as if she floated with him.

"You weren't honest with me," she said. "You said you couldn't dance. You're an expert, Creed Riley."

"Aww, shucks, ma'am, you're just bein' nice to this rough old cowboy. Woman gorgeous as you makes me look like a bumbling fool."

Her stomach fluttered at his deep drawl and she wanted to drag him away from the party. She hadn't even wanted to like him in the beginning and now his voice made the zipper on her dress itch to slide down.

What about all the other women watching and waiting for their turn to dance with him? They'd fall backwards on the nearest bed or haystack and drag him down on top of them without blinking an eye. And he would forget all about the Amazon he'd brought to the dance.

He glanced toward the ceiling. "Look there. I believe these folks rustled up some mistletoe."

She looked up and there it was, hanging from the bottom of a huge crystal chandelier. She started to say something but didn't get the first syllable out before his lips were on hers right there in the middle of the dance floor in front of Lawton, all the other ranchers, April, and even the Almighty.

She felt like a mule had kicked her in the ribs, knocked the breath out of her, and stopped her heart between beats. Then her heart gave a lurch and took off like a steam engine.

"I ain't got a no trespassin' sign to hang around your neck, but I wish I did." He breathed into her hair when the kiss ended.

The dance ended and a woman was suddenly glued to Creed's side so tight that air couldn't get between them. She had a thumb hooked in his belt at the small of his back and gazed up at him with adoring big brown eyes.

Interior decorators could say what they wanted about green being a peaceful color. It caused all kinds of fiery heat in Sage that evening and it was a very different kind of blaze than what Creed created when he kissed her under the mistletoe.

She flipped her shoulder-length blond hair back and said, "I'll take the next dance."

Creed stepped away from her and slid an arm around Sage's shoulders. "Well, ma'am, I'd be glad to dance with you but I just now promised Miz Sage that I'd go with her for some barbecued buffalo wings. I understand that Hilda makes the best in the whole county and we're about to put them up against my momma's with a taste test."

The short blonde popped her hands on her hips. "Sage, you don't play fair."

"All's fair in buffalo wings and dancing, Dee Mercer." Sage tucked her hand into his and led him toward the refreshment table.

"Did I just miss the opportunity of a lifetime or did you save me from a life of heartache?" he whispered.

"The latter," she said.

"Why's that?"

"She's a female player, Creed. She'd tear your heart out and shred it into bite-sized pieces and then feed it to her cat."

"Sounds like a vicious woman," he chuckled.

"All women are vicious," Sage told him.

He kissed her on the forehead. "Darlin', you are a sage in more than just your name."

The twinkling lights surrounding them in all the decorations reflected in Creed's green eyes, and when she looked into their depths, she and Creed were the only two people in the whole big room. There was music but it was over in the next county. There was mistletoe but someone else could dance under it and steal a kiss because she knew in that moment that she belonged with Creed.

And it scared her spitless.

"Come on, Creed. Now I've got to take you to the buffet and make an honest man out of you." She laughed to cover up her instant fear.

"Is there a preacher over there?"

She popped him on the arm and started around the busy dance floor. "I'm making an honest man out of you so that you didn't lie about going for buffalo wings."

"Well, damn!" he muttered with a chuckle.

As soon as they reached the table she put a wing on a plate, picked it up with her fingers, and held it to his mouth. She hoped Dee was watching and got the message loud and clear.

"These wings are fantastic," Creed said. "Momma's can't hold a light for them to go by, but if you ever tell her I said that, I'll swear I never said it. You've got to introduce me to Hilda."

"Not tonight," April said at his elbow.

"Why?"

"Hilda don't like big crowds. She cooks and stays in the kitchen. The caterers do the serving and toting. You can meet her tomorrow though."

Creed raised an eyebrow toward Sage.

She shrugged. "Tradition."

"What?"

April picked up a pecan tartlet. "We have church at the chapel at two thirty tomorrow. The blizzard prevented the Hanging of the Green ceremony we usually have the first of the month, but we'll have it tomorrow. Afterwards, Grand and Sage come home with us for supper. It's just the leftovers from today, but it's just Hilda, me and Daddy, and Grand and Sage. Grand ain't here so you'll have to fill in for her."

"Is that even possible?" Creed teased.

"Sure it is," April said. "You just argue with Daddy, say 'shit fire' when you are mad, and try to steal Hilda from the Canyon Rose. It won't do you any good because she's been here since Daddy was born, but that's the tradition."

"Expecting a big turnout at the church in this kind of weather?" Creed asked.

"Chapel will be packed full. Folks don't miss church and this ceremony is nice," Sage said. "I'm going to sneak back into the kitchen and tell Hilda she's outdone herself. You go on and talk cows and tractors with the ranchers."

"I'm going with you," April said.

Creed hung his head. "I'm not feeling much love right now."

April motioned toward a tall dark-haired woman wearing a black dress slit up to her hip coming right at him. "Oh, honey, you could have all the love you want. That is Lisa Reynolds coming at you. She is wild as a March hare in heat so don't let her talk you into something that will get you killed."

The woman had her eyes fixed on Creed, so he smiled and held up a buffalo wing.

April pulled Sage toward the door leading into the kitchen. "Don't worry about him. He's a big strong boy who can take care of himself."

"Why would I worry about him?" Sage asked.

"Hey, woman, I saw that kiss. It heated up the room about twenty degrees. Had Maria and Willa Sue both pantin' and wishin' they could corner him up under that mistletoe. Someday I'm going to find me a cowboy like Creed Riley and…" She stopped and blushed.

"And what?" Sage asked.

April whispered, "And we're going to do things that'll make snow boil."

"April Pierce!" Hilda looked up from the island in the middle of a big modern kitchen.

Hilda was leaning toward the back side of sixty but her hair was still black as a crow's feathers. Her round face sported a few crow's-feet around her dark brown eyes, and her body was a little rounder than it had been when she was twenty. She'd never married and lived in a small house out behind the bunkhouse. But most of her time was spent supervising the staff in the big house. And nobody that had two sane brain cells to bump against each other crossed her.

Not even April.

"Sorry, Hilda. You weren't supposed to hear that."

Sage rounded the island and bent low to hug the five-foot woman, but it didn't take her mind off what she'd heard April say about Creed, and she damn sure didn't like the look in Lisa's eyes when she pranced all prissy-like across the dance floor.

"Well, I did and I'd best not hear any more such things coming from your mouth. You are going to be the mistress of Canyon Rose someday and that's no way for a lady to talk. Now, tell me about your trip to the artist thing, Sage. Did you do well this year?"

"Very well. Enough that I get to paint another year."

Hilda wiped her hands on a bibbed apron that hung around her neck. It covered a red pearl-snap shirt and a pair of jeans. "That's good. Now tell me about this cowboy that Ada put so much trust in."

"What have you heard?" Sage picked up a finger

sandwich. "Is this your chicken salad? When I get married you've got to give me the recipe for my wedding present."

"You are marryin' up with that cowboy?" Hilda asked.

Sage fumbled the sandwich and had to maneuver fast to keep it from making a mess on her dress. "Hell, no!"

"Never knew Ada's Indian sense to be wrong. You'll bring him around tomorrow for me to meet, won't you?"

"Of course I will. It's Christmas," Sage said.

"Well, I'm glad you're home, child, and safe. Storm like we had, it's a wonder you didn't get stuck off in a bar ditch somewhere." Hilda pulled another pan of wings from the oven. "Now go back to the party. Them dresses cost too much to be standin' in the kitchen with me. Go show them off."

―――∾∾∾―――

The tall woman pressed against Creed as if she wanted to get her message of availability through to him by touch. The blizzard hadn't frozen his ability to reason and there was no way you could rearrange the aura around her to spell anything but trouble. Not even the love of the Christmas season and the mistletoe hanging above them had worked its magic to the point that Creed wanted to do more than dance with the lady. Fact be known, he would have rather been doing chores with Sage than two-steppin' the tall lady around the floor.

"I'm recently divorced. Got a pretty nice little cotton farm up in Silverton in the divorce settlement. I'll show you mine if you show me yours," she whispered.

They were directly under the mistletoe when Lisa tangled her fist into his hair and pulled his face to hers.

"Merry Christmas to me, Creed Riley. May it be the start of something hot and wonderful."

And then her lips were on his. He kept his mouth shut tightly, even when she pried at it with her tongue. He didn't shut his eyes, so everything on her face was out of focus. Her mascara had globs as big as cow patties and there were crow's-feet around her eyes. Was that a mole she'd covered up with makeup? No, it was a tiny bit of chocolate chip from a Christmas cookie.

"You don't kiss worth a damn," she said as she pulled away. "We'll have to work on that, but I do love playing the role of teacher."

"I'm not a very good student." He smiled.

"Then you might get a spanking with a ruler. I've got my ways to make you into a very good boy."

The gritty growl in her voice left him cold, as if he'd rolled in the snow strip stark naked. He'd tasted the faint remnants of cigarettes covered up by beer and chocolate. But there was no stirring in mind or body that wanted him to show her anything he had. And he was too old to go back to school, even if the teacher did promise to work with him.

Lisa stepped back abruptly and Sage stood behind her.

"May I cut in?" Sage asked.

Lisa's laugh was brittle. "Sure thing. Don't throw him back, Sage. He's not trained, but there's promise in that sexy body."

Sage's body next to his had a very different effect. Instantly, he wanted to kiss her. Hell, he wanted to do more than that. He wanted to carry her up that staircase and kick open the nearest bedroom door.

The vision of tumbling her onto a bed and letting the hot kisses take them on another wild journey stirred every nerve in his body. "How long do we have to stay?"

"Until the last dog is dead. April and I are cohostesses at the party. And why were you kissing that hussy?"

"I didn't kiss her. She kissed me. Sometimes the mistletoe is your friend. Sometimes not so much. Where did all these women come from? I thought the canyon was like a man cave."

Sage's fingers played in the hair hanging on his neck. The visual of hauling her off to the bedroom changed to carrying her into a cave with candles glowing in the corners and stretching her out naked on a pile of thick soft bearskin rugs. With Sage, he just might enjoy role-playing after all.

"But I never did like whoopin's," he mumbled.

"What did you say?"

"Lisa offered to take me home and teach me how to kiss. She'd be the teacher and I'd be the student and if I didn't get it right, I'd get a whoopin' with a ruler," he said honestly.

"That hussy! I'll show her a whoopin', but it won't be with a ruler."

"I've handled worse than her, Sage. I can fight my own battles."

The dance ended and Lawton tapped Creed on the shoulder. "We've got a discussion going about breeding buffalo with Angus. We'd like your input."

~~~

Sage made herself walk slowly up the staircase but she wanted to run. Greenery had been looped around the banister and red velvet bows were attached on every fifth rung. The sides of the landing were strung with gold tinsel garland and caught up at the top with another bow and a big ball of mistletoe.

The kissing was over. She'd already let it go way too far.

She bypassed the restroom at the top of the stairs and circled around to April's room. She stopped at the edge of the railing and looked down at the party. The feeling of Christmas was in the air. Lights twinkled everywhere. Ladies kept trying to work their way under the mistletoe as they danced. When they did, the kisses were anything from brief pecks on dry lips to downright take-it-to-the-hayloft sexy. A riot of red, green, gold, and silver decorated the whole room as well as the big tree. And then there were the two-foot trees that decorated the tables shoved away from the dance floor.

A beautiful sight with a great party, and she'd forgotten that Grand wasn't there for the first time in more than fifty years. April was sitting at a table with Willa Sue and Maria. Lawton had Creed cornered beside the Christmas tree.

Sage started to turn around and go into April's bedroom when her skin tingled like it did when Creed touched her. She looked back down and he was gazing up. He grinned and waved, then went back to his conversation.

She eased into the bedroom, turned on the light, and shut the door. The blue dress was crumpled on the bed beside her when she sat down. She pulled the phone from her tiny gold evening bag and hit speed dial. Her grandmother picked up instantly.

"Hey, are you having fun?" Grand asked.

"You are supposed to be here."

"And I'm not. Deal with it. We work hard all year and we only party at Christmas and Independence Day. If you are sitting in April's room sulking, you deserve to be miserable."

"How did you…" Sage stammered.

"I might not be there, but never doubt my Indian sense."

"Or Hilda's cell phone or the gossip hotline, right?"

"Doesn't matter how the ESP shit works. I just trust it and I don't fuss about the way it comes to me. Now get back downstairs and have fun. I understand Creed is gettin' on well with Lawton and that April didn't wear that topless dress."

"It was you that sent that to Lawton, wasn't it?"

"It was not! I sent it to her mother and she sent it to Lawton. A mother has a right to know how her girl is looking in public."

"And what if that dress had been mine?"

"You are twenty-six, Sage. You've got better sense than that."

"Don't you miss all this? It's Christmas. We only had each other all these years and Christmas was our favorite time of the year," Sage asked.

"Sure I miss it. I miss your grandpa. I miss the ranch. I miss my son. I miss your mother, who was like a daughter to me. I miss you. I miss all of it. Don't mean it's not time for a change. I'm hanging up now. Call me tomorrow after the Hanging of the Green and tell me all about the weekend."

～⁄w～

Lawton stood beside April as the last of the guests left after midnight. Hugs and handshakes and the door shut behind Lisa, the very last one to leave. She sent a wink and a kiss blown from her fingertips across the room toward Creed and gave Lawton an extra long hug. The lights still flickered. The mistletoe was still in place. The band had gone home and the caterers were cleaning up.

"Wonderful party," Creed said.

"Thank you. Hilda takes care of it every year. I just show up and make sure my daughter is dressed right," Lawton said.

"Daddy!" April hissed.

Sage hugged Lawton. "I missed Grand but it really was a good party."

"I talked to her during the party and she and Hilda were on the phone with each other most of the night. I don't think she missed much." Lawton chuckled.

"Well, we'll be leaving now. See you tomorrow at church," Sage said.

"And afterwards you will be here to help us eat up some of these leftovers, right?" April asked.

"Wouldn't miss it," Sage said.

"And you?" Lawton asked Creed.

"Wouldn't turn down another bite of those buffalo wings for anything. I'd walk through the blizzard to get at those things."

"My kind of cowboy," Lawton said.

Creed's pickup was barely warmed up by the time they reached the end of the lane on the Canyon Rose. He'd put the console up so that there was a wide bench seat and Sage had moved right up next to him.

"I feel like a teenager," she said.

"You don't look like one. Who was that last fellow you danced with?"

"Joe Rendetta. He's the vet from Claude. We see a lot of him."

"He married?"

"Was but now he's divorced. He and Lawton went to school together."

"Does anyone get married and stay married in the canyon?"

"Grand did."

"In this generation?" he asked.

"Lots of young women are workin' on that," she said. "You see anything you were interested in?"

"Yes, I did," he said.

Sage's breath caught in her chest. "Did someone introduce you to her or did you dance with her?"

"Both."

Sage hadn't wanted to share Creed, and riding home in the dark with nothing but snow still on the ground and cold wind blowing, she understood why. If he was suddenly thrown into a room full of petite, charming women eager to do whatever the hell he wanted in the bedroom, she'd soon be like yesterday's newspaper. Tossed in the pile at the end of the sofa to take to the burning barrel.

"And who is she?" she asked, but she didn't want to hear the name.

"You," he said softly.

He parked the truck in front of the house and opened the door before she could answer. He hurried around the truck, opened her door, and slipped an arm under her bottom and one around her shoulders, just like in the visions he'd had that evening. Through the pounding in her ears and the beating of both their hearts, she could hear the soft crunch of the top layer of snow as his boots crunched their way toward the house.

And for the first time in her life, she forgot all about her size.

She leaned away from him enough to open both the glass storm door and the real door and he carried her over the threshold but he didn't put her down. His lips found hers and the kiss spoke volumes. It said that all the cute little women at the party hadn't appealed to him. That she was the one he wanted to be with; she was the one he had danced with; and she was the one he carried into the house. She put both arms around his neck and her feet hit the ground just enough to give her momentum to take a gentle leap and wrap her legs around his waist.

He cupped his hands under her bottom and the tight-fitting dress hiked right up as if it had a mind of its own. He took a step forward and set her on the credenza. The zipper of her dress came down and warm air flowed against her cool skin. How had he gotten her coat off? She'd had it on and now it was gone.

Her hands went to his chest to find that his coat was gone too. The man sure didn't need lessons in how to undress a woman without her even knowing it. She unbuttoned his shirt and slowly ran her fingers across his tense abs and up across his chest. Lord, he felt good. Tight and ready and good and from the hardness pressing against her stomach, something was happening below the belt buckle.

He peeled the dress down from the top without

stopping the hard, demanding, and hot kisses. Next the bra came off and then he skimmed the bikinis from her hips slicker than skimming cream from the top of milk.

She moaned when he pulled her forward until her hips were at the edge of the credenza. When she opened her eyes, he was as naked as she was and his eyes had that soft, dreamy look in them, made even sexier with nothing but the light flickering from the fireplace.

"I want you," she gasped.

"Bedroom?"

"No, right now," she whispered hoarsely.

The washstand was exactly the right height for him to take her right where they were. Hard flesh joined hot flesh and her fingernails dug into his back. The last thing she thought before she gave up thinking about anything but satisfying the ache inside her was that she was damn glad she hadn't put the ceramic nativity scene on the credenza yet. If she had there would be shepherds and wise men smashed all over the floor and Creed might cut his feet.

The thrusts started out slow but they got faster with each kiss and groan. She couldn't breathe. She couldn't think. She just wanted release and when it came, he said her name in a ragged, hoarse breath. He backed up and she scooted forward, wrapped her legs tightly around him, and he carried her to the bedroom.

Then she was on the bed, in his arms, the covers pulled up over them, with that gorgeous thing called afterglow settling around them.

She giggled as she snuggled up next to him, sharing a pillow.

"Please don't tell me you thought that was funny," he gasped.

"No, it was wonderful... absolutely fantastic. I've never flown so high, Creed, or felt so safe afterwards. It was the place where I took flight from. I'll have to polish the top of that credenza until it shines before next week and put the nativity on it or Grand will want to know why."

He chuckled. "You don't think your Grand and grandpa ever used it for that reason?"

"Yuk! Erase that picture from my mind."

"You are so right. I'd rather have a picture of you wrapped around me in every sense of the word. You are a beautiful, sexy woman, Sage. You were the most gorgeous woman at the party tonight."

The smile that covered her face was nothing compared to the feeling in her heart. "Thank you, Creed."

"Good night, darlin'."

"Good night, Creed."

Chapter 16

WHEN SAGE SAID THEY WERE HAVING SERVICES IN A chapel, Creed pictured a small building that would seat about thirty people. But the white clapboard building in front of him was bigger than the church he'd attended his whole life in Ringgold. It had a small front porch held up by two square porch posts, a steeple on the top, and windows down both sides, not totally unlike the one in north central Texas. But there was a lot more distance from front to back than the one he was used to.

"Chapel?" he asked Sage when he parked the truck.

"That's what it's been called for years. Story has it the first Pierce who settled on the land built it because it was too far to go into town on Sunday. Each generation has maintained the building. It's probably petrified wood under those layers of white paint. Grand says she remembers when the last stained glass window was replaced, so it must have been quite the thing in the beginning."

She opened the door and made a face. "Should have worn my boots."

"Wait right there. I'll carry you inside. You'll get your feet wet in those shoes and catch pneumonia. Your grandmother will tack my hide to the smokehouse door if you get sick."

He shoved his jeans down into the tops of his boots and circled around the truck to her side. She swung the door open and he slid a hand under her knees and the other one around her midsection. "You can shut the door, please, ma'am."

She slammed it shut. "I can't believe you are doing this."

"Just don't want your Grand to skin me alive," he said.

But Creed's intentions were far from honorable. If he carried her inside the church right there at five minutes before services began, then the other cowboys would for sure see that she wasn't available anymore. And he fully well intended to share his hymn book with her too. In his part of the world, that meant that there had been an agreement of sorts met. He hoped the cowboys in the canyon played by the same rules.

The door was open a crack when they reached the porch so he stuck a toe in it and kicked. It swung to the inside and she wiggled as if she wanted him to put her down but he ignored it.

"If you'll shut that please, darlin'," he whispered.

Inside the quiet confines of the packed church the whisper carried right down the center aisle to the preacher who was just taking his place behind the podium. Lawton turned around from the front pew and grinned. April followed her father's gaze and winked. Hilda gave them a mean look.

"Put me down," Sage whispered so low that only Creed could hear it.

He marched down the entire length of the aisle and sat her down beside Hilda. Then he took his place right beside her, untucked his jeans from his boots, and laced his fingers in hers.

The preacher looked down at them, a question in his eyes.

"Excuse us, sir. She didn't wear her boots and there's too much snow still on the ground for her to plow through in those shoes," Creed said.

———— ∽∾ ————

Every woman in the church sighed.

"Well, that was very gallant. We wouldn't want her feet to get wet or for her to be sick." He smiled and said, "As you are all aware, we usually have this ceremony at the first of the month to get the congregation ready for the true reason for the season. But evidently God had other plans because we got snowed in pretty tight. So today we will celebrate all that is Christmas and begin with congregational singing. Inside the program, you will find the Christmas carols we will be singing this afternoon. We'll start with 'Silent Night.'"

Creed had a lovely deep voice that resounded off the walls. When they got to the part about all is calm and all is bright, she stopped singing. It was true that everything was bright and pretty that time of year. It was Christmas, the season of love and happiness, of giving and sharing. But what scared her was the calm in her heart since the night before.

She did not want Creed to leave. She damn sure didn't want her grandmother to move away permanently, but the Rockin' C was plenty big enough for all of them. Grand didn't have to move and Creed didn't have to go. Just admitting that had brought about the peace they sang about.

Hilda nudged her and grinned. Sage didn't know what was so delightful until she realized that she and Creed were sharing the program with the two congregational hymns printed inside. That might not mean jack shit in his part of the world, but in hers, if a woman brought a man to church and shared the hymn book, it meant something.

Sage shook her head at Hilda, but the older woman's smile didn't wane one single bit. And Sage would bet that as soon as she could find a quiet place, Hilda would call Ada and tell her all about it.

When the last piano notes of the carol ended, the preacher began the responsive reading that retold them the reason they were preparing the chapel for the birth of Christ. He read a line and then the congregation spoke their line in unison.

The preacher said that the branches of cedar and garlands of pine and fir represented never ending life because their branches were always green. The voices in the congregation joined together in the proper response. Then he said that the wreaths of holly and ivy told of the passion, death, and resurrection of the Lord and Savior.

Sage read her lines but she thought about her passion for painting and how Creed understood it. He hadn't made one small overture toward changing her but encouraged her to do more and more. She thought about the death of the anger inside her and how she'd been so determined to see him leave. And the resurrection of a calm peace when she accepted the fact that she didn't want to face the days ahead without Creed in her life.

The preacher's wife sang "Mary Did You Know?" Cold chill bumps raced down Sage's backbone. She wondered if Creed's momma had known when she had him if one day he'd leave her and move away hundreds of miles to a big hole in the ground. If she realized the effect that he would have on one woman in that canyon.

Then the preacher sat down on the edge of the altar at the front of the church and motioned for the little children to join him. A couple of little girls sat on his knees and the others gathered around him in a circle. One thing the canyon did was produce kids and lots of them had skin the color of Creed's. That lightly toasted color that testified of Hispanic blood.

He told them that the legend of the poinsettia came from Mexico and went on to talk about a little girl named Maria and her little brother Pablo and how they looked forward to the Christmas festival.

She'd heard the story so often that she could read it back to the preacher without looking at the words, so her thoughts veered off in another direction. Her hand tucked into Creed's felt right and good, but how had it all happened?

Magic, Grand's voice said in her ears.

The story ended and the preacher asked eight children to carry pots of poinsettias to various parts of the church. The other children raced back to their parents and the preacher took his place behind the podium to tell the story of the shepherds and the birth of Christ.

"And this morning the church gets dressed in its Christmas apparel. The Christmas tree has been brought to stand in our sanctuary. This day for the first time its lights will shine on us. While the children bring their ornaments to hang on the tree, we will sing 'Away in a Manger.' Let your voices resound with the glory of the season."

Sage and Creed held the program between them, their

voices blending with the other members of the church at the back side of Lawton Pierce's property. When the song ended one little boy flipped a switch and the lights on the tree sparkled.

"Beautiful," Creed whispered in Sage's ear.

The heat from his breath sent instant flutters all the way to her stomach. She nodded in agreement but her thoughts were not on the sparkling Christmas tree, but rather on the shiny surface of a freshly cleaned credenza in their house.

Their house!

Lord Almighty, and I'm not swearing right here in the church house but asking, where did that come from? She looked toward the ceiling.

The preacher talked about preparing the communion table. He removed the old cloth and replaced it with one with embroidered poinsettias on it that matched the curtain in the kitchen. Someone's grandmother from ages past had embroidered it for the season no doubt.

Then a teenage girl came forward. She wore a lovely crimson red velvet dress and cowboy boots. She took her place behind the podium and read about the lighting of the candles as three other girls her age lit candles in the windows and on the communion table. With each candle that was lit the congregation read the responsive reading from the program.

Sage was amazed at how well Creed fit right into the whole program. "Have you done this before?"

"Many times. I used to be the one who read that passage that she's reading right now," he whispered.

"As we light these candles we symbolize God, Emmanuel, God with us. His peace and joy comes through the illumination of His message of love," the young lady said and went back to her seat.

There were five more readers. Cedar branches and holly were placed on the communion table. Wreaths were hung in the windows and on the front of the pulpit. At the end of the last reading the children came forward and sang "Little Drummer Boy." Then the whole congregation stood and read the ending prayer together.

"We dedicate our lives and all that we have to the work of life, of love, of peace. Receive our gifts and lead us in wisdom and courage. Amen."

Sage felt naked when Creed dropped her hand to shake with the preacher. Half of her was suddenly gone and then his other arm was around her waist. In that moment she realized that Creed was a part of her and that he was never leaving.

"You are no stranger to the Hangin' of the Greens, are you?" The preacher pumped Creed's hand up and down. "I'm Willard Dumas. I preach up in a church in Claude on Sunday morning, but these folks needed someone to come down here, so we set up a Sunday afternoon service. Glad to see you in church with Sage. Give Ada our best when you talk to her."

"I will surely do that. I'm Creed Riley, the new owner of Rockin' C next week when Miz Ada returns from her trip and we get the papers signed."

The preacher leaned in. "Don't let your spirits rise too high, son. Ada's got a lot of memories invested on that ranch. I'm not sure she'll really sell out when she gets to thinking about it."

Sage's heart twisted up into a pretzel. What was she going to do if Grand did change her mind and Creed left the canyon? Just when she'd found her soul mate, would he be jerked out of her life?

—⁓—

Creed stood to one side and let the ladies and Lawton go ahead of him into the ranch house. It still looked intimidating even in daylight, but not so much as it had the night before with all the lights glowing brightly.

What surprised him was the intimacy of the dining room setting as compared to the big ballroom party. When he first walked inside, he noticed that the double doors to the left of the staircase were closed. He followed Lawton and the ladies down a wide hall. One door led into the kitchen, but they bypassed it and went on to the next one, a formal dining room set up for five people at the end of a table that could easily seat a dozen.

The table had been set and the women went right on into the kitchen and started bringing out dishes. Creed was amazed when his stomach growled. It was already close to four o'clock and it would be chore time in less than an hour.

"We'll have a little something and then get on about the feeding," Lawton said as if he could read his mind. "Ranchin' don't stop just because baby Jesus was born in a manger."

"It was a nice service though," Hilda said. "I couldn't believe that Amelia let her daughter wear boots with that beautiful dress."

"It's the style, Hilda," April said.

"And she didn't have a Creed Riley to carry her into church." Sage smiled.

Lawton motioned for everyone to sit down, said a quick grace, and looked right at Creed. "If Ada decides not to sell, I've got a place for you right here on the Canyon Rose, Creed."

Creed nodded. "Thank you, Lawton. But I've got my heart set on havin' my own place. I appreciate the offer, but if she backs out it wasn't meant for me to be in the canyon so I'll just go on my way and find where it is I'm meant to settle down."

Besides, before I tell Sage exactly how I feel, I want to have something to offer her. She deserves more than a hired hand.

"Offer still stands if you change your mind," Lawton said. "Now pass me those buffalo wings and help yourself first. Once April gets a hold of the bowl we won't get any."

"You got that right. I was too busy to eat very much at the party. And believe me, I don't get this kind of food in Weatherford, Oklahoma!"

"That where you live?" Creed asked.

"That's where I go to college."

Creed passed the bowl to Lawton. "And what are you going to be when you grow up?"

"A rancher. I'd like to be one right now but Daddy is on Momma's side and you can't fight City Hall." She shot a look down the table at Lawton.

"You remember that. When you get your education you can learn ranchin'. There's plenty of time."

Time, Creed thought. Not everyone had plenty of time. He had one more week and then he'd either be out of time or he'd own a ranch. His whole future hinged on whether or not Ada Presley sold him the ranch.

Creed set the milk bucket under the cow and reached for his phone before he started his final chore of the evening. His brother, Ace, answered on the second ring.

"Hey, are y'all thawin' out? Our snowman looks like a snow blob now. There's nothing left on the ground and Jasmine wanted a white Christmas so bad."

"Bring her out here. Roads are clear and the weatherman says we're having a white Christmas for sure. It'll take days and days to melt all this," Creed said.

"Oh, no. Not a chance. Momma is already carryin' on because you are gone and the whole family won't be at her place over the holidays. Why couldn't you have found something within driving distance?"

Creed chuckled. "I did. I'm only five hours from y'all and I'll try to make arrangements to be home sometime over the holidays another year, but this one, it's impossible. You got a minute?"

"Oh, boy! That tone means you've got a problem. That weird artist givin' you fits?"

"Yes, she is, but she's not weird. She's beautiful. How did you know for absolute sure, I mean without a doubt, that you had fallen for Jasmine before you married her?"

"You have a hell of a big problem if you are askin' that question," Ace answered.

"Well?"

"Thing is, I didn't. Only a couple of people know the real story of me and Jazzy. Can you keep a secret?"

"Of course."

"I didn't know I'd fallen for Jazzy before I married

her. She offered to marry me because of that damned clause in Grandpa Riley's will. He said I had to be married within a certain time and I had to stay married a year or else the whole ranch went to our cousin, Cole."

"Holy shit!"

"Don't know if it's holy even during Christmas, but you got it right. Remember when Grandpa's old lawyer died and the new one took over his files? Well, he found that part in the will and I had a week to get married or lose everything. I told Jazzy about it and she offered. We flew to Las Vegas and we intended to keep it a big secret between just the two of us. You know the rest. It was broadcast on television and the secret was out."

"Damn!"

"That's what we thought, but then we had to live together…"

Creed chuckled then. "And your three younger brothers had moved into the house with y'all. How'd you ever figure out that you'd fallen in love?"

"It just happened. One day I couldn't wait for the year to be up. The next I couldn't live without her. So tell me what's going on," Ace said.

"I think I'm to that latter place and it's only been two weeks. Things in the real world don't happen that fast, do they?"

"Sometimes in the real world they happen in the blink of an eye. When are we going to meet this woman?"

"Anytime you want to make a five-hour trip to the canyon."

Sage painted when she was nervous. It settled that antsy feeling inside her and took her mind off whatever was chewing on her nerve endings. That evening she picked up her brushes with intentions of beginning a new mistletoe picture. She'd envisioned it that morning in church. She'd already sketched in the Christmas tree standing beside the old upright piano.

The little four-year-old girl had come forward with her decoration when the preacher said it was time. She had big blue eyes, dark curly hair, and a round cherub face. She wore a denim jumper with a Christmas tree appliquéd on the bib and a ruffle of eyelet lace around the hem. Her red glittery shoes looked like they came right out of a *Wizard of Oz* Broadway play and her legs were chubby. She held a small ball of mistletoe with a red velvet ribbon on the top and she tiptoed to hang it in just the right spot.

The picture Sage sketched in didn't show that whole end of the church. It was just the corner of the upright piano, a small portion of the tree, and the wonder on the little girl's face as she carefully hung her mistletoe on a tree branch. Above it was a bright white bulb throwing off light rays that looked just like a star.

Noel sat beside the easel leg and watched her paint. Angel left her fighting triplets and watched from the middle of the living room.

"I love you both and I love your babies, but I want a little girl like that one. I want her to have dark curls and green eyes and I want her to be raised in the canyon and put a decoration on the tree at the church at Christmas," she said.

Noel's tail thumped against the hardwood floor and Angel purred.

"So we are in agreement. Your puppies and kittens will be grown by the time I get a little girl like that, but you wouldn't mind sharing the ranch with a child?"

The purring got louder and the thumping sounded like a bass drum.

"Okay, then, I'm admitting it. I want a family."

She picked up a brush and squirted several globs of paint onto a palette. As she began to paint her mind went to the wild sex on the credenza the night before. That urgent, demanding need had engulfed her and taken over her body. It was a brand new experience and the first time she'd had sex without a bed involved.

She wondered what it would be like in a hayloft or in the front seat of a pickup truck. Maybe an experience like the night before only came along once in a lifetime.

You got that wrong, her heart said. It didn't have Grand's voice but she recognized it as the sassy tone that argued with her all the time.

"Oh, yeah," she said aloud.

It can happen lots of times if you just let it. He's the one, just like your Grand knew in the beginning. Creed Riley is the one that this ranch needs to bring it back to its splendor and to make you happy at the same time.

The door opened and the force that was Creed was back in the house. Noel jumped up with a yip and ran that way. Angel stood up and stretched, yawned, and then went to rub around his legs.

"Fickle pets. They leave me when you arrive." Sage was grateful the voice had stopped and that she didn't have to deal with her newly found revelation anymore.

"It's not me, darlin'. It's the milk bucket they are interested in. We've got to go to town tomorrow and get them some proper food. Roads are clear and traffic is flowing. Let's go to Amarillo."

She cleaned her brush and laid it on the easel tray. "We can get dog food and supplies in Claude."

He set the milk on the table and met her halfway across the floor. He wrapped his arms around her waist, pulling her close to his chest, tipped up her chin with his gloved fist, and kissed her hard.

"Miz Sage Presley, would you go to dinner with me tomorrow in Amarillo? I thought we'd have dinner and then take in a matinee in the afternoon or else do some shopping after dinner. Your choice and you can pick the restaurant since I don't know what you like."

"Are you asking me on a date?" she asked.

"I am."

"Yes, I would love to go to dinner with you and afterwards I'd like to go to a little art shop and pick up some paints and then do some Christmas shopping at the mall. I haven't bought a single present."

He kissed her again and she felt the edges of that same raw need she'd felt the night before. So it wasn't a one-time thing. It had nothing to do with the season or the party and everything to do with the cowboy.

Chapter 17

CREED REACHED ACROSS THE TABLE AND COVERED Sage's hands with his. Big white cloth napkins were folded into a point and set on a red and white checkered tablecloth. To one side a green wine bottle held a bright red candle. The candle's wax melted slowly, traveling at a snail's pace toward the bottom of the bottle. The flicker from the tiny fire reflected in Sage's eyes.

Creed had seen that sweet look in them the night before when they'd gone to bed together. They'd fallen asleep after sex before and spent the night together but last night was different. They'd gone to bed together like a couple and it had been so natural, so right.

He squeezed her hands gently.

"You are beautiful," he said.

"Thank you, Creed. You look pretty damn fine yourself."

"Cowboy puts on his best for a date with a gorgeous woman." He picked up her left hand and kissed her fingertips, lingering over each one.

"Lord, that makes me hot. Reckon we could hide under the tablecloth and…" She wiggled her eyebrows.

"Probably not, but hold that thought."

The waitress appeared out of the shadows with a huge bowl of salad, two smaller bowls, and a basket of bread sticks. She refilled their wine glasses and told them their food would be out shortly.

Creed pushed his wine to one side. "No more for me today. I'm the driver but you can have all you want."

"I'd best not drink all I want. I love good wine so I'll finish this glass, but two is my limit," she said.

"It's the Indian blood."

Using the hinged tongs she filled her bowl with salad and buttered one of the bread sticks. "What's that got to do with anything?"

"They don't hold their liquor so well."

She pointed her bread stick at his nose. "Darlin', I'm only an eighth Indian. The rest of me is red-hot Irish and I can hold my liquor. I'm not having but two glasses because the third one takes all my inhibitions away and that Irish gets crazy."

Creed chuckled. "Remind me to stop by the liquor store on the way home. I'd like to see that Irish crazy come to the surface."

––––––

Sage ate slowly, not because it was her nature, but because she wanted the moment to last forever. Sitting in the dark shadows of an Italian restaurant across the table from the sexiest cowboy in Texas made her feel special, protected, and complete.

"Do you think the animals miss us?" she asked.

She could have bitten her tongue off for such a stupid question. Dogs and cats shouldn't even cross her mind.

"Don't worry, Momma. The babies will be fine until we get home," he chuckled.

Hearing him call her that startled her. Was she really ready for a little dark-haired girl to call her Momma? Or a son?

Mercy! What would she do with a son? She'd never been around little boys that much, only at church and in very small doses. She understood girls better after being around April.

Creed came from a family of seven sons. From that standpoint the odds were that she'd have boys and lots of them.

"What in the world are you thinking about? Noel and Angel will be fine, honest." Creed gently squeezed her hands.

"Tell me more about their new little houses," she said quickly.

Creed went on. "I'm buying insulation this afternoon so I can finish their houses. They'll be done tomorrow and we'll see how they do on the front porch. I think Angel is getting stir-crazy in the house. She sits on the windowsill behind the Christmas tree and I can see it in her eyes. She wants to be outside."

"And Noel?"

"She'll be happier on the porch. And pretty soon those puppies are going to open their eyes and scoot right off that blanket. Then there'll be a puddle or worse everywhere you walk."

"Yuk! I see your point."

He picked up the silver salad tongs and filled her bowl first and then his. "They'll still run in and out and you can go outside to visit them."

She took a bread stick and handed the basket to him. "What about your dogs? Will they kill the cats?"

He shook his head. "No, they might have a few issues with Noel, but they've been raised around cats. They'll bark at them, but they won't kill them."

She swallowed hard. "What kind of issues?"

He laid his fork down and cupped her chin in his palm. "They won't know if she's a dog, a bear, or a miniature alpaca."

"Never thought of crossbreeding a dog with an alpaca."

"Well, Noel is living proof that it can be done," he said.

Snowflakes the size of silver dollars drifted lazily down from the gray skies to rest on them as they left the restaurant. Creed threw his arm around her shoulder and together they hurried toward the pickup.

"More snow! We should have that white Christmas for sure." She dusted the flakes from her denim duster when she was inside the truck. She switched on the radio as Creed stomped the extra snow from his boots and settled into the driver's seat.

"Don't put up your boots or sleds just yet," the DJ said when Creed turned on the engine. "We've got another winter storm watch in effect. We won't get as much snow as last time, but the weatherman says there'll be another inch of accumulation. It will move on toward the east by morning. What's one more inch when we're already dealing with eight inches, folks? Just puts us in the mood for the season. And now for five uninterrupted Christmas songs to keep that mood going..."

Creed sang, "Sleigh bells ring, are you listenin'," along the singer as he backed out of the parking lot.

"Paint store?" he asked before he turned one way or the other onto the highway.

"It's next door to the mall. We can go there afterwards."

"And after the mall shopping, we'll hit Home Depot for insulation and Walmart for supplies and pet food, right?"

She nodded.

"Navigate for me."

She looked across the seat. "Do what?"

"Tell me when to turn and how to get to this mall. I've been in Amarillo a couple of times but it was for rodeos. We hit town, did the rodeo, went to a couple of clubs, and back to our hotel or to our travel trailers."

"Turn right at the next light, then left at the one after that, and you'll be able to see the mall on the next block. Park anywhere you can find a spot."

The light was green so he made a right. The next one was red and Sage pointed toward the mall parking lot. It looked like an enormous car dealership. He made the turns and crept up and down the lanes until a red car finally backed out not far from the mall's main entrance. He snagged the spot and unbuckled his belt. Before he could get around the truck, she was already outside with the door slammed. She grabbed his hand and set a long-legged pace straight ahead.

She had a list of presents she needed to purchase and he could tag along or he could go his own way and they'd meet up later. It was most likely the last time she'd get to Amarillo before Christmas day and every minute counted.

"Now what?" he said when they were inside out of the cold.

Christmas carols came through the central stereo system. A huge tree full of shiny decorations, gold tinsel, and blinking lights graced the center of the mall. Santa's

photo station had been set up in front of the tree and a
line of kids snaked down the corridors for at least two
city blocks.

She rose up slightly on her toes and kissed him. "I'm
going shopping."

"Me too. I haven't sent a thing home and I see a place
over there that will ship for me. I'll meet you back here
in one hour?" He looked at his watch.

Sage pushed up the sleeve of her fancy Western-cut
shirt and nodded. She could buy for everyone on her
list in that time because she already knew what she was
looking for. The lines to check out would take longer
than the picking out process.

The first store she headed for carried Western wear
and the best flannel shirts in the whole state. She chose
a red and black plaid one for Creed because she'd stolen
his and had no intentions of giving it back. Then she
picked out a blue plaid for Lawton and headed to the
ladies' side of the store for something with lots of bling
for Hilda and April. Hilda got a floral: black with red
roses, with red pearl snaps. April got a pink one with
jewels forming a longhorn bull on the back yoke.

She paid for them and was on her way to the next
store for something for Grand when she passed one of
the holiday kiosks on the way. It offered leather goods
and there was a gorgeous hand-tooled man's wallet
complete with initials. She pondered a long time but
finally picked up the one with a *C* on it and paid for
it, shoved the box it came in down into her shirt bag,
and went on.

Grand was getting a decent handbag that year. She
wouldn't ever part with the money for a good leather

bag but Sage had seen her admiring them several times that fall. The kiosk had offered a few styles but the one Grand had kept going back to was in a leather shop down one of the mall wings. Sage remembered the name of the store but not the exact location so she stopped at a mall map to find it.

It was down the wing housing Dilliard's so she set a course for that part of the mall. Once in the store she went straight to the back shelves where the handbags were kept. She didn't know she was holding her breath until she finally located the exact bag shoved behind some newer stock.

It was a hobo-type bag with a wide shoulder strap and made of the softest black leather she'd ever touched. No wonder Grand liked it. She could carry half her belongings in the thing and it would rest easy on her shoulder. She was halfway to the checkout counter when she remembered Aunt Essie.

"Shit! I almost forgot her. Well, if Grand would like this bag, then so would Aunt Essie." Sage went back to the shelf and started to hunt for another bag like the one she'd just picked out.

"May I help you?" a sales clerk asked.

"I'd like another one just like this," Sage said.

"That's our last black one. It's been a great seller this season. I do have a brown one but it's just a little smaller. We also have the matching wallets and they are on sale." She pulled the brown bag from a lower shelf and handed it to Sage.

She held them up, side by side. There they were, Aunt Essie with her lighter hair and smaller size. Grand with her dark hair and bigger-than-life attitude.

"I'll take them and the wallets. Do you have those fur-lined house shoes?"

"Yes, ma'am!" The clerk was all smiles as she led the way to the shoe shelves at the back of the store.

"I need a size eight in brown and a size nine in black in ladies," Sage said.

"They're not on sale today but they will be the weekend before Christmas," the sales clerk whispered from behind her hand.

"I won't be back again, so I'll just have to pay full price."

"Too bad. Our men's slippers are on sale this week."

Sage followed her. "Well, now that's interesting. I'll take a pair in a thirteen if you have them."

"That's a big foot. We ordered one special last week and the lady broke up with her boyfriend so we've got it. Normally we only stock up to a twelve. You are a lucky woman today."

"Yes, I am," Sage said.

Creed was buying for his younger two brothers and his mom and dad when he looked at his watch and realized he was out of time. He phoned Sage and she picked up on the first ring.

"I'm almost done. They're ringing up Grand's and Aunt Essie's presents," she said.

"Well, I'm not. I bought for each family member and then took it to the shipping place and I've still got at least half an hour before I'm done."

"Great!" she said. "I'll have time to look around and go to the paper store to buy wrapping supplies. Meet you at the Christmas tree in forty-five minutes?"

The phone went silent so he shoved it back in his pocket and went into the next shop and bought presents for his two younger brothers and his parents. He had them wrapped and took them to the shipping place and then it hit him. He had less than thirty minutes to buy something for Sage.

"God, I can't pick out something that important in that length of time," he groaned.

As if a higher being answered his prayers on the spot, he looked across the way from where he stood and there was a jewelry store. He'd never seen her wear jewelry except the night they'd gone to the Christmas party. She'd worn long dangling topaz-looking earrings and a matching necklace.

There were no customers in the jewelry store so he didn't have to wait for a sales clerk to help him. He was on his way to the bracelets or earrings when the wedding rings caught his eye. It was as if he had stepped in superglue and his feet would not budge. His boots were filled with lead and his eyes couldn't see a blessed thing but sparkling diamonds and matching wedding bands.

"Could I help you?" a petite blonde asked.

And he looked right into the eyes of Macy, his ex-fiancée.

"Creed?" she asked with a catch in her voice.

"Hello, Macy. What are you doing here?"

"Just a little job while school is out for the holiday. I teach down in Hereford, Texas, these days. What are you doing here?"

"I'm not sure."

"Well, you are looking at wedding rings, Creed. I suppose that means you are doing something in the store."

"I guess I am at that. How are you?"

He didn't want to talk to Macy and he damn sure didn't want to buy a wedding ring from her, but there it was: a set of matching bands. And right beside them was a little red velvet box with an engagement ring. One diamond set on a thin band. Sage could wear them both or just the wedding band when she was painting or feeding the chickens.

"I'm fine. My husband got transferred to this area last summer. It's not home and it's taking me a while to get used to the place, but it's only for two years and then we'll probably be going to the East Coast for a while."

"Can I see those rings and that engagement ring beside them? I'm buying a ranch in the Palo Duro Canyon," he said.

"What for? We drove through there one time. I hated it." She pulled the rings out and handed them to him.

If the man's ring fit his finger and if the woman's ring fit his pinky, he would buy them. If not, it wasn't meant to be. He picked up the smaller ring and it slipped on his pinky perfectly. The larger ring fit his ring finger just as well.

"Who is she?" Macy flipped her blond hair back over her shoulder.

"It's complicated." He put the engagement ring on with the band and held his hand up to the light.

"That's a fine diamond. One of the best we have in the store. Not the cheapest or the biggest but the best for fire and brilliance. Personally, I've always liked gold but some women do prefer white gold. That's platinum, by the way, and it's expensive," Macy said.

"I'll take them and now I need to look at a bracelet."

"Tell me about her and I'll make a recommendation."

Creed shook his head. He didn't want to buy something for Sage that his ex suggested. He wanted something very special that only he would understand the reason behind the gift.

"Tennis bracelets are here. All women love diamonds," Macy said.

He barely glanced at them before moving on. He checked his watch. He had fifteen minutes.

Macy pointed toward a plain gold bracelet and that's when he got the idea.

"Show me some of those things that dangle on a bracelet like that."

She pulled out a tray of gold and silver charms and set it before him. "Like these."

"Do you have a bracelet like that only in white gold or platinum?"

She put a tray of white gold bracelets in front of him.

She pointed to one substantial enough to hold the charms he had in mind. "Then that's what I want. Can you put these charms on it and have it ready to go in ten minutes?"

"I can put them on as you pick them out." Macy reached for a tool under the counter and held it up.

Creed picked out a dog, a cat, a Christmas tree with a sparkling diamond at the top, and a round disk engraved with mistletoe in the middle. Tiny opals created the berries. It was a perfect gift. Each year he would add a charm to it that signified something wonderful that had happened in their lives.

"Wow! That is some present," Macy said. "Really, Creed, tell me about her."

"Like I said, it's complicated. So you are happy?" he asked, changing the subject.

He hadn't seen her since she'd come home from that trip and told him that their engagement was over. But now, looking at her and hearing her talk about how happy she was and what a wonderful marriage she had, he wondered why he'd ever fallen for her anyway. Nothing stirred inside him. Not anger. Not bitterness. Certainly not passion.

She handed him the bracelet tucked inside a long red velvet box that matched the engagement ring box. "There you go."

Fingertips brushed together and still he felt nothing. She rang up his bill and he didn't even flinch.

She handed him the credit card receipt. He signed the bottom and shoved his copy into his shirt pocket.

"Creed, I never meant to hurt you. I really did think I loved you when I accepted your proposal."

"Macy, I'm over it. I've got to go now. Merry Christmas."

He looked at his watch and hurried out into the mall before he realized that the small bag had the jewelry store logo on it. He had five minutes so he went to a kiosk that sold small-tooled leather items.

"Help you?" a lady wearing boots and a denim mini-skirt asked.

"Yes, ma'am," he said. "What kind of wallet are the ladies using these days?"

She picked up one that looked like an oversized old-time cigarette case and handed it to him.

"I'll take it. And how about cell phone cases?"

She showed him a rack where dozens hung.

"This one. This one and this one." He laid three out on the counter.

She rang up his bill and he'd barely gotten the items paid for when his phone rang.

"Yes?" He expected to hear Sage telling him that she had been waiting for ten minutes, but instead she was out of breath.

"I ran into an old friend and we got to talking and I'm just now in the paper store. Give me ten more minutes."

"You got it," he said.

A window display caught his eye as he slowed his pace and took his time getting to the rendezvous place. He stopped and a wide grin spread across his face. There was the perfect gift for Sage. She'd all but stolen his favorite red and black plaid flannel shirt, and hanging right there on a mannequin was one very similar to his. The plaid was a little smaller and the flannel not as soft since it hadn't been washed a hundred times, but she'd love it for a nightshirt.

He walked into the store and bought the shirt. It was the last one so they had to take it off the mannequin. They wrapped it for him in shiny red paper and slipped it down into an enormous plastic bag with the store logo on the front. He put his leather purchase bag and his jewelry store bracelet down in the bag with the package and tied a knot in the top. The two ring boxes were in his coat pocket.

~~~

Sage was on her way to the meeting point when someone ran up behind her and touched her on the shoulder. She whipped around and came face to face with Victor Landry.

"Sage Presley! It is you!"

"Hello, Victor. What in the world are you doing in Amarillo, Texas?"

"My folks moved here last year. I can't believe after all this time that you are right here in front of me. I hear you are the next rising Western art star. I've got to be honest—when you left college, I didn't expect much."

She winced.

"Well, you did have commitment issues. I figured it was in all things, not just relationships, but I was wrong." He ran a hand down her arm. "Let's go to dinner and talk art."

Dammit!

She hadn't wanted to go to dinner with Victor when they were practically living in the same dorm room. She damn sure didn't want to go to dinner with him that day.

"Hey." Creed waved from ten feet away and quickly joined her.

"Creed, meet Victor Landry. Victor, this is Creed."

Sage felt his eyes go to her left hand but it was holding so many bags that there was no way she could shove it into her pocket.

Creed shifted his bags to his left hand and stuck the right one out. "Pleased to make your acquaintance. You live around here, do you?"

"Victor and I were art students together at college," she explained.

"I remember being quite a bit more than that," he said. "And to answer your question, no, I live in New Orleans. It's a wonderful place to feel the art."

He was a tall, lanky blond-haired man. He wore black dress slacks and shoes with tassels on the toes.

A pale pink shirt collar showed from under a pink and gray argyle sweater and his watch was a very good Rolex knockoff.

"Well, it was good to see you, Victor. We've got to get home and do chores before dark. If you see any of our old crowd, tell them hello for me." Sage's voice was so high-pitched that it even sounded strange in her ears.

He stuck a hand between the V-neck sweater and the pink shirt and handed her a card. "Call me, darlin'. We really should get together and talk art."

She pocketed the card. "Got to run. Come on, Creed. Cows have to be fed."

She didn't even look back to see if Creed was behind her but set a course out of the mall as fast as she could go.

"What was that all about?" Creed asked when they were inside the truck.

"It was about nothing. Victor and I had a six-month thing. He wanted more than I wanted to give. End of story. Now let's go home."

"Must be old flame week. I walked into the… into a store and there was my ex-fiancée working behind the counter. Her husband got transferred to this area and she's teaching school down in Hereford."

"What's she doing working in the mall?" Sage asked coldly.

"Selling stuff while she's not teaching, I guess," he said.

Sage looked out the window and bit her lip to keep back the smart remarks that were on the tip of her tongue. She'd been in such a good mood when she went into the mall, but a demon had taken up residence on her shoulder when she came outside. The devil could go by any number of names: jealousy, anger, fear. But it was there, so she turned a cold shoulder to Creed and stared out the window.

He stopped at Home Depot and asked if she was getting out.

She shrugged so he went in and bought a roll of insulation without her.

He stopped at Walmart and she was out of the truck and practically jogging inside before he could put the vehicle in park. She bought the most expensive dog and cat food in the place and three of the biggest pots of poinsettias she could find. He loaded his cart with groceries, toilet paper, and laundry soap.

She helped unload the items when she got home, fed the dog and the cat, and went to her room. She slammed the door, picked up his flannel shirt, and threw it at the wall. The nightshirt she found in her dresser drawer was old and soft but it wasn't as comfortable as Creed's shirt.

Finally she threw herself across the bed and wept even though she didn't know why she was angry or why she was crying.

Creed didn't know what in the hell he'd done to make her mad. He'd been up front and told her about Macy. After all, he'd bought an engagement ring and matching wedding bands. If things had worked out between them, he sure didn't ever want it to come up that he'd actually bought the rings from his ex.

He turned on the Christmas tree lights, sunk down

into the sofa, and picked up the remote control. He flipped through channels until he found reruns of *NCIS*.

"Understanding murder is simple compared to understanding a woman, Leroy Jethro Gibbs. You been married a bunch of times. What advice would you give me?" He talked to the character on the television.

Gibbs said, "Grab your gear."

"That's exactly what I probably need to do, ain't it? Grab my gear and go back to Ringgold, Texas."

Noel pushed the pie plate around the floor, licking the last crumbs of her dog food from the corners. Angel sat in front of the tree and washed her paws.

"All is quiet. All is calm," Creed said. "Except in my heart. What in the devil made me think I could meet my soul mate and everything would work out just wonderful in two weeks? The season made me crazy is what happened. Blame it on Christmas."

Noel jumped up on the sofa and laid her head on Creed's lap. Angel pranced across the floor and curled up on his other side.

"Grab your gear," he repeated. "Sounds like the best advice one man could give another in my predicament."

Chapter 18

THE WHIR OF THE SEWING MACHINE SOUNDED THROUGH the whole house. The thing was old as God and sounded worse than a threshing machine. Well, almost, anyway! Ada remembered when her mother bought it in 1948. She was just a little girl that year and Essie had already gotten married and moved away. It was probably just tired of working and ready to retire to the attic with everything else Essie couldn't bear to part with.

Ada cut the small squares and Essie sewed them together. The pattern, showing them which colors went together, was tacked on the wall and provided plenty of fodder for arguments.

"That thing sounds like a threshing machine. You sure you oiled it?" Ada asked.

"Three times a year. On New Year's Day. On Mother's Day to remember Momma. And on Labor Day because I've made it work so hard," Essie said.

"Why didn't you ever buy a new one?"

"Didn't need a new one and this one reminds me of Momma. We only got to go home to Oklahoma once a year at first because it cost so much to travel. And she'd always have the machine set up to make me a couple of new outfits."

Ada laid the scissors down. "I remember. She'd get so excited when your letters came, and the week before you were supposed to be there she'd cook all kinds of things."

"And send half of it back with me." Essie smiled. "We'd eat on that food all the way home. We even shared with the folks on the train until we got our first car and could travel that way."

Ada went back to cutting squares. She'd thought she could sell the ranch and she hadn't been wrong about Creed. He was the one. She'd known it in her bones that first day and they hadn't been lying.

But she couldn't leave Sage on the porch the same way that Essie had left their mother all those years ago. She just couldn't.

Essie wouldn't remember because she stayed a few days and then disappeared again. Ada was the one left behind to witness her mother's tears, long sighs, and broken heart until the next time Essie came home to Oklahoma.

"Just look what all we're getting done," Essie said. "Sage is going to love this."

"Yes, she is," Ada said around the lump in her throat.

"We'd never get it done in time if I didn't have the quilting machine. Top it out today and tomorrow and quilt it on Wednesday," Essie said as she worked.

"You ever make one of these for your grandkids?"

"Every one of them has a quilt. Gave it to them at their wedding showers. Did I tell you that Calvin's oldest granddaughter is getting married in June? That'll be the first great-grandchild to get married so we'll start one for her after the holidays are over. What do you think? A wedding ring pattern?"

Ada didn't have the heart to tell Essie that she wouldn't be there after the holidays.

"I cried every time I had to leave Momma and Daddy.

Especially after Daddy died and it was just her standing there on the porch waving until I couldn't see her anymore," Essie said. "I'm glad we're together, Ada, in our last years. Being alone ain't no fun at all and getting old alone is a pitiful damn shame. Especially on Christmas. This has been the best season since I lost Richard."

—∿—

Sage had slept little and alternated between bouts of crying and cussing all night. Grand would be home in a few days. After the cold shoulder she'd given Creed the night before for no reason whatsoever, she'd best get to work on it. He damn sure wouldn't want a thing to do with a moody woman who wouldn't talk to him.

"Oh, shit!" She wiped her cheeks and went back to cussing.

It had been a date.

A real, honest-to-god date.

He'd taken her to dinner and to shop and damn, after seeing Victor she'd forgotten to go to the art store. And she'd acted like a bitch on a PMS high. She hadn't kissed him good night; hell, she hadn't even thanked him for the day.

She hugged the pillow but it didn't hug back and it didn't wipe away the fresh batch of tears flowing down her cheeks. She had her mood swings every so often like most women, but what she experienced the previous night was brand new territory. If only she could get a line on why she was so upset, she'd face off with her demons and destroy them.

"I'm twenty-six, not fourteen," she said.

The clock flashed five o'clock when she finally gave

up and slung her legs over the side of the bed. When Sage was angry, she painted. When she was happy, she painted. She'd never tried painting through tears, but maybe if she cleared the multitude of thoughts from her head, she'd figure things out.

She pulled on a pair of sweatpants and jerked a sweatshirt over her head. The nightshirt hung out the bottom, and her dark hair looked like she'd fought with grizzly bears all night. She pulled it up into a ponytail using only her fingers for a brush.

Palette in hand. Paint squeezed onto it.

She picked up the right brush and started filling in the limbs of the tree behind the little dark-haired girl's head. Her soul settled as she worked.

When she had picked up a canvas it was white. That's the way yesterday had started. A clean slate with the promise of something beautiful just around the corner. He'd knocked on her bedroom door and when she opened it, he had been leaning against the jamb. The first thing he did was tell her how beautiful she looked and then he kissed her ever so sweetly on the lips.

"I'm here to collect Miz Sage Presley for a date," he'd said.

It was like sketching in the lines for the picture.

Then they'd had such an amazing day right up until she felt Victor's hand on her shoulder. And that's when her brush slipped and she ruined the whole picture.

She stood back and looked at the canvas in front of her. "But why?"

Then the answers came flowing so fast that she could hardly understand them.

It was painful to let go of the past. Victor reminded her

of abandonment. He'd gotten so angry when she wouldn't commit to living with him and even madder when she told him that she wouldn't be back to college that next fall.

She picked up her brush and the picture began to take shape. Creed would never understand why she'd acted so crazy. She couldn't explain in words to herself. But sometime in the night, she'd faced off with her demons and she was ready to tell Creed that she was madly in love with him.

It was eight o'clock when she looked up from her picture the next time.

Angel hopped out of the baskct and rubbed around her legs. And the puppies started whining.

"Noel, feed your babies," Sage whispered.

But there was no Noel. She wasn't on her blanket and the three puppies were crawling around crying for her.

"Must be in Creed's room," she said.

Even with Angel trying to trip her, the sound of puppies and kittens in the background, and a sparkling Christmas tree, the house felt empty. His door was wide open. The bcd was made so tight that she could have bounced a quarter on it. Yet there was no Creed and no Noel.

"Must be milking," she said. "But it wouldn't take three hours."

She reached around the door and flipped on the light. Angel jumped on the bed and a sheet of paper floated to the floor.

Her name was written on the outside and the next breath caught in her chest like a rock, refusing to move. She picked up the note and carried it to the living room where she melted into a chair. Her heart raced and her breathing returned in short, raspy gasps.

Angel jumped up in her lap and curled up for a nap. Sage made herself open the note and read it, knowing fully well what it would say before she saw the first lines.

Dear Sage,

Your grandmother and I had an agreement. If either of us didn't want to go through with the sale then we had the option of backing out. I'm calling that option and going back to Ringgold.

Chores are done for the morning. You'll only have to milk a few days. Sorry that I've left you with that job.

I love the ranch. It's exactly what I want, but I don't think the whole panhandle of Texas is big enough for both of us. You've got my number. Call me if you want to talk.

Creed

She dropped it. Her shaking hand wasn't blistered but it felt hot. She was on her feet and headed for the front door when she heard the loud thud on the front porch. The noise stopped her in her tracks and then another one hit, shaking the floor under her bare feet.

She jerked the door open and plowed right out onto the porch. Her socks did little to protect her feet from the cold porch, and the cold north wind whistled right through her sweatshirt.

Creed stood at the edge of the porch, looking at the two tiny log cabins. She wanted to shoot him and then hug him, in that exact order. Noel sniffed the larger of the houses and stuck her head in past the leather flap covering the doorway.

"You are leaving?" Sage hugged herself against the wind.

"Looks that way. I was already in the truck and pulling out when I saw the insulation in the back. I don't leave jobs unfinished. I'll drill a couple of holes to snake the electric cord into the house and put the bulbs inside the attics. You can move them out when you get ready."

"I'm not moving them. This was your idea, Creed Riley. You shove them out into the cold."

"You better get back inside. You're going to freeze to death," he said.

"What would you care? You wouldn't even know about it if I did. I could fall and break an arm and not be able to get to a doctor but you wouldn't give a damn. You'd be gone. I was a fool to trust you. I was an idiot to think we might have something. Nobody finds their soul mate in two weeks." Her voice got louder with every word.

She was shocked when he crossed the porch, picked her up, and carried her back inside the house. Her head rested on his chest and through the thick coveralls she could hear his heart thumping every bit as fast as hers. Noel raced inside the house with them and didn't stop until she was curled up around her hungry puppies, but Sage wasn't even aware of the dog.

Creed sat down on the sofa with her and grabbed a fluffy throw to wrap around her feet.

"I don't want to leave," he said.

Those five words were better to Sage than winning the lottery.

"I don't want you to go," she whispered. "I'm sorry

about yesterday. I can't begin to explain, but it all came down on my head at one time."

"Next time trust me enough to talk to me about it. Don't shut me out, Sage. Tell me what's buggin' you and we'll work through it together," he said.

"Is there going to be a next time? You are leaving."

"I think I'll stick around for a while." He grinned. "You don't like to milk cows and you are too softhearted to put the animals outside. And I'd hate to think those two perfectly fine houses will be sitting empty."

"I love you," she said softly.

Creed's kiss was long, hard, and lingering. She tried to melt her body into his and become one with him but that damn throw was in the way. She tugged it out from between them and tossed it on the floor.

She pulled back. "It's crazy. I know it is. We've known each other less than three weeks."

"Soul mates know." His kiss was more demanding, somehow hotter and sweeter at the same time.

"Did you?" she mumbled as his lips left hers and worked their way down to the hollow of her neck.

"I knew before you did."

She pushed him back and stared into his eyes. They had gone all soft and dreamy like she loved. "When did you know?"

He couldn't very well tell her that he'd finally seen the big picture in a jewelry store with his ex-girlfriend. That he'd figured out he was a lucky man because Macy didn't marry him because he had been given the time and opportunity to meet Sage, his true soul mate.

"When doesn't matter, Sage. I love you. I think I always have. I just had to look a long time before I found you."

"So this is it? We are in a relationship?"

"I am. Are you?" he asked.

"God, I can't even think with your hands touching my skin," she said.

"Want me to stop so you can think about it all day?"

"Hell, no! Please don't stop. Wait!"

He pulled his hands free and sat up. "For what?"

"What are we going to do when Grand comes home? We can't sleep together in this house with her in the other room, and I don't ever want to spend another night without you."

"I guess we'll clean out the bunkhouse for us or for Miz Ada," he chuckled.

"It's not funny. I can't imagine telling her good night and her knowing I'm sleeping with you."

"Are you proposing to me, Sage?" Creed asked.

She blushed redder than the shiny bulbs on the Christmas tree. "One baby step at a time, cowboy. I'm damn sure not proposing. I've just got one little toe in the commitment pool."

"Good, because I would have said no." He laced his fingers in hers and stood up, pulling her toward the bedroom.

"Why? Am I just relationship material and not bride material?" She didn't hesitate when he headed toward the bedroom.

"No, ma'am, but when there's a proposal, I'll do it," he told her.

She stopped in her tracks and pointed at the puppies. "Creed! Look!"

He looked down and that damned ugly mutt was smiling. And all three puppies were looking up with their little eyes opened up wide.

"Their eyes are open. Stop! We've got to look at them."

Creed was fully aroused and ready to make love to Sage. Tomorrow morning, he'd make breakfast and they'd share it in bed before they had another round of wonderful sex. Then they'd have dinner and go back to the bedroom. Things really were looking wonderful.

They'd just declared their love for each other. It should be a spectacular day. He wished he had a bottle of champagne to celebrate or even a six-pack of beer. But they had been angry with each other when they went to Walmart and neither of them even thought about buying beer or even a bottle of wine.

She dropped his hand and plopped down on the floor beside Noel.

Creed loved Sage.

He had admitted it to himself.

Rings were stuffed down into his luggage, which was in the truck.

He had told her.

Now she wanted to play with three bluetick hounds?

He chuckled and sat down beside her. "Look, Elvis can see now."

"Just like us," Creed said.

Her eyebrows knit together. "What does that mean?"

"I love you, Sage."

"Oh, I get it." She leaned forward to collect the kiss coming her way. "Symbolic, ain't it? They open their eyes on the day their house is finished and the day that we finally open ours."

Creed wanted to rush out to the truck and bring in the velvet box. He wanted to propose to her right there in the middle of the living room floor with wiggling puppies around them and the lights of the Christmas tree sparkling behind them.

But he couldn't.

Not until the ranch was paid for and his property. He didn't want her to ever think for one single minute that he'd used her precious love that way.

"So are you ready to put these critters outside? It'll only take ten minutes to put the electrical cord through a hole into the house."

She laid Elvis back down beside his mother and took his hand. "That can wait. I want you to take me to bed, Creed."

She reached out a hand and he helped her to her feet. She led the way to the bedroom and shut the door behind them.

Sage unbuttoned his shirt and slid it from his shoulders. She wasn't in a hurry. They had all day to put the icing on their declarations of love. And she didn't care if the *M*-word wasn't mentioned for several months. She already knew how she would answer when it did come into play.

His hands trembled as he pulled her sweatshirt up over her head, taking the nightshirt with it. She rolled up on her toes so that their eyes were level and sunk into the depths of his soul.

"Merry Christmas to me," she singsonged.

"Ditto," he rasped.

She unfastened his belt buckle and zipper and slipped her hand inside. He groaned. "I don't want foreplay. I want to feel you, Creed. Make love to me."

She stepped back and shimmied out of the rest of her clothing and left them lying on the floor. She was already under the covers when he joined her, his lips and body joining hers right along with their hearts and souls.

"I'm so ready and you feel so good," she said.

"So do you, darlin'. Have I told you in the past two minutes that I'm hopelessly in love with you?"

"Don't ever leave me, Creed. Promise that you won't ever leave me."

"Wild horses couldn't drag me away from you."

With that promise he was inside her and the rocking motion of beautiful lovemaking began.

"I love you," she said, and the words came straight from her heart.

Chapter 19

SAGE SET A POINSETTIA ON HER GRANDFATHER'S GRAVE.

"Merry Christmas, Grandpa. Grand is selling the ranch. I'm okay with it now but it took a while for me to come around. She won't be able to stay away very long because this is where your spirit is. I couldn't ever stay away from Creed so I know she'll be back often to visit. She'll be here in a few days and I'm sure she'll be around to tell you all her news."

She went back to the tractor where Creed waited and picked up the next two pots of bright red flowers.

"You okay?" Creed asked.

"Yes, I really am," she said.

She set one plant in front of her father's grave and one in front of her mother's.

"Merry Christmas, Momma and Daddy. Every Christmas I wished I had a momma and daddy like all the other kids. I never told you that, did I? I'm sorry. I should have told you that even though I can barely remember either of you that I did miss you in my life. Grand has been a wonderful parent, but there was a hole in my life and in my heart. Momma, you'll be glad to know that Creed took care of that, and Daddy, don't worry, he's a good man. He'd have to be. Grand picked him out special for me."

"Thank you," Creed whispered as he slipped his arms around her from behind and drew her back to his chest.

The sweet strains of "Silent Night" on the tractor radio drifted across the cemetery and filled the canyon.

"Sleep in heavenly peace," Sage said the words. "Fitting, ain't it?"

"Yes, ma'am, it surely is."

The sun setting over the west bank of the canyon cast the last glorious golden rays of the day down upon the three graves. A day had ended but the ones ahead held the promise of something beautiful and real.

Creed had expected tears but Sage had handled things better than the first time they'd visited the cemetery. Whatever she said before he joined her had brought peace into her heart and it showed in her face.

She hummed along with the Christmas carols playing from the country station on the radio and kept time by tapping her foot. He still couldn't believe that she loved him, a plain old cowboy. And she had said it first. To Creed, that meant the whole world. It wasn't just an answer back to what he had said but it was going out on a limb and saying the words with no idea of how he would respond.

"Chores done… check. Flowers out… check," he said.

"Supper to be cooked… no check. Making love before supper… definitely," she teased.

"Which one first? Kitchen or bedroom?"

"Kitchen," she answered without hesitation.

He cocked his head to one side.

"Has to be that way even if it's one of my gourmet bologna sandwiches. Once we hit the bedroom, we won't be finished until morning."

The deep chuckle turned into laughter. "Honey, I'm not nearly that good."

She ran a hand up his thigh. "Darlin', together we really are that good."

He pulled the tractor through the double doors of the barn and started to turn the engine off but the DJ was talking about tomorrow's weather so he waited.

"And tomorrow the weatherman says we can look for more of the same. Low temperatures. Sunshine. Some icicles. Not much in the way of melting the snow. It's looking more and more like we'll have a white Christmas in the panhandle of Texas, folks."

"Well, that's a big surprise," Sage said. "Hey, I'll wait for you beside the doors and race you to the house. Loser has to cook supper in the nude."

Creed turned the key and everything went silent except for the mooing of the cows out back. He'd turned the milk cow out with the herd that morning so the whole barn was empty.

Sage swiped a kiss across his cheek. "I can already see you without a stitch of clothes on because I'm going to win this race."

"I can't even keep my boots on?" he asked.

"Not even your socks."

"Just remember that when I win. The floor is cold without socks. Want to revise the rules?" he asked.

"Nope, nude as the day you were born," she answered.

"Okay, let's shut the doors then and get to it. I'm lookin' forward to supper now. Have you ever had a cowboy make love to you on the kitchen table?" he asked.

She slid off the seat and shivered. "No, I have not."

"How about the credenza right inside the door?"

"One time. Man that was some hot sex."

"Could be again if you'd move that nativity scene you put up there the next day," he said.

She giggled and helped slide the doors shut.

Creed stretched one long leg out and said, "One for the money. Two for the show. Three to get ready, and four to…"

She leaped and he reached out and grabbed her by the seat of her coveralls. "I didn't say go."

"You don't play fair." She moved away from him at least four feet. "I'm calling it. Three to get ready and four to go!"

Dusk settled on a blur of mustard-colored coveralls and long legs making a dash for the house. She was keeping up with him, step for step. Then he sidestepped twice and tackled her, but instead of bringing her down in the snow, he threw her over his shoulder like a bag of chicken feed and kept running toward the house.

The sizzle of chicken frying filled the whole kitchen.

Essie cut out biscuits and put them into a big round cast iron skillet. Ada slid them into the oven and checked the potatoes. They would be ready to mash at the same time the biscuits finished cooking. Green beans with bacon simmered on the back of the stove and a loaf of freshly baked pumpkin bread cooled on the cabinet.

"I'll set the table while you fix up a fruit salad," Essie said.

Ada nodded.

The day before, she had made up her mind. She was

giving Creed back his escrow money and backing out of the deal. She'd hire him to stay on at the ranch and even clean out the bunkhouse for him, but she couldn't leave the canyon. Now she wasn't so sure that was the right decision.

She looked at the Christmas tree and then at Essie. Surely to God, something would give her a sign. Anything to point her in the right direction. She liked living in Pennsylvania and she would love it when summer came and it wasn't hot as hell. She loved bantering with Essie and remembering the old times. But she missed Sage.

"Can't have your cake and eat it too," Essie said.

"You talkin' to me?"

"I am. I know it's been botherin' you these past few days and I kept my mouth shut. I don't want you to ever regret leaving, Ada. You know where I stand, but time is getting pretty damn short. You've got to make up your mind and not look back."

Ada swallowed twice, but the lump in her throat refused to budge.

I've relied on my Indian sense all these years. Don't fail me now. Give me a sign. All I want is one little sign to show me how to make this decision. A star floating over the fried chicken with a long banner trailing behind it would be nice. Or writing on the wall. I don't even care if it's in orange Crayola.

The back door flew open with such force that Essie grabbed her heart.

Sage's butt popped up in the air above Creed's shoulder. Her words came out one at a time between giggles and gasps. "You cheated. Now I don't get to see you make supper in the…"

He quickly swung her around and her face popped up. She gulped twice and said, "In the kitchen."

Ada Presley had her sign.

―⁓―

"Grand, you are early! And you talked Aunt Essie into coming with you!" Sage hurried across the room and grabbed them both in a three-way hug.

"Surprise," Essie said. "But I don't know who got the real surprise. Girl, y'all about scared the bejesus right out of me. You're supposed to come in gentle-like, not like a tornado blowin' the door down."

"When did you get here? Or better yet, how did you get here?" Sage asked.

"We flew into Amarillo and got a taxi to bring us home," Ada said.

"We would have come and got you, Miz Ada," Creed said.

"Hello, Creed, I'm Essie, Ada's sister. She's told me all about you. We didn't mean to be rude and not include you in this homecoming surprise."

Creed stuck out his hand, but Essie bypassed it and hugged him.

"Aunt Essie, you said y'all instead of you'ens." Sage laughed.

"You scared seventy years off of me and I reverted back to my Okie days," she said. "Now go get washed up. Supper will be ready in ten minutes."

"Grand, a taxi must've cost a fortune. Why on earth didn't you call us?" Sage asked.

"Wanted to surprise you, and besides, money ain't nothing but dirty paper with dead presidents on it. The look on your face when Creed hauled you in here like a sack of feed was worth every dime. Do I want to know why you got carried in that way?" Ada asked.

"We were racing. Loser had to cook supper," Creed answered. "It looked like I was going to lose so I evened the odds. That is one long-legged granddaughter you got, Miz Ada."

"From the smell of this kitchen, I'd say we both won, and neither of us has to cook," Sage said.

"We been here an hour and thought we'd go on with the supper. Place looks nice all decorated up," Ada said. "You didn't even forget the nativity on the credenza."

Heat popped out on Sage's face and neck like a red-hot sunburn. "No, ma'am, I did not."

"I like it better there than on the mantel. Creed, did she tell you the story of that credenza?" Ada asked and went on before he could answer. "It belonged to my mother's grandmother. Started out as one of those old washstands that folks put in their bedrooms. There was a bow on the back with a rod across the two ends to hang a towel on. And the washbowl and pitcher set on the top. The doors underneath opened up for a chamber pot."

"Grand!"

"Well, they did. Momma said that when she inherited it she set it on the screened-in porch and opened the doors for a whole summer just to air it out. She gave it to me for a wedding present and it has set right there ever since Tom brought me down into this canyon. He laughed when he brought it in and said we was uptown now because we had a credenza."

"Well, it's a nice piece of furniture. Good and sturdy," Creed said.

Essie gave Sage a push toward the living room. "Stop talkin' about old furniture and go wash up. We can talk over supper."

Creed held it in until they reached the bathroom and then he chuckled.

She unzipped her coveralls and let them fall down to her waist, pushed up the sleeves of her knit shirt, and turned on the water. "Lord, if you hadn't turned me around when you did I'd have embarrassed the tee-total hell out of us both."

"Credenza?"

She looked in the mirror at his reflection and grinned. "I know. She's psychic, I swear she is. Why else would she bring up the credenza?"

"You going to tell her?" Creed asked.

Sage shivered. "Hell, no! Not even on her deathbed."

Creed unzipped his coveralls and let them fall to his waist, pushed up his sleeves, and stuck his hands under the faucet with Sage's. Would there ever come a time when his touch, even with her grandmother so close by, didn't give her naughty thoughts?

She wrapped her soapy hands around his fingers and washed his hands for him. "Oh, I'd slippy and I'd slidey over Creed's little heinie. Oh, I wish I was a little bar of soap."

"Shhh." Creed caught her fingers. "You want to get me in trouble? And besides, that's not the way the song goes."

"That's the way it went in my head right then. And besides, I don't get to see you cook supper in the nude," she whispered.

He burst out laughing.

"It wasn't that funny," she said.

"Not that. It just dawned on me. The credenza."

She blushed. "What about it?"

He stopped laughing and kissed her on the cheek. "We had sex on top of the outhouse. Bet you never thought you'd say that, did you?"

Sage's eyes popped so wide open that they hurt. "We did, didn't we? Oh my God!"

They finished washing up and Creed stood to one side so Sage could go ahead of him. She made it to the middle of the living room floor when she stopped so suddenly that he plowed right into her back. She started to fall forward but he grabbed her from behind and held on until she got her balance.

"Where's Angel and Noel?" she whispered.

Ada poked her head across the bar and said, "They'll be outside in those fancy log cabins. I plugged in their lightbulbs and you should have seen those two animals. They carried on together in the snow like a couple of kids. You'd have never believed that they were supposed to hate each other."

"Cats don't like me and I ain't none too fond of them either," Essie yelled. "I'm mashing these potatoes and then we're eating."

"It's okay," Creed whispered. "They helped us out. Neither one of us could have carried the puppies or the kittens outside. We'll go check on them after supper."

"That is one ugly dog," Ada said. "I would have bought you something a little prettier than that. Them bluetick pups of hers is even better looking than she is."

Sage patted Creed's hands, which were still firmly

around her waist, and took a step forward. "She grows on you. In a week, you won't think she's ugly because she is so sweet."

It wasn't that the sofa was uncomfortable. There had been times when Creed had slept on the hard ground with nothing but his saddle for a pillow.

It wasn't that he was hungry. After that supper, he probably didn't need to eat until Christmas dinner.

The tossing and turning was because he missed Sage. He missed the feel of her back pressed against his chest, his hand wrapped around her ribs, and her hair tickling his nose. He missed the sweet smell of soap on her skin and her cold toes warming against his feet.

And there was that other thing.

Ada hadn't brought up the sale or what she'd decided in her almost three weeks, but the time had come. Creed wanted the Rockin' C and he wanted Sage right along with it. He didn't know what he'd do if Ada had changed her mind and didn't want to sell. He couldn't ask Sage to leave her home, but his heart would shrivel up and die without her.

He pulled the quilt up over his shoulders and shut his eyes tightly. It didn't work but it did provide a blank screen for him to imagine all kinds of pictures of Sage. There she was in the kitchen that first morning looking like she could chew up nails and spit out staples. And in the mall with the same expression on her face the day they went on their only date.

His eyelids flew up so fast that he couldn't focus for several seconds.

He couldn't ask Sage to marry him. They'd only been on one date.

Don't be stupid. What was that little ride through the pasture the day that Noel had the puppies? What was that trek through the snow to show her the icicle on the mistletoe?

The quilt fell on the floor when he sat up and stared at the fireplace. He was so deep in the inner argument with himself that he didn't hear Sage padding across the floor. He felt a movement and there she was, pulling his arm around her and the quilt over both of them.

"I can't sleep. Hold me," she mumbled.

He kissed her on the forehead and rested his chin on the top of her head. "Me neither."

———※———

Essie awoke the next morning long before dawn and tip-toed to the kitchen to make a pot of coffee. She stopped in front of the Christmas tree, turned around, and went right back to the bedroom she and Ada were sharing. She pulled the cover off Ada and slapped her on the shoulder.

"I'm awake," Ada said.

"Then quit wastin' daylight."

"I'm not. Can't waste what ain't here."

"Yes, you are. You can get the chores done and use the daylight to do what you can't do in the dark."

Ada sat up and yawned. "What put a burr in your butt this morning?"

"Put on your housecoat and come with me."

Ada slung her legs over the edge of the bed and Essie handed her a faded blue chenille robe.

"Shhhh!" Essie motioned for her to follow.

They stopped in the middle of the living room floor and stared mesmerized at Sage and Creed. One quilt covered both of them. Her head rested on his shoulder. His chin rested on her head.

"Ada, they couldn't sleep without each other. You've got to loosen up and tell them they can sleep in the same bed."

"The hell I can. This is still my house and if she wants to sleep with him in a bed under my roof, she can marry him."

Chapter 20

SAGE SAT ACROSS FROM HER GRANDMOTHER AT THE kitchen table. Essie had claimed a rocking chair in front of the blazing fireplace and was crocheting something pink. Creed had suited up and left to do the chores.

It was time for the argument that Sage had looked forward to and planned for the past three weeks. And she was speechless.

"Well?" Ada asked.

"You first," Sage answered.

"I was right."

Sage shrugged.

Dammit, anyway! It wasn't easy admitting defeat before she'd even spit on her knuckles and drawn a line in the snow.

"I liked that cowboy from the start and you've fallen in love with him," Ada said.

"You were right, and yes, I have."

"Then why the long face this morning?"

Sage stretched her hands across the table and laid them on Ada's. "Grand, I don't want you to leave the Rockin' C. I can live with the sale now. Got to admit when I dropped down into the canyon on those slick roads all I wanted to do was bust in here and have a big fight with you, but you were right about Creed."

"You can't have your cake and eat it too," Essie said from the living room.

"She's been spoutin' off that brand of bullshit for days," Ada whispered.

"I can hear you," Essie singsonged.

"She's probably right but it pains the hell out of me to admit it," Ada said.

Sage gently squeezed her hands. "Why? You and Aunt Essie can live here. The ranch is plenty big and I can take care of you when you get old."

"When? Honey, we done passed the time of if and when. We *are* old," Essie said.

———— ✦ ————

Creed fed the cattle and worried.

He scattered chicken scratch in the henhouse and worried.

He opened the chute and poured a mixture of sour milk and cornmeal into the hog's trough and worried some more.

Sage was in the kitchen with Ada and it didn't take the intelligence of a rocket scientist to know what they were discussing. His whole future, hell, his whole heart was laid out on that old kitchen table between them.

His boots felt like they'd been filled with concrete as he trudged back to the barn. The brown and white milk cow waited for him as if she understood that he didn't need any further distractions that morning. He led the way to the milk stall and she followed obediently.

"I'll hire some help so Sage can have more time for her painting. Lord only knows I don't want her to give that up." He pulled up a three-legged milking stool and sat down.

The first milk made pinging noises as it hit the

bucket, and whirls of steam arose until the bottom was covered. "Besides, I love to watch her paint. It's soothing to a cowboy's soul. Rye mentioned one of his cousins was looking for work. I met several of his family at his and Austin's wedding reception. I can't put names with faces, but if he's an O'Donnell, you can bet that he knows ranchin' and horses."

The cow mooed.

"Sounds like a good idea, does it? I can clean up the bunkhouse and start with one hired hand this year and if the calf crop and the hay makes good, I can maybe hire a second one next year."

By the time the bucket was full, he'd envisioned more than one year into the future and every one of them involved Sage and the rings still hidden in his coat pocket.

"Well, shit! If Ada gets to snooping around in the closet, she's liable to find the rings. That would be a disaster."

He let the cow back out with the other cattle and carried the milk back to the house, dreading what lay ahead.

His eyes swept the kitchen first looking for Sage, but she wasn't there. He peeked around the bar but she wasn't working on the newest painting. Essie was doing something with pink yarn in front of the fireplace. Ada had just pulled a pan of spicy-smelling cookies from the oven.

She tossed oven mitts on the cabinet, poured two cups of coffee, and motioned for him to sit down. "I'll strain the milk while you get out of those coveralls and we'll talk."

He unzipped his coveralls. "Where is Sage?"

"She's out on the porch playing with her pets. I got to hand it to you, Creed Riley. I knew you was the cowboy

I'd been waiting for when you knocked on my door. I could feel it in my bones but I never figured that you'd talk her into animals. That's a pretty nice momma cat; kinda pretty with all that long fur and I can see Sage falling in love with her. But that ugly dog? God Almighty, that took a pure miracle."

Creed didn't want to talk about animals. He wanted to talk about the sale of the Rockin' C. "Yes, ma'am, but Noel wormed her way into Sage's heart real quick."

He kicked his boots off and joined Ada at the table. A plate of fresh cookies sat between them and the coffee was still steaming.

Ada pushed the cookies his way. "Help yourself."

He bit into the soft gingerbread and nodded. "Very good."

"Christmas tradition around here. I like that y'all put the tree up and the lights around the barn and that you made sugar cookies and gingerbread. I had to make fresh for today though because this is an important day."

It took two long gulps of hot coffee to swallow the gingerbread. "Yes, it is."

"I'm going to sell you this ranch, Creed. I'm not backing out of the agreement. Are you?"

He shook his head. Had he heard her right? Would Sage be able to really live with the decision?

"Good."

"Well, damn!" Essie said. "Now she'll lord it over me that her damned old Indian sense is real."

"Oh, hush. You want me to sell the ranch and you know it. Put that yarn down and tell Sage to come in here. We need to talk amongst the four of us because there are some conditions."

Essie obeyed but she muttered something about her sister being too bossy.

Creed smiled at Sage when she came back into the house. Her nose was scarlet and her knit cap was set off to one side. No doubt Noel had been extra friendly.

She smiled back and winked.

The stone in his heart dissolved completely. She was okay with the sale and their relationship was fine.

"Okay, Sage, get out of that coat and pour some coffee for you and Essie. We're going to lay out the terms of this sale amongst us."

Sage stopped long enough to brush a kiss across Creed's cheek. "Good morning."

He grabbed her hand and pulled her down onto his lap where he kissed her properly. "Good morning, darlin'. Your grandmother has not backed out of the sale."

"I know. I chose eating my cake."

A puzzled expression crossed his face.

Essie laughed out loud. "So did Ada, thank God."

"I'm sure it'll all make sense someday," Creed said.

He would have preferred that Sage sit in his lap through the whole discussion of the terms but she stood up. Once her coat was removed she took her place and reached under the table to squeeze his thigh.

"Okay," Ada began. "I'll go first. Essie and I had a long talk last night after we went to bed. When I left the canyon I was positively sure about this sale but then the doubts came creepin' in on me. So we made arrangements to come a few days early so that I could tell Creed I'd changed my mind and wasn't going to sell out. Seemed only right to give him time to go home to his family for the holidays and I wanted to be with you, Sage."

"She was an old bear," Essie said. "Wanted her cake and wanted to eat it too, just like Sage did."

Ada shot her sister a dirty look and went on. "Essie and I want to be together in our old age. She wants to be in Shade Gap because that's her home. I want to be here because this is my home. We couldn't have it both ways until we got to studying the matter. This is what we've come up with and if you are in agreement, we'll call the lawyer and have him meet us at the courthouse in Claude this afternoon."

"Why the hurry?" Sage asked.

"Courthouse will be closed on Monday. Tuesday is Christmas, and besides, Essie and I are going back to Shade Gap on Sunday evening. Had to get a red-eye home because all the planes are booked full during the holidays."

"But Grand, if you were going to back out of the sale, why did Essie come with you? She would have had to fly home all by herself," Sage asked.

Essie put up a palm. "That was my idea. If I let her out of my sight for a minute she makes the wrong decisions. I had to come along to keep her in remembrance of the fact that I need her to help me."

"Bullshit! Woman who can climb on the roof don't need nobody to help her," Sage said.

"Okay, you caught me. I don't need her but she needs me," Essie giggled.

"That's a load of bullshit for sure," Ada raised her voice.

"Oh, hush the bitching and tell them the plan," Essie said.

"Okay, I'm selling you the ranch for the price we agreed upon. But I want to buy this house back from you for the same amount. Not the land it sits on, just the house."

Creed's brows knit together. "Explain please."

"You are going to give me the rest of the money for the ranch. I'm going to tear up the check because I'm buying my house back from you. Understand that much?"

"But why?"

"Essie and I are going to spend our winters here and our summers at her place. We've even written it down on the calendar. We'll go to Shade Gap after Easter and we'll come back here after Halloween each year. All but this first year which we plan to spend in Shade Gap. We will come back to Texas for Easter this year and for July Fourth," Ada said.

"But I'm staying under the air conditioner and knitting. I'm not going outside in that sweltering heat," Essie declared.

"Then we'll come for the winter after Halloween. By then I expect you two to have your own house built with the money I'm paying you for this house. There's over a thousand acres here so you've got lots of choices to make about where you want to build and what size house you want, but I don't want to give up my house."

Creed nodded. "But you can have this house and we'll build one, Miz Ada. You don't have to pay for it."

"See, Sage, I told you he was a good man." Ada grinned.

"Stipulation number two coming up," Essie said.

Ada looked from Sage to Creed. "You've got to hire some help. Sage can't leave her career in the dust to be a rancher's wife. She'll resent it in her old age."

"Agreed," Creed said without hesitation.

Sage blushed. "No one said anything about a marriage."

"Any more conditions to the sale?" Creed asked.

"That's it," Ada said.

"Then I think the terms are more than generous and I want to add my stipulations to the deal," Creed said in his slow Texas drawl.

All eyes were on him.

"When I drove up in the front yard three weeks ago, I knew I'd found home. Don't know if your Indian sense had found its way to me by osmosis or what, but I was at peace for the first time in years. All I wanted for Christmas was a ranch of my own. I didn't have any idea what all went with the ranch." He grinned and leaned over to kiss Sage on the cheek.

"Here's my only condition, Miz Ada. When you two are too old to make the trips back and forth, I want your promise that you will settle here on the Rockin' C with us and let us take care of you."

Ada looked at Essie, who nodded.

Tears flowed down Sage's cheeks.

"See, I told you he was the very cowboy to take over the Rockin' C." Ada's voice cracked.

Essie leaned over and whispered in Ada's ear. Her younger sister shook her head emphatically and said, "Hell no, it's my house!"

"Where are y'all going?" Sage asked when Ada and Essie headed around the house toward the barn.

"Out to the cemetery. I want to visit with Tom and see your folks while I'm here. I won't be back until Easter. You did get flowers put out, didn't you?" Ada asked.

"Yes, ma'am. Poinsettias. The biggest pots that Walmart had to sell."

"I'll take you, Ada," Creed said.

"No, you won't. There's only room on the tractor for two people and Essie wants to go with me. Three weeks didn't knock out my ability to drive that tractor, son. You go on in the house and get to thinkin' about what kind of house you want and where you are going to put it. I don't intend to share mine when I come back at Easter."

He nodded. "Yes, ma'am."

He waited by the kitchen window, standing under the mistletoe still hanging on the curtain, for the sound of the tractor's engine starting up. Sage slipped her arms around his waist and together they watched Ada back it out of the barn and head down the plowed path to the cemetery.

"I love you," Sage said.

"Wait right here. Don't move."

"You're supposed to say that you love me," she said.

"I do but… no, stand right here." He walked her backwards until she was standing in the exact same spot where she'd been when he first saw her. She had been wearing sweats that day. Today she wore jeans and a bright red sweater with a Christmas tree knitted into the front. Christmas bulb earrings dangled from her ears and her hair was loose around her shoulders like Creed liked.

"What are you doing? Taking a picture to remember this day by?" she asked.

"Something like that."

It felt strange opening the door into the bedroom where Ada and Essie had taken up residence. It wasn't his even though that was his television on the chest of drawers and his things in the closet. He dug into the pocket of his coat and found the right ring box and carried it to the kitchen.

"I didn't move. Where's the camera?" she asked.

He kissed her hard and passionately.

She threw both arms around his neck and hugged him tightly. "You got it backwards, darlin'. You don't go to the bedroom before you kiss me like that. We go afterwards and have a wild hour of sex before they get back."

He removed her arms and stepped backwards, dropped down on one knee, and looked up at her. "I never figured on falling in love, didn't even know what real love was until I fell for you. You breathe life into this ranch, but more importantly, you give life to me. Sage Presley, will you marry me?"

The ring box popped open and she squealed, "Yes!" without a split second's hesitation.

Chapter 21

"ALL WEEK I'VE STRUGGLED WITH A SERMON. FIRST I thought I'd preach on the birth of Christ, but we covered that in last week's Hanging of the Green. Then I thought I'd preach on the chapter about love in Corinthians, which we're all familiar with, but nothing came to me. And then I got a call on Saturday morning from Ada Presley and everything was clear as a church bell ringing out across the canyon on Sunday morning. This afternoon, instead of a church service we are having a wedding. There is no better way to celebrate Christmas than new beginnings," the preacher said from the pulpit.

<hr />

Sage bent her knees so she could see her reflection in the mirror above the vanity in the bathroom of the church. She'd dressed at Canyon Rose, where she spent the night before with April. Grand had declared that they'd follow tradition even if they didn't have time to plan a big wedding. The groom wasn't to see the bride on the day of the wedding and nothing was going to change her mind.

The woman looking back at Sage looked happy, but was it for real? Was she really, really getting married just three weeks after meeting Creed?

He'd proposed and she'd said yes without even thinking about things. Then Grand and Aunt Essie came home from the cemetery and everything went into high gear.

"When is the wedding?" Grand had asked.

"We thought we'd go over to the courthouse this afternoon or maybe sometime next week," Sage had answered.

But that wouldn't do. No, sir! If they were getting married that quickly then they could do it on Sunday before Grand and Essie flew out. Sage had argued that it couldn't be arranged in that length of time.

"What are you thinking about?" April asked.

"How tiny this bathroom is."

"You don't lie too good, Sage. You're worried that you are going too fast and that you'll have regrets later. If you wanted a big wedding with all the trimmings you should have put your foot down," April said.

"I didn't even want this much. I wanted to go to the courthouse."

"Not me. I want the whole ten yards. That's even more than the nine yards thing. I'm having the big white dress with a train that reaches from the top of the stairs all the way to the bottom and a reception out on the ranch lawn after the wedding in the ballroom."

"I just wanted to dash into the courthouse and come out married, but Grand wanted something else and I let her have her way." Sage straightened up.

"Well God bless Grand! I'd rather be a bridesmaid and flirt with Creed's handsome brothers than yawn through a sermon today."

Sage looked at the clock above the vanity. "Five minutes."

"Nervous?" April asked.

"You'll never know."

～ᵥᵥ～

The preacher nodded at his wife who played the piano that morning and her fingers went to the keys. Creed and his brother marched down the center aisle and took their places at the front of the church.

Creed could hardly believe that a wedding could be arranged in forty-eight hours, but then he'd never known anyone like Ada, Essie, and Hilda. Ada had sent him and Sage to the courthouse on Friday afternoon to purchase a marriage license. And she'd given them strict orders that if they came home already married she'd never come back to the canyon to visit them again.

On the way back home, he'd called his brother Ace and asked him if he could drop everything and be his best man for the wedding. Evidently the ball got to rolling pretty fast in Ringgold too, because more than half of one side of the church was filled with his family and friends. They had arrived late the previous evening, checked into a hotel in Amarillo, and then come straight to the Rockin' C.

Women gathered around Sage, and surprisingly enough, she didn't let his mother or any of them intimidate her. And the ranchers wanted a tour of his new ranch. Now they were all in their Sunday best, supporting him on his wedding day.

—◦—

"I hear the music," April said.

"What do they really think of me? Do they think I married him so I could keep the ranch?" she whispered.

"Honey, a blind man could see how much Creed loves you. And his sisters-in-law and mother were very nice."

Ada pushed inside the tiny bathroom. "Your momma would have loved this day and she would have really liked the idea that you are wearing her wedding dress."

"See you at the front." April slipped out the door before Ada asked her any questions.

"It doesn't look too old hippie does it?" Sage laughed.

"It was beautiful on her and it's even more beautiful on you. I don't think she would have even minded that you cut it off. There's our cue and I hear people standing up. It's our turn." Ada grabbed her granddaughter's hand and together they stepped out of the bathroom.

Sage's dress had been white when her mother had worn it but it hadn't been stored in one of those non-yellowing containers so the satin was a rich ecru color. However, the illusion covering the satin and billowing out from the skirt that ended right above her knee was still snowy white. The scoop-neck bodice was covered in white beads and sequins that had also escaped the aging process. Long fitted sleeves ended in points and had one dozen buttons each on the underside of her hand. The dress had fit her just fine but her mother had been six inches shorter than Sage so the hemline had stopped at midcalf. Hilda had spent Saturday afternoon cutting it off and hemming it for her.

They hadn't had time to think about flowers or bouquets but somehow Grand and Essie had made a trip to Claude and picked up two potted plants at the grocery store. A bouquet of poinsettias tied up with red satin ribbons lay on Sage's left arm and April had carried a nosegay of tiny rosebuds. Both had been arranged by Creed's mother, Dolly, in between supervising baking a wedding cake in Hilda's kitchen.

She had bought a brand new pair of white cowboy boots for her gallery showing in Denver, so she opted to wear them. Grand had wanted her to wear the veil that went with the dress but she'd drawn the line there. She had styled her dark hair high on her head and fastened a sprig of the mistletoe from the kitchen window into one side. Another piece had gone into making the boutonnieres that Creed and Ace had pinned to their black Western-cut jackets.

"Grand, I'm nervous," she whispered when they were going down the aisle.

"Don't be. Just look at Creed and forget all these people."

Sage looked down the aisle and caught Creed's gaze. And nothing else mattered. She was getting married. She was going to have a family and live on the Rockin' C until she and Creed were both too old to play games on that credenza.

He smiled as if he could read her thoughts and she blushed.

———

Creed pinched his leg and it hurt like hell, so he wasn't dreaming. That really was Sage coming toward him and she wasn't wearing his red and black plaid flannel shirt like she'd threatened.

Just looking at her floating down the aisle in that beautiful dress made his mouth so dry that he wasn't sure he'd be able to utter his vows. He wanted her to have a wedding to talk about with the other sisters-in-law, but he wished they had just gotten married at the courthouse. Right now they could be naked as newborns under a quilt in their bedroom or better yet, playing games on the credenza.

And that's when she looked up at him. He smiled because there was no doubt from the pink in her cheeks that she was thinking the same thing.

———

"Who gives this woman to be married to this man?" the preacher asked when Sage and Ada reached the front of church.

"I give Sage into Creed's hands." Ada lifted her granddaughter's hand and gave it to Creed. "Love her. Respect her. Or you'll deal with me," she whispered.

"Yes, ma'am," he said seriously.

"You may be seated," the preacher told the congregation.

"You are so beautiful," Creed whispered. "I'm glad you decided not to wear my flannel shirt."

"Honey, that is reserved for the honeymoon, right along with that lovely quilt Grand and Aunt Essie made," she whispered back.

"Dearly beloved, we are gathered here today to witness the union of Creed Davis Riley and Elizabeth Sage Presley," the preacher began the traditional ceremony.

In one sense the ceremony lasted an hour and in another it was over in less than a minute. Time stood still for Sage. She heard the words but what she felt was the true uniting of her heart and Creed's. Two soul mates that had been floundering around for years were bonding and no one else even felt it.

She exchanged vows, put a ring on Creed's finger, and he put one on hers and then the preacher pronounced them man and wife. It was time for their first kiss as husband and wife. When his lips touched hers they promised her the moon, the stars, and everything in between.

"And now I present to you Mr. and Mrs. Creed Riley. They, along with their families and friends, invite all of you to a reception at the Canyon Rose. I hear Hilda made the cake and also the buffalo wings, so me and my wife will be the first in line."

April insisted on a first dance, so Creed two-stepped his new bride around the floor to an old George Strait song, "I Cross My Heart." Creed sang softly with the words, telling Sage that his love was unconditional. He promised to give all that he had to give to make all her dreams come true.

"I do, Sage Presley Riley." He stopped singing and looked at her.

"And I do, Creed Riley. I promise to give all I have to give to make your dreams come true too."

"I don't want you to ever stop painting," he said. "Come spring, I'm planning to hire one full-time cowboy and when summer comes, maybe a part-time teenager to help us on the ranch. You'll always have time to paint."

"I couldn't stop painting if I wanted to, Creed. It's part of me."

"And I love every single thing that makes you who you are. I wouldn't change a single thing about you, darlin'."

Before the song ended, Creed's dad tapped him on the shoulder and took his place with Sage and Creed's mother slipped into her son's arms.

"Welcome to the Riley clan, Sage," Adam said. "I'm glad to see the light back in Creed's eyes and we all thank you for putting it there. We hate to see him live this far from the rest of us but we're so happy for you both."

"You're invited to visit us anytime. The door is always open. We'll be starting a new home soon and we're making it big enough for lots of company."

"We'll take you up on that," Adam said.

The song ended and Lawton tapped a knife against the side of a glass and welcomed everyone to Canyon Rose. "I'm kind of sorry to see Ada sell the Rockin'. C to this feller. I wanted to hire him as my new foreman but I'm glad to have him for a neighbor. Raise your drink in a toast to our new couple in the Palo Duro Canyon."

"My turn." Ace stepped up beside Lawton.

He sure didn't look like he belonged in the Riley family. All of Creed's other brothers had dark hair and shades of brown eyes, but Ace had blond hair and the prettiest blue eyes. Creed said he got it from Grandpa Riley. Sage thought it would be wonderful if her bit of Irish and Creed's produced a little blond-haired boy with blue eyes.

"Welcome to our family, Sage. We're glad to have you. I could tell you stories about my brother that would make you tear up that marriage license, but I'll wait until you are married a year."

Everyone laughed and had another sip of their drink.

Creed slipped his arm around his wife's waist. "Darlin', don't pay no attention to him. He won't tell a single thing because I know too much on him."

"Oh?" Jasmine, Ace's wife, asked. "Maybe you should be talking to me."

"Not a chance." Creed laughed.

"Hilda says we're cutting the cake now," Lawton said.

She pushed a three-tiered cake on a wooden cart from the kitchen. Mistletoe with streaming red ribbons rested on the top and around the base. "Y'all didn't give me time to go rustle up a bride and groom for the top."

Creed laid his hand on top of Sage's as she cut the first piece of cake. "I like the mistletoe better anyway."

"Fits us, doesn't it?"

Later that night, Creed carried Sage over the threshold and stopped right inside the door.

Both of them noticed the credenza at the same time.

An envelope the size of a greeting card was propped up in front of the nativity scene.

He set her down and she tore into the envelope. "It's from Grand. She's says this piece of furniture is our wedding present from her and that when she comes back, it's the only piece of furniture that had better be missing from this house."

Creed chuckled and picked her up, carried her to her bedroom, and set her on the bed. "I love you, Mrs. Riley."

"I love you. Kiss me again and let's start a honeymoon that will last the rest of our lives." She unpinned the mistletoe boutonniere from his lapel and laid it on the nightstand.

"Yes, ma'am," he drawled.

Dear Readers,

Welcome to the Palo Duro Canyon. Creed Riley has found the ranch of his dreams in the big crater out in the Texas Panhandle and just in time for Christmas. There are a couple of little stipulations in the deal. He has to live on the ranch for three weeks before he and the owner sign the legal forms and he has to agree to let her granddaughter live on the ranch as long as she wants.

No problem!

And then the snowstorm blows in, shuts down the electricity, and roads are closed into and out of the canyon. He and the granddaughter are stuck in a small house together with an ugly stray mutt and a momma cat. He's determined that he is buying the ranch; she's determined to change her grandmother's mind about selling and his about buying.

Husband and I discovered the Palo Duro Canyon when we were out on a research trip south of that area. A little town called Post, Texas, was the place I had in mind to set this book, but something about it wasn't the "right" place for *Mistletoe Cowboy*. So we drove on, and on, and on, until we reached Silverton. I almost had a "feeling" about that place, but when we drove north toward Claude (mentioned in *Darn Good Cowboy Christmas*) and found the canyon, I knew I'd found the setting for *Mistletoe Cowboy*.

Husband and I made several trips to the canyon before this book was actually finished. It is an amazing place with its rock formations rising up like castles or huge chimneys to heights so tall that the eagles nesting at the tops look like tiny toys. It's a desolate, lonely land dotted with mesquite and scrub oak and cows, but there was something about it that said love and romance could be found there with the right characters at the right time.

Mistletoe Cowboy is the fifth book in the Spikes & Spurs series. If you are enjoying the series, keep your boots on—there is more on the way. Gemma O'Donnell finally gets her story told in *Just a Cowboy and His Baby* in December, and sometime in 2013, Dewar O'Donnell will finish up the Spikes and Spurs series with his story.

Special thanks, as always, goes to the awesome Sourcebooks staff for their dedication and work on this book. To all those behind-the-scenes folks whose names I don't even know—thank you. A really big thanks to my amazing editor, Deb Werksman, for all she does.

To all of you who continue to read my books, tell your neighbors and friends about them, review them in your book clubs, and pass your used copies on to your best friend, please know that you are appreciated.

Happy Reading!
Carolyn Brown

Read on for an excerpt from

JUST A COWBOY AND HIS BABY

Coming December 2012 from Sourcebooks Casablanca

EVIL SHOT FROM HIS DARK EYES. THE AIR AROUND HIM crackled when he raised his head and glared at her. He'd been bred, born, and raised for that night and she didn't have a chance against his wiles. He was bigger than she was and he knew it. He was meaner and he'd prove it.

Gemma O'Donnell didn't give a damn how big or how mean he was. She intended to be in control from the minute she mounted him. The message from the set of his head and unwavering stare said that she was an idiot not to shake in her cowgirl boots. She glared right back, her dark green eyes meeting his near black ones and locking through the metal bars separating them.

He dared.

She challenged.

She hiked a leg up to the first rung on the chute, and two hands circled her waist from behind to help her. Her heart slipped in an extra beat at the cowboy's big hands touching her, but she attributed it to nerves. She glanced over her shoulder into the sexiest brown eyes she'd ever seen, all dreamy and soft with heavy dark lashes.

"Thanks," she said.

"My pleasure. Go get 'em, darlin'." His voice went with the rest of the package: a deep Texas drawl that sounded like it should have been singing country songs in Nashville, not riding wild broncs on the PRCA Million Dollar Rodeo Tour.

Dammit, Trace Coleman. You pulled a slick one, but it's not going to work. You are not going to throw me off my game, she thought as she slung a leg over the top and locked eyes with the wild creature again. She had a horse to ride and even though his coat was as white as the driven snow, the look in his black eyes said that he could run Lucifer some serious competition when it came to meanness.

His name was Smokin' Joe and he was a rodeo legend. Cowboys said that he could see right into the soul of a rider and could feel the fear he'd struck in their hearts. Well, Gemma wasn't afraid of Smokin'-damn-Joe. He wasn't a bit meaner than the bronc out on Rye's ranch that she'd trained on, and she'd shown him who was boss. Smokin' Joe was just the next bronc in a long line, so he could take his evil glare and suck it up. Tonight she was the boss. She didn't care if the other riders had made bets about how quickly into the ride he'd throw her off into the dust. She'd show them all, cowboys and bronc alike, that a *cowgirl* had come to town.

She had two options.

Number one: Stay on his back for eight seconds and show him she was the boss.

Number two: Wreck.

There was no in between, and "almost" did not count. Gemma didn't allow herself to think the word *wreck*, not even when the almighty Trace Coleman produced a smile that would part the clouds. He was well over six feet tall, dark haired, and light brown eyes. She'd done her homework on all the cowboys. She knew most of them personally from the rodeo rounds, but she'd only known Trace by picture and reputation. Both of which

intrigued her to no end. When she'd seen him in action
in San Antonio, the heat level of the whole great state
of Texas jacked up twenty more degrees. His swagger,
his broad chest, and his body had said that Gemma was
in deep trouble. But it was that deep sexy Texas drawl
that brought on images of tangled sheets, lots and lots
of heat, and a warm oozy feeling called an afterglow
flitting through her mind.

Trace might have just meant to be charming and help-
ful, holding his hand out to assist her in climbing the
chute, but Gemma wasn't buying his brand of bullshit.
He wasn't stupid, and the twinkle in his eye said he
knew exactly how his touch affected a woman. Besides,
his gaggle of rodeo groupies were proof positive of that.
In San Antonio, Austin, Redding, and Reno, Gemma
had seen them circling him like a chocolate addict set
loose with free rein in a candy store. Oh, yes, without a
single doubt Trace knew how to turn a woman's mind
to mush, and she'd lay dollars to horse apples that he
played it to the nth degree.

Just like Smokin' Joe, Trace Coleman had met his
match. Gemma intended to win that big shiny belt
buckle in Las Vegas come December and leave Trace
Coleman along with his scanty-dressed groupies in a
cloud of dust. She had a big construction-paper lucky
horseshoe tacked to the door of her travel trailer, and
every time she won, she rewarded herself by pasting a
small shamrock on it. After the final ride, it would be
matted and framed and hung in her beauty shop, and all
the cowboys who'd given her a hard time could crawl up
under a mesquite bush and lick their wounds.

Any other time and any other place she might have

flirted with Trace. Cowboys were definitely her thing, and he sent out vibes that dug deep into her gut. But this was the rodeo circuit. For the next six months, Gemma O'Donnell had her job cut out for her and there was no room for Trace or any other cowboy.

Damn his sorry old hide, anyway! He was the top-seeded contestant in the tour and ten thousand dollars ahead of her. Staying on Smokin' Joe's back a full eight seconds could knock Trace off that pedestal in a tailspin—if thinking about his dreamy eyes didn't ruin her score. She took a deep breath and put him out of her mind. If he thought his cute little grin and deep voice could mess her up, then he could smear ketchup on his chaps and eat them for supper. And slap a little taco sauce on his spurs and have them for dessert.

She closed her eyes.

He will not bother me. He will not get into my head. He will not throw me off my game.

She kept the three sentences running on a continuous loop as she slung a leg over the top of the chute and got ready to mount old Smokin' Joe. She couldn't very well ride with her eyes shut, so she opened them, only to see Trace standing beside the bucking chute with a cocky little grin on his face. Light-brown chaps parenthesized a package locked behind his zipper that looked so inviting that Gemma almost drooled. She envisioned peeling his tight jeans from his body, leaving him wearing only boots, that cute grin, and a Stetson that sat just right.

"God Almighty," she whispered.

Someone called his name and he turned and walked away. But the backside was just as hot as the front with his chaps framing the cutest butt she'd ever seen. Lord, if she could stay on the horse eight seconds it would be a miracle. If she got a score high enough to beat him, it would be pure damn magic. She blinked and imagined Trace tossing his hat toward a pitchfork in a hayloft and coming toward her with those brown eyes speaking volumes about how hot that hayloft was about to get.

Stop it this minute! You've got to stay on this horse eight seconds. Sweet Jesus, you haven't ever let a man upset you with just a touch before. What in the hell is the matter with you? Get it together, Gemma O'Donnell!

The familiar whoosh filled her ears. When she had first started riding, her brothers had told her to focus on the ride and block everything else out. She'd imagined holding a conch shell up to her ear. Nothing could break through her concentration once she got her whoosh mojo going. And she was almost in the zone.

Folks around Cody, Wyoming, were big rodeo fans, so the stands were packed with a loud, rowdy crowd that night. But Gemma didn't look up into the crowd, even though a rider likes a whole arena full of noisy fans as much as a country music band likes to play to a lively audience. If she looked, it would break her focus, and she'd already drawn the meanest damn horse in the rodeo. Which was good because if he bucked hard that meant more points. She rolled her neck, limbering it up for the ride and reminding herself to keep it loose. It only took one drop of fear to lock it in place and then *boom*, whiplash would put her out of the next ride over in St. Paul, Oregon.

The announcer's voice was full of excitement. "Gemma O'Donnell, our only woman contestant in saddle bronc riding, will be coming out of gate six. Gemma comes to us from Ringgold, Texas, and I hear she can ride anything with four legs. She told me this afternoon that her big regret in life is not pursuing this dream before now and letting Kaila Mussell take home bragging rights to being the first woman to show the boys how it's done. Keep your eyes on gate six and let's make some noise for Gemma, who intends to be the second woman ever to win the bronc riding contest when the dust settles in Las Vegas in December."

When she settled back into the saddle, she was fully well in her riding zone. The announcer might as well have been reciting poetry, because all Gemma heard was each heartbeat in her ears as she eased into the saddle. She tried to psych Smokin' Joe out. It wasn't against the rules, and he'd done the same thing when he glared at her through the bars. She leaned forward and whispered softly in his ear, "You do your damnedest, old boy. Buck the hardest you've ever done and I'll do my damnedest to stay on your back. I need the scores, so give me your wildest ride. Don't you hold back a thing because I'm a woman, darlin'. I could ride you with my eyes shut and eating a hamburger with my free hand."

She measured the hot pink and black rein and got a death grip on it. Her saddle had been tweaked by her brother Dewar and the rein braided by her brother Rye. The gold lucky horseshoe pin had been fastened to her hot pink hat by her brother Raylen. All of it was important but especially the saddle. To a bronc rider, a saddle or stirrups can be off one-quarter of an inch and it might as well be a mile. It has to be absolutely perfect, in tune with the rider and so comfortable that she could sleep in it.

She shoved the heels of her boots firmly down into the stirrups and put everything out of her mind but the "mark out." The heels of her boots had to be above the points of Smokin' Joe's shoulders before the horse's front legs hit the ground. After that it would be an eight-second line dance. Smokin' Joe would buck. Gemma's legs would go back and come forward, spurring him on to buck even more. In the end one of them would win, and Gemma was absolutely determined that Smokin' Joe would lose.

If she missed the mark out she'd be disqualified, so she got ready.

Rein in hand.

Determination in her heart.

"Eight seconds!" Trace's deep voice said from the top of the chute.

She could have shot him, dragged his sorry carcass out to the back side of the O'Donnell ranch, and poured barbecue sauce on him for the coyotes. She vowed that she would get even. He had the next ride of the evening and paybacks were a bitch. He should have thought of that before he broke her concentration.

She pulled up on the multicolored rein.

Everything stopped and she was in a vacuum. Even the dust out in the arena was afraid to succumb to gravity and fall back to earth. The noise of the crowd hung above the arena like a layer of foggy smoke in a cheap honky-tonk, but Gemma couldn't hear it.

She settled her straw hat with the lucky gold horseshoe pin attached to the brim on the back of her head, touched the horseshoe for good luck, and nodded. Three rodeo clowns stepped away from the gate. The chute opened and a blur of white topped with snatches of hot pink whirled around the arena, kicking up dust devils in its wake.

Time moved in slow motion. She could hear the crowd going wild and the announcer's excitement, but the roar of blood racing through her veins kept all of it at bay. The dry dirt clouds filling her nostrils were like drugs to an addict, and with every breath she took in more, the exhilaration so great that her heart was on the brink of explosion. The horse attempted to twist itself into a pretzel, but her body responded with the right movements instinctively. The next move put both his back legs into the air and she felt like she was on a little kid's slide. The dirt arena came up to meet her and then *boom*, Smokin' Joe was a damn camel with a big hump where his back used to be. But she stayed loose in the saddle, moving her legs the right way for balance as if she'd been born to ride Smokin' Joe that day in Cody, Wyoming.

About the Author

Carolyn Brown is a *New York Times* and *USA Today* bestselling author with more than sixty books published, and she credits her eclectic family for her humor and writing ideas. Her books include the cowboy trilogy *Lucky in Love*, *One Lucky Cowboy*, and *Getting Lucky*, the Honky Tonk series, *I Love This Bar*, *Hell Yeah*, *Honky Tonk Christmas*, and *My Give a Damn's Busted*, and her bestselling Spikes & Spurs series with *Love Drunk Cowboy*, *Red's Hot Cowboy*, *Darn Good Cowboy Christmas*, and *One Hot Cowboy Wedding*. She was born in Texas but grew up in southern Oklahoma where she and her husband, Charles, a retired English teacher, make their home. They have three grown children and enough grandchildren to keep them young.